Open Doors may be ordered via internet on:

Amazon.com, Createspace.com, or

NafessaCollins.com

Mrs. Precious Books

Philadelphia, PA 19128

First Printing 2017

ISBN 978-09963774-2-3

Printed in the United States of America

Acknowledgements

Thank you God for allowing me... to release a piece of me!

& of course, thank you...to YOU... for reading!

Peace & Blessings!

Open Doors

Chapter 1- Lesson: Good Things & Bad WILL Happen in Life...

~Friday: June 5, 2009~

"Ok, kids! I'll see you all on Sunday," smiled Angelica looking at her three children as they entered her mother's car.

"Bye mom," yelled Kendall, Gavin, and Hailey in unison as they settled in the car.

Angelica quickly pointed her finger toward Kendall, "Don't forget to brush your teeth, Kendall."

"I won't!"

Angelica's mom smiled and laughed at her grands before looking at Angelica. "Angelica, I'll call you before I bring them home on Sunday," said Mrs. Delores.

"Ok mom, be careful!"

"Oh, I will baby," she said while she adjusted her rear-view mirror. "If you *DO* decide to go out, have fun!" Angelica's mom put the car in drive and pulled off down Webster Street. As she turned, the kids yelled their loud goodbyes out of the window.

It was around 8:45 pm and Ian, Angelica's husband, was on his way out as well. As soon as the springtime brought in summer like weather, Ian played out in the streets just about every weekend. When he left the house, he would usually return home around 5 o'clock the next morning. They argued about it many times, but Angelica was sick and tired of arguing with him. Angelica re-entered the house to see Ian immaculately dressed. He stood in the living room looking at himself in the mirror while adjusting his shirt, "Angel, I'm out. I won't be out too long."

"Yeah you always say that, but whatever," she muttered to herself. "Have fun," she said out loud.

Ian kept his eyes fixed on the mirror. "Are you going out," trying, but failing, to sound genuinely interested in her plans for the evening.

"Maybe," she said walking up the stairs. "Can you lock the door on your way out?"

"Yeah! If you go out, don't forget to charge your phone," again failing to sound concerned.

"Ian," she said chuckling, "Be careful and I'll see you in the morning." Angelica went into the bathroom and ran some water in the bathtub.

"Why you gotta start that shit again! I told you I wouldn't be out that long," he yelled standing on the bottom step.

Angelica went to the top of the stairs so that she could see his face, "Ian, I'm not starting shit! Just stop trying to act like..." she paused mid-sentence and just closed her eyes. "Never mind...just go!" Ian cursed underneath his breath and left out of the house while slamming the door behind him.

Angelica went back into the bathroom, turned off the water, and began to take her clothes off. As she eased each foot into the warm water, she didn't care less about where Ian was going or when he was coming back. All she wanted to do was take a bath, watch a movie, and relax for the rest of the night. While Angelica washed her body, she listened to an episode of Law and Order: Criminal Intent which was playing on the Bravo channel in her bedroom. While trying to hear the conversation between Detective Goren and Detective Eames, Angelica thought she heard the downstairs front door opening. "Ian," she yelled.

The house stayed silent except Detective Eames and Goren on the television. Angelica just stared at the floor trying to concentrate on where that sound came from. Then she heard a knock coming from the direction of the house next door. Angelica figured that the noise was coming from the new neighbor. Someone finally bought the house that had been on the market for about two years! She shook her head and thought that maybe they were moving some things into the house. Angelica quickly dismissed her thoughts of the house next door and began to cleanse her body. After ritualistically washing her upper torso before the lower portion of her body, she just laid in the tepid water. She so longed to immerse her whole body in the water, but the tub wasn't big enough! As she let her head sink into the water, she tried so hard to rinse away the anxiety she felt within.

After fifteen minutes or so, she rose out of the tub, enveloped herself in her soft yellow towel, and walked into her bedroom to get dressed for bed. It was almost ten o'clock and Angelica couldn't wait to lay down. While smoothing Shea Butter all over her body, she watched the remainder of the Criminal Intent episode. By the time the credits were scrolling down the TV screen, Angelica was underneath the sheets. Twenty minutes into the next episode, Angelica was fast sleep.

~BANG!~

Angelica was startled out of her sleep as she sat up quickly in her bed. She stared at the television, but the volume wasn't that loud! She rubbed her eyes so that they could focus better. The noise sounded like a glass had fallen onto the floor. Angelica wiped her eyes again. She looked around the room from where she was now sitting feeling drunk from her slumber. The television was showing another Law & Order episode within the Criminal Intent marathon que. Since it wasn't the T.V., she thought that maybe the noise was from the new neighbor's next door. Her bed *was* positioned close to the adjacent wall. So, it would make sense that the noise seemed to be close-by. She shook her head and quickly glanced at the alarm clock's display of 1:28. Angelica turned the television off with the remote and laid back down in her warm, cozy spot.

What seemed to be minutes later, Angelica felt Ian tapping her on the shoulder. Angelica ignored him. She was so sick of him and his lame ass ways of trying to make love to her. Would a real man seriously tap their wife on the damn shoulder in the middle of the night wanting to make love to her? He then glided his hands from her ankles all the way up to her neck giving her a sensual massage. Angelica laid there on her side motionless. She felt him adjusting his position so that his body laid alongside the length of hers. Her body shivered as he began to kiss her from her neck all along the length of her back. His hand gently caressed her waist as he began to pull down her panties. Angelica couldn't believe how sensual he was with her. She just knew he was drunk! Ian never kissed her like that unless he was drunk! He inched his way underneath the covers. While underneath, he grasped her hips and turned

Angelica on her back. While keeping his body hidden underneath the covers, he slowly opened her legs and began to devour her from the inside out. Angelica moaned from being in pure ecstasy! He rarely EVER did THIS, and when he did, he was never REALLY into it. But he was definitely into it tonight!

Although he pissed her off earlier, he was making her feel as if she was floating on air! She decided to stop ignoring his forthcomings and put her hands on his head. Her body went numb, and her heart began to beat rapidly! As she tried to catch her breath, she moved her fingers slowly against a rough, cottony- material on his head! He instantly stopped licking her and raised his head up from underneath the covers while simultaneously covering up her mouth with his hand. It wasn't Ian!

She attempted to scream and went ballistic trying to break free from his grasp, "Stop it! Stop it! I'm not going to hurt you," he whispered. Angelica's eyes were so wide as she stared at the eyes staring back at her in the darkness! She kept struggling like crazy trying to escape! When she tired herself out and couldn't overpower him, she cried hysterically.

"Shh! Shh! I'm not going to hurt you! I'm not...going... to hurt you," he said assuredly. Angelica started to cry harder as the man tried to soothe her. "Please don't cry. Please! I'll make you feel all better...ok? Please don't cry! It's ok! It's ok! I'm not going to hurt you. I'm not...going...to hurt you. I'm here to love to you...not hurt you! I promise! I promise!"

Angelica was in shock. Everything he said, everything he did was being mentally recorded. "I'm going to take my hand from your mouth. Do... not...scream." The man removed his hand, and Angelica just kept on crying as her body trembled from head to toe. "Don't cry. Please don't cry!"

He slowly kissed each one of her eyes and wiped her tears away as they kept falling down her cheeks. She desperately tried to make out his face but couldn't! It was too dark. She couldn't see, but she could feel that she was completely naked. Angelica couldn't figure out how he removed her nightgown while she was asleep!

He slowly raised each one of her arms above her head after tenderly kissing each hand. He then placed one hand over the other as her arms

8

extended above her head. While holding them in place with his left hand, he kissed her on her neck and moved down to her breasts. He grasped them one at a time and roughly sucked on them while tantalizing her nipples with his tongue as if he were starving for her. She could feel that he didn't have a shirt on and could only see his eyes and mouth through his ski mask.

After he sucked on her breasts, he went up to her face, "I have to blindfold you. Don't move," he whispered. Angelica was so afraid! She didn't know what to do! He released her hands, got off the bed, and pulled something from his pocket. He then quickly tied the blindfold material firmly over her eyes. His face was now close to her ear, "Don't move, ok?" Angelica fearfully nodded her head yes and didn't move. She kept her arms above her head and firmly held them where he placed them.

Angelica could hear his belt unbuckling. Then she heard what sounded like his pants dropping to the floor with keys jingling. She tried to think of something to do but was so afraid to move. She felt so bad! Hopeless! All she could do was cry underneath the blindfold. She prayed to GOD that he wouldn't hurt her. He put his hand on her face and kissed her on the cheek, "It's ok. It's ok. Baby, please don't cry. I'm here for you. I'm here to make you feel better. Don't cry. Please don't cry," he soothingly pleaded. Angelica smelled his familiar Burberry cologne and just hoped for a minute that maybe it WAS Ian. She prayed to God in her mind over and over again. Angelica mentally pleaded to Him to forgive her of her sins and to allow her to enter heaven once he was done with her. The man took her left hand and kissed her bare ring finger, "Open your legs."

Angelica began to pant as her breathing became erratic! She began to cry out loud but did as she was told. The sheet was then removed from her body. He took her arms and placed them alongside her legs. She could feel him climbing onto the bed. He then positioned himself between her legs again and continued licking her down below while holding onto her hands at her sides. The man devoured her for what seemed like forever. She just laid there listening to the slurping sounds from his mouth enjoying the taste of her. "I'm here to make you feel good. I'm here to make love to you."

Angelica just laid there motionless, "I want you to enjoy me. Enjoy me...while you have me here with you."

He rose from between her thighs, gently grabbed her arms, and raised them over her head again. As he held them down to the bed with his left hand, she could tell that he was close to her face. She could feel his breath, "I want you to enjoy me." Angelica turned her head to the side and just kept still. She felt his fingers rubbing up against her. The man then made licking and sucking noises as if he were licking his fingers, "Mmmmm...You taste so good...even better than I thought you would." Angelica's body became rigid as he blanketed her body with his. She shuttered and sobbed louder knowing what was about to happen. "I love you," he said while slowly entering Angelica.

She gasped for air, "Please...Please stop," she cried.

He instantly stopped moving. "Am I hurting you?" Angelica just continued sobbing trying not to think about what was going on. He kissed and licked her neck, "Angelica, am I hurting you?" Angelica shook her head yes. He sighed heavily,

"Tell me the truth. With what I am doing to you right now, am I hurting you?"

Angelica slowly shook her head no. She didn't understand why he even cared about her being in pain in the first place! Sick motherfucker! Angelica just *knew* he was going to kill her afterward. She was being raped in her home and felt completely helpless and weak. She didn't know when or if Ian was even coming home! THIS was all Ian's fault!!

He took his time entering her, savoring her inch by inch. "Angelica, you feel so good. I hope you're enjoying this as much as I am." The man laid his full body weight on top of her and sucked all over her neck once he completely filled her. He began to moan as he slowly pushed himself in and out of her. "I would love to feel all of you, but I'm not gonna take the condom off," he whispered in her ear. "Am I making you feel good?" Angelica didn't say a word.

The man stopped and just laid on her body. His body was wet with perspiration. He was enjoying every bit of it! "While tasting you, I felt your body trembling...and it wasn't from fear. I know you like what I'm doing to you," he said kissing her neck. "I know it's fucked up...because I'm taking you...but I know...deep down inside; you're enjoying it." He started moving, and Angelica started sobbing again. "You feel so good! It's unbelievable! Your nut-ass husband is too weak to be your man. He doesn't deserve you. He doesn't fucking deserve you, Angelica!"

He sucked a little harder on her chest and all around her breasts and neck. Angelica couldn't do anything but listen to him and the smacking-wet sounds from him moving inside of her. He was breathing frantically! Drops of something wet fell onto her face and neck with almost every movement of his hips plunging deep within her. He was sweating! His mask was off! "I want you to come for me. If you don't come, I... will... NOT... stop... making love to you. I'll be here all night and all morning," he whispered in between breaths. He continued moving with a slight circular motion and increased his tempo just a bit, "Are you going to come for me?" Angelica vehemently shook her head no. He sighed, "I guess I'll be spending the night. Who knows when your dumbass husband will be coming back!"

"Please...just stop," she sobbed.

He slowed down, "Why? Aren't you tired of being alone all the time? He doesn't love you, and you know it! You deserve this! You deserve to be made love to, and I'm the only one who is ABLE to do it." He slowly increased his movements but pushed deeper inside of her causing her to take deeper breaths. "So...are you going to come for me?"

"Please...don't do this," she begged.

"Are you going to come for me Angelica," he asked sucking all over her neck and ear lobe. "I want you to be mine so fucking bad," he whispered. "Come for me," he said digging deeper. Angelica didn't know what to do or say. He seemed to be getting more agitated by the moment. She didn't know if he was about to get more violent or if he was just really turned on. He groaned, "God, I wish you belonged to me! I love you so fucking much! Come for me!"

Angelica took a deep breath, "Ok."

He stopped, "I'll know if you're faking it. Don't do that to me... ok?" Angelica shook her head yes while he commenced pushing deeper and going faster. He softly bit the nipple on her left breast and Angelica screeched. She could feel his lips smiling as he released her nipple, "I want to feel you so bad. Please move for me." Angelica shook her head no. "Please...please move for me." Angelica sobbed and did as he asked. He loved every bit of it, "Yes...yes...more! I need to feel you!" Angelica moved a little bit more hoping that he would be satisfied. "More!"

"I can't," she whispered, "I can't."

He stopped. The man took his left hand off of her arms and kissed them, "Lift your sexy ass up off of the bed."

Angelica didn't know what he was about to do, "I can't! You're too heavy!"

He then pushed himself deeper inside of her! She instantly raised her hips while he placed her hands against the small of her back. He held on to them with his left hand and grabbed her behind with his right. "If you don't give me some more, I'm going to come...and then I'm going to make love to you again... and again..."

"Ok," she growled. She moved her hips and gave him what he wanted.

"Oh my God! Angelica, I need you to come for me."

"I can't," she yelled!

He stopped moving, "Why are you yelling? Am I hurting you?" Angelica didn't say anything. He moved his head closer to her ear and sucked on her earlobe, "Am I hurting you?"

"No...but you are raping me," she said in a very aggressive tone.

The man sighed quite a few times and dropped his head into her neck. He shook his head as if he had some sort of remorse. He raised his mouth to her ear, "I'll stop if you come for me." Angelica sobbed even more. "Do this for me, and I'll stop. I promise."

Angelica laid there as if she was frozen solid. She could feel his body hovering over hers. He kept his body still while he stayed firmly inside of her.

He softly licked her breasts and continued making love to her very slow. He whispered in her ear, "I'll never tell a soul. Just let your body feel me. Let me take you there...please." He kissed and sucked all over her neck. "All those nights alone...all those nights that he leaves you here ALONE! Let me have you! Let me show you how love feels!" He took a deep breath and kept his stride, "Feel me, Angelica! Feel me and come for me, baby! I love you so much! Oh, God...I love you!"

Angelica felt his chest heaving. He placed his head in the crook of her neck repeating how much he loved her while moving inside of her. She felt a warm wetness coming from his face. It wasn't heavy like spit or like the other drops of sweat. He was crying! Angelica inhaled as much as she could with her stuffed-up nose, "Ok."

The man released her arms from underneath her lower back. He then interlocked his fingers with hers above her head. "Is this ok?" Angelica nodded her head yes. "Can I go deeper?"

"Don't," she pleaded.

"Can I go deeper?"

She shook her head from side to side, "I can't do this."

"Yes, you can! I feel you! Don't stop!"

"Why are you trying to make me like this? I don't want to like this," she yelled.

The man stopped and said nothing for a few minutes. Angelica couldn't see him, but she knew he was staring at her. She was scared! She cursed at herself for making him mad. He then started moving again but didn't say anything to her. He separated his hands from hers and held her arms down with his left hand like he did before. Then he tucked his right hand underneath her lower back pushing her pelvis flush with his. "I guess I have to MAKE you come then." He moved deeper and deeper inside of her.

Angelica moaned, "Please," she pleaded. He didn't say a word. Angelica just moaned louder.

"Angelica, I need you to come with me." Angelica couldn't say anything. He was so deep inside of her! She just kept on moaning hoping that he couldn't hear her: but he could! He knew she was getting closer by the way her body drastically

18

loosened up and the way she was rocking her hips. He quickly released his right hand from underneath her, raised one of her legs around his back while still holding her arms down with the left. He then took his right hand and grabbed her ass. Angelica moaned a little louder while he stayed completely silent. Drips of sweat landed one by one onto her neck. He moved his hips faster making sure that he was deep inside of her.

"Please don't," she whispered.

"Don't what?"

"Don't do this to me...please," Angelica begged.

"Don't do what," the man asked sounding as if he was angry.

"Don't...do THIS!"

"Wrap your other leg around my back!" Angelica quickly did as she was told. The man then resumed placing his right hand on her bottom. He squeezed her ass compressing their pelvis'.

"Why are you doing this to me?"

The man sucked on her neck some more, "Because."

"Stop moving, please! Just get off of me," she whispered.

He slowed down, "I won't tell... if you won't tell." He released the hold that he had on her ass. The man then used both hands to hold each arm above her head. He interlocked their fingers, "Kiss me." Angelica shook her head no. The man placed his lips so close to hers that she could feel his breath floating over her mouth. "Kiss me."

She cried, "Please...please don't."

"Kiss me...please." He then began kissing her neck, right ear lobe, and cheek. He paused and then gently kissed her lips. "I love you. Kiss me." Angelica kept her mouth closed. He quickly pushed once deep inside of her. As soon as Angelica let out a wail, he began to envelop her with his mouth and tongue quieting all her sobs. "I love you, Angelica!" He circled his hips with every stroke going deeper and deeper inside of her.

"Stop," she cried.

"Come for me." Angelica's body began to quiver like never before. "Yes, baby! Yes! Come for me Angelica! I love you so much! Come for me!" The man was incessant with his grinding and pounding. Their bodies were gliding effortlessly because of the sweat and tears. Angelica couldn't help but groan louder and louder. "Come for me!" He began to suck all over her neck until she yelled and cried for dear life! Her insides gave way to the biggest orgasm she ever had. "Angelica, I love you," he whispered while trembling and twitching inside of her.

Angelica cried as he laid on top of her while still inside. "Did I hurt you?" Angelica stayed silent. "Did I hurt you? Please answer me."

Angelica cried, "You got what you wanted...please leave...please."

He kissed all over her face, neck, and breasts, "I love you, Angelica. Damn I love you!" He lowered her legs, backed out of her, and kissed her neck again. Angelica felt him moving from the bed. A couple of minutes went by, and Angelica began to panic! She started sobbing out loud as her body began to shake. He touched her hand, and Angelica snatched it away! "Take my hand."

"Please don't kill me! Please," she begged.

"Have I hurt you at all this evening?" Angelica didn't answer. He placed his hand on top of hers, "Take my hand." Angelica took his hand as he helped her to sit up in the bed. After helping her to stand, he hugged her close while breathing deeply. Angelica just tried to stay calm while keeping her arms by her side. He kissed her neck and then her lips as if she were fragile. The embrace was so close that Angelica could feel that he was getting excited again! He was positioned right in between her legs, and she could feel him getting harder by the second. Angelica tried to break the hold! "Shhh! If I get back inside you, I won't ever leave."

Angelica relaxed a bit. She could smell something sweet. It smelled like cookies and vanilla. "We're going to take a nice hot bath together." The man walked her into the bathroom and helped her into the tub. He helped her to sit down and then sat down right behind her. He made her lean back onto his chest as he massaged her arms and played in her hair. The man gently kissed the back of her neck while caressing her breasts. Angelica could feel him getting excited again! She slowly reached for the sides of the tub but, he quickly grabbed her hands and kissed them, "Just relax."

He washed her back and then told her to stand up while he washed her body from head to toe! He then instructed her to sit back down in the tub. She sat there emotionless while listening to him wash his body. Minutes later, she felt him rise out of the tub. A few moments went by and then he grabbed her hand. The man helped her to her feet, wrapped her in a towel, and carried her back to the bed.

As soon as he placed Angelica on the bed, she sat upright. "Lay back." Angelica slowly laid back on the bed. He unwrapped her from the towel and slowly collected the water that was left behind with the soft towel. He then began to smooth Shea butter all over her body. She felt the bed dip as if he were now laying on the bed. She was right! "I'm leaving...but before I go, I'm going to give you something so that you will go to sleep, ok?"

Angelica didn't say anything she just shook her head yes. The man helped her sit up and put a pill in her mouth and let her take a swig of water. "It's just going to allow you to go to sleep." She moved the pill underneath her tongue. "Open your mouth."

Angelica opened her mouth and closed it quick. "Open your mouth and lift up your tongue." She opened, raised her tongue, and revealed the pill resting underneath. "I'm giving you some more water, and I want you to swallow it." She drank the water and took the pill as he demanded. He laid her back down on the bed and helped her to lay on her side. He laid right alongside the back of her body and kissed her on the back of her neck. "I love you so much. I'm going to miss you so much, Angelica." He repositioned her head so that she was now laying her head on his other arm. She was now cocooned within his embrace, "I love you...I love you, Angelica...I do...I love you so much." Angelica sobbed herself to sleep as he continued to hold her close...kissing her neck...playing in her hair...

~

Angelica tried to open her eyes, but her lids were massive. She finally managed to open them and to keep them separated. She was relieved to see that she was still in her bed and alive! Angelica looked down at her body and quickly wrapped a sheet around her. She frantically looked for her phone around the room! It was in her underwear drawer!

She began to sob and tremble as her mind immediately began to replay the events from what had happened! Angelica pressed 911 but then heard a noise on the other side of the room. She quickly turned toward the sound and wondered if it was coming from her closet. Angelica held on tight to the sheet around her, along with the phone, and peeked into the closet. There was nothing there!

"911! What's your emergency?"

Her mind was indeed playing tricks! She was awake, but her mind recalled the noise from the broken glass that happened in the night!

"911! What's your emergency?"

She was startled by the woman's voice and turned to see where it was coming from. Angelica was so disoriented and a little dizzy that she bumped into the dresser! The phone dropped out of her hand, onto the floor, and underneath the bed.

"Angelica...what's all that noise up there?"

Angelica was in shock! Was that Ian? Angelica apprehensively walked out of the room. "Ian?" she whispered. "Ian!" she said louder. "Ian...Ian," she yelled.

Ian looked up at the ceiling, sighed, and shook his head, "Yeah...I'm down here! Why are you yelling like that," he snapped?

Angelica was so drowsy from the drug that the man gave to her. All she could do was cry as she staggered down the stairs. She reached the bottom step and just sat there staring at Ian while holding the sheet around her body.

Ian was pissed. He stayed laid out on the couch looking at her from winced eyes, "Why are you sitting there like that?" Angelica didn't say a word. She just sat there on the step and looked at the front door. It was ALL his fault!

"Did you hear me? What's wrong with you?" Just then there was a hard knock at the door. "Who the hell is that knocking on the door!" Ian angrily hopped off of the couch, went to the door, and opened it. He was surprised as hell to see that it was the police. There were about four squad cars on the block! "Yes," Ian said sarcastically.

The officer frowned and looked inside the house from where he was standing. He could see a woman sitting on the bottom of the stairs, "Sir someone called 911 from this residence."

Ian turned his head to Angelica, "Did you call 911?" Angelica didn't say a word.

"Can we come in please," the police officer asked while walking through the doorway.

"Sure," Ian said looking confused.

The policeman walked straight to Angelica who was still sitting on the bottom step staring at the floor. "Ms. what is your name?" Angelica looked at the officer.

"Angelica Kings."

The officer looked at Angelica and smiled. He noticed that she had been crying and that there were a couple of visible marks around her neck. He offered his hand, "I'm Officer Roman Callowhill and this is my partner Christopher Straight. We're here to help you. We're not going to hurt you in any way."

Angelica silently began to cry. She released the hold she had on the sheet covering her body and tucked it underneath her armpits. She took both of her hands and firmly grasped his hand. "Please get me out of this house! Please!" She stood up slowly and clung to his body while crying and shaking hysterically. "Please take me out of this house!" Ian was still confused but started getting upset at how she was holding on to the policeman.

"Angelica what are you doing?"

Ian walked up to her and was about to say something, but she beat him to the punch! She spoke to him in a deep, menacing, tone of voice, "You fucking asshole! This is all your fault! If you hadn't been running the fucking streets, he wouldn't have even came in here and raped me! You left the fucking door open again, didn't you! Didn't you," she said screaming and crying her eyes out. "I hate you! I fucking HATE YOU! Look at what he did to my body...LOOK!!!" She pulled the sheet

28

completely off showing Ian, and the policemen, her body. The man left passion marks on the lower part of her neck, all over her chest, breasts, stomach, arms, back, ass, thighs, and lower legs.

"Oh Shit," said Ian holding his hand up to his mouth. "Angelica, I'm sorry...," Ian took a step toward her and wanted to cover up her nakedness.

Angelica screamed while waving her hands in the air, "Get...the... FUCK away from me! You did this! You did this to me, and I fucking HATE YOU!"

Officer Callowhill stepped in front of Ian, "Just back up," he commanded shielding Angelica.

"Mr. Kings," interjected Officer Straight trying to calm the situation down. "Can you please get her some clothes and shoes to put on so that we can take her to the hospital?" Ian nodded and went upstairs to grab the things Officer Straight asked of him. While scrambling around for some clothes and shoes, he heard the busy signal from the phone underneath the bed. He reached underneath the bed, picked up the phone, and just stared at it in disbelief of what had happened. Ian looked at the bed, which had been stripped of its sheets, comforter, and pillows and just shook his head.

"The ambulance is on its way ok," Officer Callowhill said picking up the sheet and placing it around her. He heard the other officers coming into the home and started to walk away from her to debrief them on the situation but, Angelica forcefully pulled on his hand.

"Don't leave me...please," she cried hysterically.

"Ok, Ms. Kings...just calm down. Everything is going to be just fine." Ian came downstairs with the clothes. He gave them to Officer Callowhill, and he handed them to Angelica. She walked in the kitchen slowly as if she was a zombie. Angelica let the sheet drop to the floor. She dressed her naked body right in the middle of the kitchen. Ian was shocked at her behavior and just stared at the marks on her back while she dressed. She walked back in the living room and put on the Crocs that Ian brought from upstairs. Angelica then walked right up to Officer Callowhill. She stood behind him as if that were the only place that she could stand.

"So where are you taking her," Ian asked looking completely bewildered at Angelica's behavior.

Officer Straight looked at Callowhill and then to Ian. Both officers picked up on his reference to just 'her' going somewhere. Ian didn't intend on going to the hospital with Angelica. Officer Callowhill stared at Ian, "We're taking her to the hospital...University of Penn. Are there any children in the home?"

Ian stared at Angelica who blankly stared at the floor, "No they're at my mother-in-law's house until Sunday." The ambulance sirens were piercing outside of the door.

Officer Straight shook his head, "Good. The detectives are on their way inside. They will take your statement as to what happened. The ambulance will give you the telephone number to the hospital so that you can be informed about what's going on."

Angelica snapped out of her zombie-like behavior and grabbed onto Officer Callowhill, "I don't want them to see me!"

31

Ian walked over to her and handed her his jacket, "Here baby...put this on..."

Angelica stepped back, "Get the fuck away from me," she screamed.

Officer Callowhill moved him aside, "It's ok. There's a blanket in the ambulance." Officer Straight went into the kitchen to get the sheet while Angelica buried her head in Officer Callowhill's chest. Ian was mad at how she was clinging to the officer.

Officer Callowhill wrapped his arm around her and tried to calm her down. "It's ok," Callowhill said while respectfully patting Angelica on her back so that she could calm down, "Remember...me and Officer Straight are here to help you. Are you ready to go to the hospital?"

"Everybody's going to know," she said crying like a lost child. Tears started to form in Ian's eyes. He had never seen her cry like this before.

Officer Callowhill released her from his embrace and put his hands on her arms, "Just hold my hand and we'll walk to the ambulance ok?"

"Ok."

Officer Callowhill, Angelica, and Officer Straight walked out of the house while the detectives walked in. As Callowhill and Angelica walked down the front steps, she wrapped her arms around one of his and buried her head in his chest. Callowhill took his other arm and held her close. Straight stopped walking and began speaking with the incoming detectives as Callowhill and Angelica continued walking toward the ambulance.

Callowhill and Angelica walked to the rear of the ambulance where the female and male EMT's were standing. Roman started the introductions, "Hey, this is Ms. Kings. Ms. Kings, they're going to take you to the hospital ok?"

Angelica looked at the officer with her red, bloodshot eyes. "Aren't you coming with me," she asked sniffling through her stuffed-up nose.

"Ms. Kings, they are going to take good care of you. She...," he said briefly looking at the female EMT and then back to Angelica, "...will make sure that you have..."

Angelica wouldn't look anywhere else, "Please...Please don't leave me," she said with tears running down her face, "...just until I see the doctor...please."

Callowhill nodded his head, "Ok." He called Straight on his cell while the EMT's helped her in the back of the truck. "She wants me to go with her. Alright...follow us...ok...thanks, man." Callowhill took a deep breath and looked down the street at all the police that were around the house. He looked up at the sky and closed his eyes as he took another deep breath. He wiped his face with his hand and walked to the truck.

"We're ready," said the male EMT while getting into drive.

Callowhill climbed in the back of the ambulance and sat across from the gurney. Angelica held her hand out to him as tears fell from her puffy red eyes. "I feel so bad."

"Everything will be ok," he said rubbing her hand politely.

"My kids..."

Callowhill interrupted her, "Ms. Kings, try not to worry about those things right now. Just breathe." He looked at her breathing while still crying. "That's it. Whenever you feel overwhelmed, just take a couple of deep breaths, and that will make you feel a little better."

Angelica squeezed his hand, "I'm sorry."

"This is my job! This is what I do," he said smiling.

Angelica tried hard to smile a little, but it didn't come to the surface. She gently pulled her hand away from Callowhill and turned her body away so that she was facing the opposite wall of the ambulance. She just laid there with her eyes closed thinking of what she did that made this happened. Callowhill sat back on the bench and looked out the front glass windshield to see where they were. He knew that they were getting close to Civic Center Blvd and that it would only be a short amount of time before they would arrive to the hospital. "We're almost there," he murmured.

"Ok."

"Ms. Kings?"

"Yes?"

"The hospital is not too far away." Angelica turned over and looked at him. "When we get inside, the EMT's and the doctor are going to escort you to your room while they perform some tests."

Tears began to form in her eyes, "Are you going to leave?"

"Yes."

The tears began to run down her face, "Can you just...ummm...," she bit her lip trying not to completely break down. "Do you think you can come back...later on?"

Callowhill had a look of uncertainty on his face and looked at his watch, "I'll try."

"I...Please can you come back?"

Callowhill heard the desperation in her voice and tried to soothe her, "It's ok. I'll come back as soon as I can."

"Ok." Angelica turned her back to him again feeling embarrassed and ashamed. Ten minutes later The EMT's pulled up to the ER entrance way. When she heard the sirens cease, she turned toward him, sat up, and just stared at the floor of the ambulance. The EMT's jumped out of the ambulance and Angelica looked up at Officer Callowhill, "If you can't come back, it's ok."

He took her hand and lightly squeezed it, "I will be back. They're going to take good care of you." Angelica started crying again.

The female EMT opened the door and smiled, "Ms. Kings, I'll be taking you inside to see the doctor ok?" Angelica instantly became frantic. She just stared at the EMT and shook her head no. She knew what was to come from watching Law and Order: SVU and she began to breathe abnormally fast. The female EMT saw what was about to happen and intervened, "Ms. Kings," she said in a motherly tone, "...just relax and breath slowly. We will not harm you in any way, I promise." Callowhill grabbed her hand while Angelica slowed her breathing down. The EMT put her hand on top of Officer Callowhill's so that Angelica could get the idea that they were all on the same side, "Let's go and see the doctor so that they can take care of you." Angelica looked at Callowhill, and he slightly nodded his head giving her the assurance that the EMT was safe.

Angelica started to cry and looked at them. She took the EMT's hand, rose from the gurney, and stepped out of the ambulance. As the EMT walked with her inside the Emergency Room, she looked back and saw Callowhill standing by the ER entranceway. Callowhill gave her a faint smile. Angelica was able to do the same.

Chapter 2- Lesson: Guardian Angels are Real

Officer Straight came in the ER entranceway and saw Officer Callowhill, "You good?"

Callowhill shook his head, "Yeah. She wants me to come back and see her. I'll check on her after work."

"I talked to Cap. and let him know what was up. He was cool. Mr. Kings wanted me to give them her insurance card. Yo', I'm hungrier than a mug...let's get something to eat," he said laughing.

Callowhill laughed right along with him, "Alright man!" As Straight went to the ER's nurse's station, Callowhill sat down and closed his eyes. He couldn't help but think about the marks that were on Angelica's body.

Straight walked up to him, "Callow, you ready?"

"Yeah, let's go."

~

While Callowhill and Straight were on their way to get something to eat, Angelica laid on a hospital bed while the doctor probed her vagina for possible DNA from her attacker. The female doctor had explained everything to Angelica about the tests that were going to be performed and how they were going to take some pictures of her body. Angelica understood what they had to do. She just wanted to lay down for a while without being bothered by anyone. After the doctor had finished taking sample after sample, she took picture after picture! Angelica just kept her eyes closed the whole time as if she weren't even there.

"Mrs. Kings, we're all done here. There are some detectives here to speak with you."

Angelica opened her eyes, "Can I just rest a bit."

The doctor sat down beside her and held her hand, "Mrs. Kings, I understand how you are feeling. The detectives would like to speak with you while the incident is still fresh in your memory. They want to get as much information as possible so that they can get this guy. What do you think," asked the doctor who left the choice up to Angelica.

Angelica took in a deep breath, "Ok."

The doctor nodded and smiled while releasing her hand, "You can take a shower over there. Here is a hospital gown, some disposable underwear, and the sanitary napkins are in that drawer over there if you need them." The doctor went to the drawers and opened them so that she could see what was inside. "...there are also some pajama pants in this drawer here if you want to wear them. Towels and cloths are over here, and soap and shampoo are already in the shower. I'll make sure the nurse brings you something for your feet."

"Can I have a toothbrush and some toothpaste?"

The doctor went over to Angelica and grabbed her hand again, "I think we can do that!" As soon as the doctor left the room, she gathered the things she needed for the shower and hopped in. The water was nice and warm just like she liked it. As she washed her body, she thought of how the man cleaned her in the tub. She cried thinking of how she thought he was going to kill her. She let the water run across her face hoping that the water drops would overpower her eye's ability to release any more tears. Thoughts ran through her mind of how he kissed her practically everywhere on her body.

After she washed and got dressed, she looked at the sanitary napkins. Angelica frowned up her face and then remembered that the doctor told her that she might bleed a little from the tests. She went back in the bathroom to put the pad on when she heard a knock at the door.

"Mrs. Kings, it's Nancy, your nurse. I'm just bringing you some socks, a toothbrush, and some toothpaste."

Angelica came out of the bathroom and tried not to make eye contact with the nurse, "Thank you." She put the socks on and took the toothbrush and toothpaste.

"When you're ready for the detectives to come in, just press the call button and we'll let them know to come on in ok?"

"Yes, thank you," she said looking out the window.

The nurse walked over to her and put her hand on Angelica's shoulder, "Would you like a little something to help you get settled? The doctor put an order in for some medication to help you to get some rest."

Angelica looked at the nurse, "Yes, thank you Nancy." The nurse smiled, nodded her head, and left the room. Angelica went to the bathroom and brushed her teeth. As she looked in the mirror, she thought about how he sucked on her breasts and neck repeatedly as if he had an un-relinquishing hunger for her. Angelica tried not think about it, until she looked in the mirror and saw her neck and chest. She had red passion marks all over the lower part of her neck. Some were small and faint while others were big and dark red. She took a deep breath and finished brushing her teeth. Angelica wiped her mouth with her washcloth and sat down on the bed. After taking a few deep breaths, she pressed the call button.

There was a knock at the door, and two detectives came into the room along with Nancy. The nurse immediately gave Angelica her medicine and a cup of water. She helped Angelica to lay down and tucked her in the bed. The nurse tilted her head and smiled at Angelica, "Press the call button when you are finished ok?"

"Yes."

One detective was female, and the other was male, just like on SVU. The female walked up to Angelica, "Hi Mrs. Kings, my name is Detective Smith, and this is my partner Detective Stockton. We're here to ask you some questions about what happened."

"Ok." Angelica ran the events down to them starting from when she said goodbye to the kids. As she talked, they wrote notes and asked her questions along the way. After she had recalled the whole story for them, she felt the medication creeping in. "He put the blindfold on, raped me, and then he made me take a bath with him. He gave me a pill so that I could go to sleep. When I woke up he was gone," she quickly concluded hinting that she didn't want to talk about it anymore.

"And you said that he used a condom right," asked Detective Smith.

"Yes," she said as tears streamed down her cheek.

"So, he only had intercourse with you one time," asked Detective Stockton.

"Yes."

"And you didn't catch a glance at him at all, is that right," Detective Smith confirmed.

"Yes, I couldn't see his face."

"Did he mention anything else while talking to you," continued Detective Smith.

"He said all kinds of things. He told me that he was there to make me feel good, and he didn't want me to be scared. He knew my name...and he knew I was married." Angelica started crying and pressed the call button.

Detective Smith kept on writing, "Did he hit you?" Angelica shook her head no. "Ok."

"Is there anything else that you want to tell us," followed Detective Stockton.

"No, I don't think so."

The doctor knocked on the door and came into the room to check up on Angelica. "Detectives, are you finished here," she asked smiling.

Detective Smith turned to the doctor, "Yes! We're finished. Mrs. Kings if you need to contact us for any reason, please feel free to call. I'll leave my card on the desk here."

"Thank you." Angelica wiped her face with some tissue and laid down on the bed as the detectives left the room.

The doctor walked closer to Angelica, "Your husband is out there in the waiting room for you. Would you like to see him?"

"No. I don't want him anywhere near me. I do not want to see him!" Angelica's tears were streaming down her face.

The doctor sat on the bed beside Angelica and consoled her. "It's ok. You don't have to see him. I'll tell him that you're not feeling well enough right now ok?" Angelica shook her head yes.

Angelica looked up, "Officer Callowhill said that he would come by to check up on me. I want to thank him for his help."

"I'll tell you what. If he comes, I'll let him come in. Since I get off at 7'o'clock tonight, I'll leave a note in your chart and at the nurse's station to let the staff know what you and I have discussed."

Angelica smiled, "Thank you for everything."

"No problem. Are you hungry?

"No."

The doctor smiled, "I know you're not hungry but try to eat something. Lunch will be here soon."

Angelica shook her head yes, laid back down and pulled the blanket over her as the doctor walked to the door. "What time is it?"

"It's 3:48."

Angelica yawned, "Thank you." Moments later Angelica welcomed the medication's hold over her eyes. She fell fast asleep.

.

~

"Ms. Kings...Ms. Kings." Angelica opened her eyes and focused. "Ms. Kings, It's me Officer Callowhill." Angelica smiled. "You *do* remember me, right?" Angelica shook her head yes. Callowhill started to back away from the bed, "I'll come back tomorrow when you're feeling a little better. I just came by because I told you that I would."

"Please... stay." Callowhill just looked at her. "I mean...I'm sorry. I know you probably have a family and everything...I don't mean...You can leave...I'm sorry!"

Callowhill smiled, "Ms. Kings, I'm not married but I do have a daughter."

Angelica's face brightened thinking of her own kids, "What's her name?"

"Winter."

"Awe! That's so pretty! How old is she," she asked feeling a little woozy.

"8."

Angelica looked down to her hands, "I just wanted to thank you for helping me."

Callowhill nodded his head, "Just doing my job."

Angelica looked up at him, "But you're doing more than your job...with you being here right now," she said softly.

He smiled at her, "I brought you a little something to eat just in case you didn't like their food."

Angelica smiled, "Thank you."

He opened the bag and pulled out a Turkey and Cheese Hoagie. "I asked them to put mayo, hot, and sweet peppers on the side. I bought you Sour Cream, Barbeque, and Plain Chips since I didn't know which one you preferred."

Angelica frowned her face at him, "You didn't have to do this Officer Callowhill."

"It's the least I could do. I know that hospital food isn't always good." Angelica smiled. She sat up and Callowhill positioned her wheeled tray over her lap so that she could eat. As he placed the tray closer to her waist, he could see a couple of marks on her neck.

Angelica caught him looking at her neck. "It's ok...they don't hurt."

He stepped back and looked at her face, "I apologize for looking."

"He...," she couldn't finish her sentence.

Callowhill raised his hand up in the air, "Please you don't have to explain."

"If they do catch him, I won't be able to help out because I don't even know what he looks like. I have no idea who it could be."

Callowhill stepped closer, placed the items on the tray, and looked at her, "Ms. Kings, just let the detectives do their job in trying to find out who did this to you."

She looked down at her hoagie, "I know you have to go. You don't have to stay any longer."

"I'll leave if you want me to leave." Angelica looked at him and tried to smile. "Do you want me to leave?"

"No, I don't. You're my guardian angel." Callowhill laughed while he unwrapped her hoagie. "I will be forever grateful to you for helping me."

"Well since I'm your guardian angel, you can call me by my first name...Roman."

"I'm Angelica." Roman smiled as she closed her eyes to pray over her food. "Did you eat already?"

"No, I didn't."

Angelica opened the hoagie and parted the halves, "Well, here take this other piece. I can't eat it this whole thing by myself."

"No, you go ahead and eat what you can. I'll eat something later."

"Please, I insist." Roman went into the bathroom and washed his hands. He sat down in a chair that was not too far from the bed. He reached over, took the other piece along with a napkin, and bit into the hoagie. "Thank you so much Roman."

"No problem. When do you think you will be able to go home?"

"Tomorrow." She put the hoagie down and stared at her hands. "I don't want to be anywhere near my husband." Roman looked at her and kept a serious face. "Roman, he is a huge reason why that man got into my home."

"Ms. Kings...I mean Angelica...we all make mistakes. I'm quite sure he didn't mean for that to happen."

Angelica ignored him and took another bite of her hoagie. "The nurse gave me a couple of Ginger Ale's to drink if you would like one."

"Oh," he said reaching to the floor. "I forgot...I brought a Tahitian Treat, Sprite, and a Cherry Coke...which one would you like?"

"I would love a Cherry Coke," she said smiling.

He opened the bottle for her and put it on her tray while she took a couple of gulps. Roman continued eating his half of the hoagie and opened the barbecue chips.

"If you don't mind me asking, are you and Winter's mother divorced?"

"We were never married. We broke up, and she met someone new."

"Why did you all breakup," Angelica asked with her mouth full of hoagie and sour cream & onion chips.

Roman smiled, "We broke up because she wasn't ready to get married."

"Do you think you all will ever be together again?"

"No," he said finishing up his half of hoagie.

"Why? I mean...I can tell that you're a good man. She'll come to her senses!"

Roman smiled at her, "She's already involved with someone else, and I got tired of waiting."

"I hear that! The woman you're looking for will come to you real soon." Roman laughed, "Roman, I'm serious! She'll come your way and all you'll have to do is open your arms and welcome her."

"What fantasy books are you reading these days!" Angelica laughed a little and Roman noticed that she was in a pleasant mood.

"I'm just saying. One of the women you're dating now is probably the one! You never know!"

Roman looked at her and ate some of his chips. Angelica ate a couple of her chips as well. "Have you talked to your husband yet?" Angelica looked at her sandwich and kept eating her chips. She totally ignored him. "Angelica, have you talked to your husband since..."

"I don't think it's going to work out between my husband and me. I think this was just the icing on the cake! We have been miserable for years and... I don't want to be with him anymore," she said in a matter-of-fact tone. She took another bite of her sandwich and looked out the window.

Roman tried to encourage her, "You know...marriage is for better or worse. The both of you can get through this and work things out."

Angelica nodded her head, "Thank you for the pep talk but our marriage died a long time ago." She started tearing up, "It will never be the same. I will never be the same. I cannot get over this one. I understand our marriage vows, and I have tried to remind him of them over the years...and I just...I can't stay anymore. I'm tired," she said crying.

"I'm sorry, I shouldn't have said anything about it," he said handing her some tissues.

"It's not your fault that my husband is the way that he is. Don't be sorry...please." Roman smiled at her. Angelica drank some of her Cherry Coke and burped unexpectedly. Roman laughed out loud and Angelica apologized, "I'm so sorry!"

"That's ok."

Angelica shook her head in disgust, "I look a mess. I sound a mess..."

"You do not look a mess, Angelica."

"Yes, I do! -All of these marks...my body looks..."

"All of the feelings that you are having now will most likely go away over time. Just give yourself time to heal. You'll work on those things in therapy so don't beat yourself up about it. The hospital has a great support network, and you will get everything you need."

"I want to get away for a little bit you know? Just for a few days so I can get myself together."

Roman agreed nodding his head, "Talk to your husband and I'm sure you all can make it happen."

Angelica shook her head, "No, I need to go away and just be with my kids...just me and my kids."

"Oh, that sounds like a good idea. Where would you want to go?"

"Maybe to the Poconos...I think I'll leave on Monday night to Atlantic City," she said daydreaming while looking out the window.

"I have a time-share in Atlantic City if you would like to use it. "

"I couldn't do that. You have already gone above and beyond the call of duty!"

Roman laughed, "I thought I was your guardian angel."

"Yeah, you are but..."

"So, if I am your guardian angel, why aren't you accepting the gift that I'm giving to you and your family?"

"That is too much," she said frowning. "No...you..."

Roman looked at her, "I'll call them tomorrow. How long would you like to stay?"

Angelica shook her head, "No...that's..."

"I'll book the room for four days."

"Roman please...no! You..."

Roman looked at her, "This is my gift to you...and your family."

"Thank you," she said crying.

"Everything is going to be ok! Trust me!" Angelica shook her head yes. Roman handed her some more tissues and cleaned up the mess while she laid back on the bed. "I'm going to head out. I have to take care of some business in the morning."

"Thank you for everything."

"Sure. That's what guardian angels do. They help to make a way out of no way!" Angelica smiled and turned on her side facing him.

"You know what?"

"What?"

"Can I talk to you for a minute? Not the policeman but my guardian angel."

Roman sat back down. "Sure."

Angelica took a deep breath, "Even though the man raped me, and violated me in the worse way...," she paused and closed her eyes. "I feel so bad even thinking...let alone saying this...," she said as the tears fell through her closed lids. "But...the way he treated me is the way that my husband should have been treating me."

Roman frowned up his face, "Why are you saying that? That man raped you. How can you even compare that to your husband?"

"Even though he had sex with me, without my permission, he *wanted* me...and as sick as that sounds...."

"Angelica, you didn't deserve to get raped! The man forced you to have sex with him!" Angelica stopped looking at him and looked out the window. "Don't say that you deserved to have someone hurt you like that!"

Angelica looked back at Roman with tears falling down her face, "He didn't hurt me...at all. He didn't physically hurt me...at all...in any way. I wish he had...I wish he had..." she said crying.

Roman walked up to the bed and put his hand on her arm, "Everything is going to be just fine."

~ Knock, Knock! ~

Another nurse on duty came into Angelica's room, "Mrs. Kings how are you feeling?

"Just tired."

The nurse nodded her head, "Just to let you know, you will be discharged tomorrow morning around 8 am. Do you have someone who can take you home?"

Angelica just stared at the nurse. Roman interceded, "Yes, I will be taking her home tomorrow."

The nurse smiled, "Great! Ms. Kings, I'll be back to check on you in about 15 minutes."

The nurse looked at Roman, and he knew what she was going to say, "I'll be leaving shortly."

The nurse smiled and left out of the room. Angelica looked at Roman, "Thank you. Thank you so much," she said crying.

He gently patted her hand, "It's ok. Just get some rest."

Angelica smiled at him, "Thank you."

Roman went in his pocket to make sure that he had his keys and checked his watch, "I'm going to head out, but I'll be here in the morning to take you home. Please call your husband."

Angelica's tears kept streaming, but she smiled, nonetheless. She sniffled a couple of times, "You have plans for tonight?"

"Yes."

"Well enjoy yourself. Life is too short not to," she said smiling at him.

"I will," he said offering his hand for a handshake.

Angelica stared at his hand. She then enveloped his hand in the both of hers.

Roman smiled, "8 o'clock?"

"Yes sir," she said staring at him. Roman walked to the door when she called him, "Roman."

He turned around, "Yes."

"Have a good time and enjoy yourself ok?"

Roman shook his head yes, "8 o'clock." Angelica waived her hand goodbye. He left out the room as the nurse came in.

Chapter 3 – Lesson: Try to Be Strong; Even When You're Not!

~Sunday 7:30 am~

Angelica woke and immediately reflected on the conversation she had with Ian after Roman left the hospital. They talked for some time about what happened and about their relationship. He begged her for another chance. He promised that he would go to marital counseling and be willing to do anything if she would just stay with him. Ian tried to ignore her request to be separated from him and just kept on begging throughout the conversation. Angelica didn't give in this time.

After showering, she brushed her teeth and thought of how often Ian said that he was sorry during their marriage. She looked at herself in the mirror. Angelica was tired and she looked tired. She jumped when she heard a knock at the door, "Yes."

"Angelica, it's Roman. Can I come in?"

"Yes," Angelica rinsed her mouth and wiped her face off. She adjusted her robe and opened the bathroom door. Roman was standing there by the bed with a bouquet of all kinds of bright colored flowers. "Thank you, Roman." He handed her the flowers, and she smelled them smiling at how fragrant they were. "They're beautiful." She placed them on top of the small dresser beside her bed.

"I brought you some sweats to wear if you didn't want to wear the clothes that you wore yesterday." Roman handed her the plastic Target bag.

"Roman, thank you! That was very thoughtful of you to do that." She went over to him and gave him a friendly hug. As they broke the embrace, Roman looked at her, "So, are...," his eyes dropped from her face to her chest. Her robe was partially open at the top exposing some of the marks below her collar bone.

Angelica looked down at her chest and quickly backed away, "I'm sorry. I didn't mean to..." She tucked her robe in around her neck.

He didn't know what to say, "Look... I'm sorry for..."

Angelica broke the tension, looked inside the bag, and wiped away her tears, "So what size did you get?"

Roman sighed and rubbed his forehead, "I figured you were a medium, but I bought you a large so that you would feel comfortable."

Angelica smiled, "Yeah right! You look nice. You're off today?"

"Yes, today and tomorrow."

"Wow. So, who's the lucky lady for tonight?" Roman laughed. "What? Don't be shy! What's her name?"

"Monica."

"Ok," she said taking the clothes in the bathroom. She closed the door, "How long have you all been dating?"

"Almost two months."

"And what do you think? Is she a candidate or just a good stand in?"

Roman laughed out loud, "Time will tell!"

"What's the run down? Kids, divorced, separated, what?"

Roman shook his head at her forward questions just as she walked back into the room, "She's divorced."

"I'm sorry," she said looking at his face. "I didn't mean to pry! I just wanted to talk...about something good."

"That's alright."

"So, you have one daughter. Do you want more children?"

"Yes."

"Can she have more?"

Roman frowned his face, "Yes! Are you about ready to go?"

Angelica could sense that he was annoyed with her, "You know what? That's ok. You go ahead! I'll catch a cab home." She waived her hand trying to downplay her emotional state, "You enjoy your day off. I need to gather my thoughts...but thank you so much for coming...and for the clothes...and flowers!"

Roman's face frowned even more, "But I'm already here. Why would you catch a cab when I'm right here to take you home?"

"Because," she said starting to tear up, "I have a lot of negative shit going on right now, and I don't want to...contaminate you...so to speak."

"Angelica, wait..."

Angelica put her things in the Target bag and put her shoes on, "Roman, I'll be fine. I'm alive, I have my children, I'll be ok...really. You go and enjoy your days off from constantly protecting and serving others," she walked over to him, "Enjoy your two days of serenity. Now go..."

"Angelica, I'm already here. It's ok."

"It's not ok Roman. Thank you for everything," she said hugging him. "Thank you. Now go, please."

"Angelica, you only live about 15-20 minutes away. I'll take you there, and that will be that." Angelica went in the bathroom and fixed her hair while looking in the mirror crying. Roman walked over to her, "I'll take you home ok," he said with his

66

hand on her shoulder. She turned toward him while keeping her head down and shook her head yes. He lifted up her head with his fingers, "I'm your guardian angel, right? This is what I have been assigned to do!" Angelica smiled as Roman tugged her hand, "Everything will be fine. You'll see!"

They agreed that she would finish with the discharge process while he went to get his car. After receiving her instructions, where to call for her results of the tests, counseling, support group information, and her prescriptions, she went out to the front of the hospital to wait for Roman. She stood out on the curb thinking about going back into that house, talking to her parents about what happened, and trying to hold it together for the kids. They had a lot of talking to do. She heard a horn going off and looked up. Roman was double parked in the street walking up to her, "Do you have everything?"

"Yes."

Roman walked with her to his truck and opened the door for her as she stepped in. He closed the door, walked over to the driver's side, and got in the truck. As he put his seatbelt on, he glanced over to Angelica, "Don't forget your seatbelt." Angelica looked down and put her seatbelt on. Roman started up his black Yukon Denali XL and pulled off. He looked at her from time to time while she just looked out of her window. "What are you thinking about?"

"Everything and nothing." Roman made a left off Civic Center Blvd and drove toward the Gray's Ferry Bridge. Angelica noticed that he was going further away from where she lived, "Where are you going?"

Roman looked at her, "Did you eat anything this morning?"

Angelica smiled a little, "No...I really don't have an appetite for anything right now."

"Well...," he said making a left at Grey's Ferry and heading toward Washington Ave, "You have to eat something. Do you like pancakes?"

"You don't have to..."

"Do you like pancakes? Yes, or No?"

Angelica looked at him and smiled, "Yes I do."

"Me too!" Roman turned on the radio so that they could listen to WRNB on 107.9. Phyllis Hyman's 'Meet Me on the Moon' was playing. Roman looked at Angelica while she continued looking out of the window. His phone started ringing, "Hello...hey, how are you...good...look, I have to call you back...ok...that's what's up...ok...bye."

Angelica overheard the woman's voice on his phone. She looked at him after he hung up, "Roman, I really don't want to go."

"Why?"

"Because, you obviously have plans for the day! I feel bad as it is already! I don't want to feel bad about infringing on someone else's time..."

"We're going! We're going to sit down, have some breakfast, and then I'm going to take you home." Roman reached Washington Ave & Columbus Blvd and made a right to go to IHOP. "Did you call your husband to let him know that I would be bringing you home?"

"Yes I did," she said looking out of the window.

"He was ok with that?"

Angelica looked at him, "Who knows and who cares. I'm done with all that analyzing and wondering why he's doing this or why did he do that! I don't want to feel like that anymore." Roman shook his head while smiling. "Why are you shaking your head?"

"No reason."

"Yes...there is a reason! Please tell me," Angelica turned her whole body toward him so that he could explain.

"It's nothing really."

"So, you don't want to say?"

Roman looked at her face and focused back on the traffic, "I just thought that in time, maybe your feelings will change about your marriage. You and your husband will probably work things out, and your marriage will be better than it has ever been. Maybe if you give him one more chance, things will work out."

Angelica looked out of the window, "Thanks for the support Officer Callowhill."

"Now we're back to Officer Callowhill? I thought that we were becoming friends."

Angelica looked at him and frowned.

Roman smiled, "Yeah, you know FRIENDS? People who talk to each other, go out, have fun, support one another...friends."

"What's your middle name," Angelica asked.

Roman looked at her and smiled, "It's Xavier."

"My guardian angel and friend, Officer Roman Xavier Callowhill! You have a very strong name."

"Thank you," he said pulling up to the parking lot. He put the truck in park, turned the car off and turned to her. "What is your middle name?"

"My whole name is Angelica Sofia Bryant...married name Kings." Roman grabbed his phone, keys, and was about to get out of the truck when she grabbed his arm. He looked at her hand on his arm and looked at her face.

Angelica removed her hand, "I'm sorry for grabbing you like that. It's just that..."

"Angelica, please stop being sorry for this or sorry for that. It's ok! It's not like you bit me or anything. We're here together! One guardian angel is having breakfast with a ...another angel!" Angelica smiled at him. "What's wrong?"

Angelica looked at her hands, "I just need a minute before I go in. You can go ahead, I'll..."

"Take your time. If you want me to go in, I will."

She shook her head, "Ok," she whispered tearing up.

Roman got out of the truck and walked toward the IHOP doors. He turned and looked at her from where he was standing. Angelica's forehead was resting on the dashboard. Roman slowly walked back to the truck. He could hear Angelica wailing as he walked closer. He lightly knocked on the door. Angelica wiped her nose with her sleeve and looked up. "It's been a minute!"

Roman opened her door and held his hand out to help her out of the car. She took his hand and nervously stepped out. Roman closed the door behind her while she just stood there looking at the ground. He put his hands on her shoulders and stooped down low to look at her face. Angelica felt like shit! She felt dirty, used up, ugly, embarrassed, and humiliated. He pulled her in and gave her a hug, "Everything will be ok. Take one minute at a time for now. Then maybe tomorrow you can do ten minutes, then thirty, hours, and then you can work your way up to days!"

"Thank you."

Roman glared, "Stop thanking me."

"No...that's the least that I can do. I hope Monica knows that she has a special man on her hands. I wish you and her all the happiness a couple can have."

Roman nodded his head, "Let's eat, shall we?"

"Yes, we shall!" Roman and Angelica went to the IHOP and was seated immediately. Angelica ordered three pancakes, three scrambled eggs with cheese, and three pieces of turkey sausage. Roman had the exact same thing. He then looked at Angelica and stared for a moment. "Why are looking at me like that? Can you see the marks," she asked trying to pull up the neck portion of her sweatshirt.

Roman shook his head, "No. I'm just admiring your strength that's all."

Angelica changed the subject, "So where are you taking Monica today?"

The waitress brought their food to the table, "...and here's your turkey sausage! I'll bring you some hot maple syrup and some more butter."

"Thank you," they said in unison.

As soon as the waitress left, Angelia bowed her head and said a silent prayer, "Amen."

Roman smiled, "Amen." Roman looked to his food and commenced eating, "I'll probably take her to the movies and out to dinner."

Angelica put some pancakes in her mouth, "That'll be nice! She should enjoy that. Have you introduced her to your daughter?"

"No," Roman answered frowning his face while adding more syrup to his pancakes.

Angelica looked at his face and tried not to take his reply personal. She changed the subject feeling really awkward, "Oh. Do you have any brothers or sisters?"

Roman laughed, "I have one brother. His name is Paul. How about you?"

"I have a sister named Linda. She lives in Florida. What about your mom and dad?"

"My mom and dad live here in Philly. My dad just had a heart attack not too long ago, though."

Angelica put her fork down, "I'm sorry to hear that," Angelica said touching his hand. Roman looked down at her hand on top of his and Angelica quickly pulled away. "I..."

Roman had a frustrated look on his face, "Don't start apologizing! It's ok to touch my hand and to give me a hug...always remember that!" Angelica gave him a fake smile and looked out of the window, "What are you thinking about?"

She shook her head, "Everything and nothing."

"One minute at a time...one minute at a time. Try not to overwhelm yourself with the world right now. Just try to concentrate on getting yourself back on track." Angelica smiled and continued to look out of the window. "Is your husband at home right now waiting for you?" Angelica shrugged her shoulders without looking at him. "Did you change your mind about going away?"

"No. But I think I just might go and see my sister at some point instead of inconveniencing you with your timeshare."

Roman stuffed his mouth with pancakes, "It's really ok Angelica! I booked your room and everything already!"

Angelica looked at him and quickly wiped her eyes, "What! Oh, my goodness! How much do I owe you?"

"Nothing." The waitress put extra napkins on the table, "Thank you." Roman smiled,

"Angelica, you don't owe me anything! Just enjoy yourself."

"This may sound kind of crazy but, I don't think I can leave Philly right now. Maybe next month," she said biting a piece of sausage.

"Why," he said frowning up his face, "Jersey is not that far and you all would really enjoy it."

"I just don't think that I can deal with being too far away." Roman just looked at her. "I just need to be close to those who are for me...right now..."

Roman interrupted her, "I understand."

Angelica continued to explain as if he didn't understand what she was trying to say. "I just don't feel that safe. I would like to but...," she said looking out of the restaurant window.

"Angelica," Roman said smiling, "...its' ok!"

"Thank you," she said tearing up.

Roman put his hands over hers, "No problem." Roman squeezed both of her hands and Angelica looked at him. "Angelica, I am your friend.

I'm here to help you and your family in any way that I can."

Tears were falling down Angelica's eyes, "And I am your friend." She pulled her hands away, "I have to go to the restroom." She got up and went to walk to the restroom when he grabbed her arm. Roman stood up, walked closer to her, and opened his arms. Angelica put her head on his chest and held him close.

He rubbed her back, "It's ok. Everything is going to be ok." Roman let her sit back down next to him in the booth. When he sat down next to her, she put her head on his chest, and he put his arm around her. "Angelica, let's eat the rest of our food before it gets cold."

"Ok." As they ate their breakfast, Angelica laughed at his jokes and stories about his daughter. She entertained him as well with stories from her own children.

The waitress gave Roman the check about twenty minutes later, "I'll take that whenever you're ready."

"Thanks. That was really good. I'm stuffed," he said rubbing his stomach.

Angelica nodded her head, "I think that will be the only meal for me today," she said smiling.

"It better not be! I'm quite sure your husband will cook for you over the next few months or so." Angelica didn't say anything. "Are you ready to go?"

"Yes."

Roman pulled out his wallet and put the money for the bill and tip on the table. He got up and then helped her out of the booth. They walked to the truck, got in, and Roman drove on his way to drop Angelica off at home. Angelica fell asleep 10 minutes into the ride. Roman stared at her when he arrived at a red light on Washington Ave. She was sleeping so peacefully. It only took him twenty-five minutes to get to her home. He pulled up in front of her house and gently nudged her on the arm, "Angelica, we're here. Angelica?"

"Yes," she said with her eyes still closed.

"We're here," he said putting his hand on top of hers. She opened her eyes and looked at him. "You're home." Angelica looked at the front of her house and she wished she did not have to go in right then. "Angelica...here," Roman gave her a card with his name and contact numbers on it. "I want you to call me from time to time to let me know that you are alright...if you want to. If not..."

Angelica took the card, "I will call you. I won't bug you though...I..."

"Angelica, I'm your friend. Call me whenever you like."

Angelica gave him a hug, "I know God is going to get me through, because he sent me a friend." She then looked very scared.

He grabbed her hand, "Tell me."

"I'm so scared! I don't want you to leave," she said crying really bad. Roman held her as she cried. A few silent moments passed by while he just held her. Angelica slowly pushed him away, "Roman, thank you." She grabbed her bag, got out of the truck, and quickly closed the door.

Roman rolled the window down, "Angelica...one minute at a time," he said smiling. Angelica turned around and gave him a fake smile. She waved her hand goodbye, walked up the steps, and into the house. She closed the door without looking back. Roman waited for a few moments and then pulled off.

Chapter 4 – Lesson: Real Friends are There When You Need Them!

~Sunday @10:49 pm

After speaking with the kids, Angelica dialed Roman's cell number. The phone rang a few times but, she hung up because she didn't want to leave a message. She tried calling again and chickened out! She laid back on the bed and held on to one of the new pillows. Angelica was glad that Ian *at least* bought new linen for the room. He never lifted a finger before. She appreciated his help, even though it was years too late. Her cell phone rang, "Hello?"

"Angelica, it's Roman. Are you ok?"

Angelica began to tear up, "No not really. I can't sleep...I just wanted to..."

Roman interrupted her. He was extremely upset, "Didn't your husband get your prescription filled?"

Angelica looked at the ceiling feeling stupid, "Ummm..."

"Well... did you tell him that you need

them?"

Angelica could hear that he was upset. It made her feel even worse, "No...I..." Roman sighed loud enough for her to hear. Angelica started crying. She felt horrible about calling him in the first place! He wasn't her husband. He was just a damn stranger! She became angry at herself for even allowing her sick mind to think that a damn stranger would have her back after knowing each other for two days! "I'm sorry. Forget I called." Angelica pressed the end button and closed her phone. Roman called right back, but Angelica didn't answer. After ten more calls, Angelica decided to answer, "Hello?"

"Talk to me! Don't hang up on me. Just talk to me," Roman said trying not to yell, but failing miserably.

"Just forget it ok! I'm sorry for hanging up on you. I'm sorry! Just forget that I called you. Don't call me back. Just forget it." Angelica hung up the phone.

Roman called back, but Angelica didn't answer. She just laid on the bed looking out the window with the television off. As her cell phone continued to ring, she just laid there crying. She tried to go to sleep, but the phone just kept on ringing and ringing. Angelica looked at the clock, and it was now 11:55. She thought that he would have stopped calling, but he didn't. She answered her phone but took a few moments before she said anything, "Yes?"

Roman kept his cool and spoke gently, "Did you eat dinner?"

She sighed, "Yes."

"What did you have?"

"Some chicken noodle soup," she said getting comfortable in her bed.

"Are you in the bed?"

"Yes."

"Where is your husband," he asked sounding irritated.

"He's not here."

Roman sighed, "How do you feel about that?"

"Look," she said taking a deep breath. "I...I just don't feel safe. I'm sorry for calling you. I shouldn't have called you in the first place. You've done more than enough already! I'm so sorry."

Roman sighed, "Stop Angelica, please! I understand what you're going through. I am here to help you in any way that I can."

Angelica was quiet, "Did you see Monica today or speak to Winter?"

Roman laughed, "I'm with Winter now. She's in her room sleep."

"Awe!! I thought that you were going out with Monica today."

"No. What are you doing tomorrow?"

"Well since my kids are going to stay with my parents for the week, I'll be here."

"You might want to get some fresh air," he suggested.

"If I do, I'll open a window!" Roman laughed along with her. Angelica changed the subject, "What are you all doing tomorrow?"

"I might take Winter to the Zoo and then out to get some ice cream."

"She'll definitely enjoy that! Look Roman, you a have a good day tomorrow ok."

"You try and do the same."

"I will! Good night Roman."

"See you tomorrow."

"What," she said laughing.

"I said see you tomorrow. What, you don't want me to stop by and say hello?"

Angelica shook her head, "It's not that, it's just that you have your daughter, and I don't want to..."

"Angelica, I'm going to drive down your block, say hi then I'm rolling out! It will be a ten-minute visit at the most!"

Angelica laughed, "Ten minutes?"

"Ten minutes and you can meet Winter if you like!"

"That sounds great! Goodnight Roman and again thank you."

"Can you do me a favor," Roman asked.

"Anything," Angelica said.

"Stop thanking me!"

"I'm trying to! Just don't be mad if I say it ok?"

"I won't. Don't forget to remind your husband about your medicine ok?"

"I'll see you tomorrow."

"Yes, you will Angelica! Bye."

"Bye." Angelica hung up her phone and put it underneath her pillow. She took a couple of deep breaths and fell asleep.

~

"Angelica...Angelica?"

Angelica opened her eyes. Ian was sitting on the bed next to her smiling. "I made you some breakfast. Would you like to eat?"

"No thank you."

"It's almost 11:30. I just came by to pick up a couple of things," he said staring at her.

Angelica stretched, "Can you pick up my prescription please?"

"Sure. Did you want anything in particular from the store?"

"No thanks."

"Alright. I'll be back shortly," Ian put his hand on her back and left out of the room. Angelica closed her eyes and tried to fall back to sleep. She thought about Ian and the conversation they had last night about their marriage. When she told Ian how she felt, he was completely supportive of what she wanted. He didn't even try to fight for the marriage. Although she was hurt that he didn't say his famous 'we can work it out' or 'don't do this to our family,' Angelica was at peace with knowing that at least he was honest. Ian looked so peaceful this morning as if a weight had been lifted from his life. She was happy for him. Angelica changed positions and felt her phone vibrating. She forgot that it was underneath her pillow! When she opened the phone, she had two missed calls and one text. One was from her sister Linda. The other call and text were from Roman. She opened the text:

Good Morning! It's Roman. I'm just checking up on you! Talk to you later.

Angelica smiled and went to her voicemail to listen to her messages. Her sister left a message asking Angelica to call her when she got a chance. She deleted the message and moved on to Roman's message:

Hey, Angelica, It's Roman. I was going to come by if that's ok with you. It's now 11:15 and we're headed to the Zoo. Give me a call and let me know if you want me to stop by. Talk to you soon. Bye!

Angelica deleted the message and called Roman!

~

Roman and Winter were walking past the Elephants, "Daddy, they smell! Can they give them baths before the zoo opens so they won't smell so bad?"

Roman laughed along with Winter, "Baby, they do smell! But we might smell different to them too. -Give them a bath before the zoo opens, that's funny!"

"Daddy, your phone is ringing," she said taking his phone out of his back pocket and handing it to him.

"Thank you," he said smiling. "Hello?"

"Hi, Roman it's Angelica."

"Hey! How are you," he said keeping an eye on Winter.

"I'm ok."

"Still in bed?"

Angelica chuckled, "Yeah."

"Did you still want me to stop by? I can shoot over there after I take Winter home this evening."

"That would be great."

"Alright, I'll see you around eight ok?"

"Sure."

Winter tugged at Roman, "Daddy, can I have some cotton candy?"

"Sure baby." Angelica smiled hearing Winter through the phone. It made her miss being with her kids. Will they see her differently too? "Did you eat yet?"

"No."

Roman sighed and said something underneath his breath.

Angelica thought she heard him curse, "What did you say?"

"Nothing...I'll see you at 8," Roman hung up the phone and tended to Winter.

Angelica stared at the phone. Did he just hang up on her? She had a feeling that she might be getting on his nerves, so she decided to call him back. "Hello, Roman?"

"Yes."

"I don't mean to bother you again...but am I getting on your nerves?"

"No! What would make you say that?"

"Well, since you just hung up on me...and the fact that you said something smart underneath your breath made me..."

"Angelica, I'm sorry. You are not getting on my nerves," he laughed. "Are we still on for 8?"

"Yes, sir!"

"Alright! I'll see you then!"

"Bye."

Angelica got out the bed, plugged her alarm clock into the socket. She set the time and alarm so that she could wake up at 7. Angelica laid back down and felt so much better. Her nerves were at ease. She just needed to try to get some more rest. Angelica tried to meditate by counting the deep breaths that she inhaled. After about 15 breaths, she fell asleep.

Beep, Beep, Beep!

Angelica opened her eyes and got up in a frenzy to turn the alarm off. It was getting dark outside, and she could tell that Ian wasn't in the house. She looked at her phone and Roman called her at 7:14. It was now 7:27. She hurried up and pressed the call button on her phone, "Hello, Roman it's Angelica."

"Hey, what's up. You still want me to come pass?"

"Yes. Did you and Winter have a good time at the zoo," she asked trying to find something simple and comfortable to put on.

"Winter loves the zoo! I have a yearly pass so that we can go whenever she wants."

"That is so cute."

"Did you eat yet," Roman asked drying his body off. Angelica was purposefully quiet because she slept through the day. "Angelica, are you still there?"

"Yes. I'm still here. No, I didn't eat anything. I'll grab something from the fridge before you stop pass."

Roman was quiet. "Angelica, is your husband there?"

"No."

"Have you been in bed all day?"

Angelica was reluctant to answer and thought about lying, "I'm fine."

Roman sighed, "I'll be there in fifteen minutes to pick you up."

"Where are we going?"

"Just be ready in fifteen minutes ok?"

"Ummm...ok." Angelica took a shower trying not to look at her body. As she cleaned herself in the near-scalding water, she stared at her breasts. She couldn't help but laugh at her body and how she looked like a fucking Dalmatian with red spots! She then started crying! Angelica cried out her fears, her anger, and frustrations with her husband and with the man who came in her room Friday night. She calmed down after her chest ached from crying so much. After turning off the water, she dried herself off.

Angelica put on her underwear, a sports bra, black workout pants, and a gray long sleeve shirt. She looked at herself in the mirror and put her hair in a ponytail. While staring at herself in the mirror, she slowly put on deodorant and simple silver balled-post earrings. Angelica held back her tears promising herself, and God, that she would take one moment at a time. Her phone started vibrating on her dresser, and she smiled when she saw that it was Roman. "Hello?"

"Hey! I'm right outside your door."

"I'll be right there." Angelica grabbed her phone and her purse and left out of the house, leaving the lights on in every room except the children's.

Roman was standing on the curb in front of her home smiling, "You missed the sun today! But let me tell you it was beautiful!"

"Oh yeah," she said laughing, "How did Winter enjoy the sun today?"

"I'll tell you all about it on our way to eat," Roman put his hand on her back and guided her to the passenger side of the truck. He opened the door for her while she sat down. Roman walked over to his side, hopped in, and pulled off. "It was so beautiful out today, it was crazy! We woke up, I cooked her pancakes, eggs, and turkey sausage..."

"Now that sounds familiar!"

Roman smiled, "After breakfast, we got washed, dressed, and went to the zoo. We went out to lunch, got some ice cream, took a nap..."

"You all took a nap?"

"Yes, we were so tired from all that walking that we had to go to sleep!"

"I know what you mean," Angelica said smiling.

"So, I cooked some dinner and then I took her home."

Angelica stared at him, "What did you cook?"

"I made some spaghetti, and she made the garlic bread."

"What did you put in the spaghetti?"

Roman looked at her suspiciously, "A little of this and that."

Angelica acted as if she was offended and held her mouth wide open, "Oh you can't share your recipe with me?"

Roman stopped at the red light and turned to her, "I put some onions, green peppers, garlic, mushrooms, and ground turkey in the sauce."

"Now that sounds good," she said looking out the window.

"What would you like to eat?"

"Where could we go to eat really quick at this hour without eating fast food?"

"I do have a whole pot of spaghetti at the house. We could eat out on the front porch if you feel comfortable enough to do that."

"What? Roman please! Let's go and eat some spaghetti at your place." Roman looked at her smiling. He continued down 60th and made a left on Walnut to the Cobbs Creek Parkway. "Where do you live?"

"I live in Overbrook."

"Dag! You're only a hop-skip-and-a-jump away!"

"So, your husband didn't come back?"

"Let's not talk about that please," she said smiling at Roman. He looked upset and shook his head. He didn't say anything to her for a while. Angelica felt his negative vibes, "Maybe this wasn't a good idea. We can do this another time," she said with a fake smile on her face while nodding her head.

Roman looked at her angrily. He changed lanes, pulled off to the side of the road, and put the truck in park. Angelica knew he was upset, but she didn't feel threatened by him. Roman turned his whole body toward her so that she could clearly see him, "Angelica I don't know your husband. I'm just going to say that I'm here if you need me ok. That's all I'm going to say. I'm not going to say how I feel about a man who doesn't take care of his wife. I'm here if you need me."

"I appreciate that," Angelica said smiling. Roman just stared at her face. Angelica looked away. "Why are you looking at me like that?"

"Sorry." Roman turned his head to look at the traffic. He adjusted his position, put the truck in drive, and pulled off. They arrived at his home about 10 minutes later. As they pulled up to his house, Angelica looked out the window at the neighboring homes. He pulled into his driveway and turned off the truck. "You ready?"

"Yes, sir!" Angelica got out of the truck by herself and followed him to the front porch. Roman opened the front door and let her in first. Angelica went right on in and could smell the spaghetti. "It smells so good in here!"

"The sauce is still a little warm. Do you still want to eat out on the porch?"

"We don't have to. I mean... we can eat in the living room." Roman just looked at her. "Do you need help in the kitchen?"

Roman laughed, "No, I'm good. You just have a seat on the couch, and I'll bring you a bowl of spaghetti." Angelica nodded her head. Roman turned on the television, handed her the remote, and walked in the kitchen. Angelica took off her shoes and sat back on his comfortable couch. She grabbed one of his pillows and hugged it as she watched a movie on HBO. Roman peeked in on her to see what she was doing as he fixed her bowl. He then walked back into the living room, "What would you like to drink?"

"What do you have?"

Roman smiled, "What do you want?"

"You are a mess! I'll have some tea please," Angelica said laughing.

"What kind? Hot, Cold?"

"Hot, with lemon and sugar please," she said smiling and batting her eyelashes. Roman smiled back at her and shook his head.

A few moments later, Roman brought the bowl of spaghetti to her, "Here you are. The water is warming for your tea."

"Thank you so much," she said scooting up to the coffee table so that she could eat. Roman sat down on the opposite side of the couch. She bowed her head, said her grace, and began to eat. "Mmmm! Roman, this is so good! I mean this is really good," she said with a mouth full of spaghetti. Roman laughed at her. She chewed up her food smiling, "What's so funny?"

Roman moved next to her, took one of the napkins he put on the table for her and wiped her nose. "You have spaghetti sauce on your nose," he said still laughing. He looked at her laughing and slowly stopped laughing. He put the napkin on the table and moved back to where he was sitting. Angelica saw the change in his mood and just focused on eating the rest of her food. She finished the last bit of spaghetti in the bowl and wiped her mouth with one of the napkins. The tea kettle in the kitchen started to blow, and Roman got up to make the tea.

"You know what, don't bother with the tea. I'll just have a quick cup of water. Thank you."

Roman quickly went in the kitchen and turned off the stove. He returned to the living room with a frown on his face, "Angelica it's ok. I can make you a cup of tea. It's not a problem."

"It is. I'm sorry."

"I don't know why you feel like that," Roman stared at her without blinking.

"Why do you look at me like that," Angelica asked feeling herself getting upset.

"I look at you like that because...," he stopped talking and looked at her neck.

Angelica looked down and knew he was staring at the marks that were peeking around her collarbone. She was infuriated! "Roman, thank you for the food and for being there for me over these past two days. I really appreciate all that you have done but, if you don't mind...I would like to go home."

"Why, you don't have to leave."

"Roman thank you for dinner. I just need to go home."

"Angelica, what's wrong?" Roman said getting close to her.

"Please!" Angelica looked at him and started crying. "Thank you for being nice to me. I am really grateful for all the things you have done for me...really." Angelica stood up and stood by the front door to leave.

Roman sighed, "I'm sorry for staring at you like that."

Angelica waved her hand at him while smiling. She tried her best to appear as if she was fine. "It's ok. I just need to go home and get some rest," she said fighting back the tears.

Roman walked over toward Angelica. Angelica looked at him walking toward her and felt uneasy. "You know what? You did a lot today, just let me call a cab."

"What?!" Roman started to get a little upset, "Angelica, it is late, and there is no way I'm putting you in a cab when I can just take you home myself!"

"Roman, please! You have done more than enough and again... I am thankful for all that you have done. To be totally honest with you, I can't just expect you to help me through what's going on in **my** life! You have a life, a very dangerous job, a child, and a woman...and I barely even know you!" Roman walked closer to her, and Angelica backed up, "I'm sorry!" She walked over to the couch, grabbed her purse, and headed for the door.

Roman went over to her, grasped her arms, and hugged her, "Angelica, its ok. It's ok." Roman rubbed her back and rested his chin on the top of her head. "I'll take you home ok."

Angelica pulled away, "No, I'll catch a cab!"

"No, you won't! I brought you here, and I'll take you back home. Come and sit down for a minute." Angelica reluctantly followed him back to the couch. He sat down on one end, and she sat on the other. Roman moved closer to her, put his arms around her, and just held her. After thirty minutes, she fell fast asleep. Roman tried to wake her, "Angelica. Angelica?"

"Yes," she said sitting up.

"I have to take you home."

Angelica's eyes slowly closed on their own, "Can you take me to a hotel for the night, please? I don't want to go back there tonight. How...'bout..." Angelica fell back to sleep while talking.

Roman smiled and rubbed her arms trying to wake her up again, "Angelica, I have to take you home."

Angelica's eyes wouldn't open! They were too heavy, "Roman...please. Just tell Monica I slept on the couch. I promise I won't be in the way. Please don't take me back there." Angelica fell fast asleep again. Roman smiled, picked her up, and took her upstairs in his room. He took off her socks and laid her underneath his thick comforter. He then turned off the light and started to walk out of the room. "Roman," Angelica called out in a terrified tone.

"Yes," he said turning on the light.

"Where are you going," she asked frantically.

"Downstairs."

Angelica sat up looking frightened, "I know you and Monica have something special...and I'm in no way trying to get in the way of that...but..." She stopped talking because Roman turned off the light and walked over to the bed. "Roman?!"

"I'm right here." Roman laid right next to her on his back. She snuggled up to him and laid her head on his shoulder. Roman felt her body go limp after about twenty minutes. As she began breathing heavily, he tried to pull himself away from her so that he could adjust his position.

"Roman...please...stay," Angelica said while sleeping. Roman pulled away from her and went downstairs. He grabbed her purse, opened her cell phone, and looked for Ian's cell phone number. He sent a text message to Ian:

> *I fell asleep over a friend's house. I'll be home in the morning.*

He put her phone back, went to the bathroom, and laid back down next to Angelica. As soon as he got comfortable in bed, she moved closer to him and put her head on his chest. Roman put his arm around her and fell asleep.

Chapter 5 – Lesson: All We Need is a Little Love!

~Tuesday, June 9th @ 9:38 am

Angelica sat up quickly, looked around, and glanced at the clock. She saw an envelope on the nightstand by the bed with her name on it. She opened it up:

Good Morning! Angelica, I tried to wake you last night to take you home, but you kept saying that you didn't want to leave. I sent your husband a text message telling him that you fell asleep over a friend's house and that you would be home in the morning. There are some bagels and muffins on the kitchen table for you so help yourself. Call me after you have eaten!

Roman

Angelica put her socks on and went downstairs. She opened her cell phone, and there were no messages or calls. She called her mom's house and Hailey answered the phone, "Hi mom!"

"Hey, baby! How are you? Why aren't you at camp?"

"We were too tired from playing late last night. We just woke up a couple of minutes ago!"

"So did I!" They both laughed. Angelica missed them so much, but she knew she needed this week to get herself together.

"Is daddy there?"

"No, he's not. Where are Kendall and Gavin," she said walking in the kitchen.

"They're upstairs watching a movie. Mom-mom is in the kitchen cooking."

"Ok. I just wanted to check up on you guys. Tell mom-mom I'll talk to her later ok? I love you!"

"Ok, mom. Love you too! Bye!"

"Bye!" Angelica looked at the table and was in awe at how he set up the different flavored bagels and muffins on the table. She then called Ian on his cell phone.

He picked up on the third ring, "Hey stranger! Everything ok?"

"Yeah, how about you?"

"I'm good."

"Look, Ian, I'm going away for a couple of days. I'll be back before the kids come home. I'll give you all the information later this evening."

"Ok." Ian paused and sighed, "The doctor...called and said that all your tests came back negative."

Angelica looked at the ceiling giving thanks to God, "Thanks, Ian. I gotta go. I'll talk to you later."

Ian stayed silent for a moment not exactly sure of what to say next, "Ok."

"Alright, bye."

Ian closed his eyes knowing that he should have said something other than 'ok.' "Bye."

Angelica picked up a muffin and a bagel and took it upstairs in Roman's bed. She pressed Roman's name on her cell. He answered on the first ring! "Hi."

"Good Morning!"

"Good Morning! Thank you for letting me stay. I really appreciate it! Just to let you know, I'm going to take a quick nap and then I'm going to head out."

"Angelica, take your time. It's no rush. I get off at 4:30. If you're still there, I'll take you home. Did you talk to your husband?"

Angelica was quiet, "Yes. If it's ok with you, I'll chill out here until you get off."

Roman smiled, "Sure! Make yourself at home. You can't be spending the night like this, or else Monica will get jealous!"

Angelica laughed, "Just tell her I'm family, and I needed a place to stay for the night...and part of the day!"

Roman laughed, "I'll see you when I get home."

"Yes, you will!"

"Angelica, you doing ok this morning?"

"I'm doing great now that...," Angelica caught herself and stopped talking.

"**That** what?"

"Nothing. I'll see you when you get here. Be safe out there!"

"Did you eat yet?"

"Noooo, but I'm about to," she said looking at the bran muffin and the cinnamon-raisin bagel.

"There's plenty in the fridge for snacks and lunch so help yourself."

"Thanks, dad!"

Roman laughed, "I'll check up on you later."

"Bye."

"Bye."

Angelica ate the bran muffin and laid back down in Roman's bed. His bed was so comfortable, and it smelled just like him. She fell asleep ten minutes after laying down. Her mind dreamt of all kinds of crazy events as if she was Alice in Wonderland. It was as if she was watching a video of what she was actually dreaming! She dreamt of arguing with Ian in their living room. Then the scene switched to her holding a machete over his head while he was sleeping in their bed. As she swung the machete to cut his head off, the scene switched to her being in bed with...the man. He had on the same mask with his eyes and mouth exposed. He started eating her pussy while squeezing her thighs. In the dream, Angelica was blindfolded, like they were that night, but her hands were bound to the bed. He kept eating her pussy so good that she tried not to come, but she did. His mouth was moving indicating that he was talking to her, but in the dream, the sound was muted out. The man grabbed his penis and put it inside of her. In the dream, he didn't have on a condom, and she could definitely feel the difference.

She kept trying to scream but she couldn't. He wasn't fucking her. He was making love to her nice and slow. In the dream, Angelica started crying because it felt so good and she knew she shouldn't be enjoying it. Then the scene switched to him holding her up legs while he pushed his dick inside. Suddenly he put her legs down and laid on top of her. The sound suddenly came in, "I want you to come with me!" She kept saying no and shaking her head while he continued making love to her. Then the scene switched to him still making love to her, without her hands being tied to the bed. The volume suddenly turned up! Angelica was moaning and begging for him to come inside of her. Although he was saying something to her, his voice was now muted. Angelica was making all kinds of loud noises. As he raised his head up to the ceiling and slowed his tempo, Angelica could feel the come inside of her. He lowered his head to her face, and she put her hands on his black-clothed mask. She started pulling on it...then opened her eyes.

Angelica sat up and had tears still on her face and the pillow. She looked at her phone, and it was 4:53. She hopped out of bed, looked in the hall closet, and grabbed a towel and washcloth so that she could take a quick shower. Angelica looked at her body while she washed and kept repeating to herself, "This is still **my** body." She finished up showering, turned off the water, and turned on the faucet so that she could brush her teeth with her washcloth. She hadn't done this since she was little. Her mom would always tell her to use her washcloth if she forgot her toothbrush while spending the night at someone's house. Angelica smiled as she finished up. She opened his mouthwash and poured a capful. After she swished, gargled, then spit, she turned off the water. She looked in the mirror making sure she didn't miss a spot on her face. Angelica smiled, grabbed her cloth, and opened the bathroom door.

Roman startled her as she bumped right into him. She put her hand on her forehead, "Oh my God! Roman, you scared the shit out of me! I didn't even hear you come in!" Angelica looked at him from head to toe in his uniform.

Roman smiled, "I called you on the phone twice, and I called your name when I walked in the door. When you didn't say anything, I figured you were still asleep." He looked at her from head to toe, "I see you found where the towels were!"

"Yes I did," she said walking in his bedroom. Roman walked behind her and could see marks on her back. "How was work," she said turning around looking at him.

"Work, was good."

"Yeah...as long as you're safe, right?"

"You know it. So, what's the plan," he asked taking off his shoes.

"Well, I'm going away for a couple of days," she said watching him.

"Where to?"

"I'm going to stay at a hotel. Probably at the Hilton on City Line Ave."

"When," he said unbuttoning his shirt.

Angelica stared at him taking his shirt off revealing his white tee shirt and his bulletproof vest, "I'm going to try to check in tomorrow afternoon." She kept looking at him while he put his uniformed shirt and the bulletproof vest on a hanger. He kept his tee shirt on, though. "Did you speak with Monica today."

"Yeah she called me not to long ago," he said emptying his pockets in his dresser drawer.

Angelica's eyes were glued to his every move for some odd reason, "What did she say about me spending the night last night?"

"She wasn't so happy about that," he said shaking his head

Angelica continued to study him, "Why didn't you tell her that I was a family member?"

"Monica and I are friends, but we're not committed to one another," he said looking in his wallet. "I'm quite sure she has friends too, even though she tells me that she doesn't."

Angelica frowned, "I'm sorry Roman."

He walked up to her, "What did I tell you about that," he said smiling.

"Sorry daddy!" Roman squinted his eyes at her and shook his head. "What's with the look?"

"Don't call me daddy."

"Are you getting mad at me," she said standing up to him, "Whatcha' gonna do about it Officer?" Angelica laughed and pushed him in the chest.

Roman stared at her and looked down at her towel and then back to her eyes, "Just don't call me daddy ok." Angelica poked her tongue out at him. "And you can't do that either!"

"Roman please..." Angelica caught him looking at her chest with numerous red marks. She pulled up on the towel, "I'm sorry." She grabbed her clothes and purse and went to the bathroom to get dressed so that she could leave. Angelica quickly closed the door. As soon as she entered the bathroom, she closed the lid on the toilet, sat down, and started to cry quietly.

Roman walked to the door and sighed, "Angelica, I didn't mean to..."

"Roman, it's ok really," she said turning on the water trying to keep him from hearing the noises she made while crying.

"Can I come in?"

"Ummm, I'll be out in a minute ok. I'm just getting dressed. I'll meet you downstairs," she said standing quickly. She went over to the sink and just hung her head low trying to get herself together.

"I'm coming in," Roman opened the door, and she was just standing there leaning on the sink. "Please don't be upset."

"It's ok. I'm fine. I'll meet you downstairs." Roman went up to her to give her a hug, and she pushed him back. "I'm fine, really," she said looking at him with tears running down her face, "It's me, not you. I'll be fine."

"Can I have a hug then?"

"Roman I'll be down in minute ok. Give me ten minutes."

"If your fine and if it's ok, why can't we hug on it?"

"Roman," she sighed, "I'm...I don't think..."

Roman hugged her close. Angelica laid her head on his chest and closed her eyes. She stopped crying and held on to him. They held each other without saying a word until Roman pulled back and kissed her on the cheek, "Do you feel better?"

"Yes. I'm going to leave after I get dressed..."

"No, you're not! We're going to eat dinner because I know you didn't eat any lunch...and then I'll take you home."

"Roman, I'm serious."

"I'm serious too," he said hugging her again, "I'm your guardian angel you must do as I say!" Roman leaned back but didn't break their embrace, "Let me see your face." Angelica just buried her face in his tee shirt. He put his finger under her chin and lifted her face, "I'll take you home after we eat." Angelica smiled, and Roman held on to her and kissed her on the cheek again. They stared at each other for a minute then Angelica stepped back breaking their embrace. Her towel fell to the floor, and Roman stood there staring at her body.

"Oh my God," she said wrapping the towel back around her. "I'm sorry! I got...I'm sorry...I gotta go," she said getting upset. Roman just stood there staring. "Why are you looking at me like that? I know my body looks horrible, but you could have at least turned around! Not...just stand, stand there staring at me like that," she said stuttering angrily.

Roman reached out and gently stroked her arm, "I'm sorry Angelica but…"

"But what? I look like a fucking freak, right? I know," Angelica yelled.

"Angelica, I already saw the marks at your house remember?"

"Oh God," Angelica screamed. She grabbed her clothes and went into his bedroom and closed the door. After getting dressed in record time, she grabbed her phone and opened the door.

Roman was standing in the hallway blocking her way to the stairs. He walked up to her, "Your body is beautiful Angelica. **That's** why I was staring at you like that."

"Roman, excuse me! Can you please step aside so that I can leave?"

Roman pulled her close to him again, "Believe me, Angelica. I'm not lying to you. Your body is absolutely amazing…despite the marks! Trust me. You and your body…are beautiful." Angelica looked at him with tears in her eyes. He backed up a little and put his hands on her face.

"You are a wonderful, beautiful woman. I feel honored that you want me to be in your life...even as a friend!" Angelica continued to let the tears fall as she listened to him. Roman moved his face in close to Angelica as if he were about to kiss her.

Angelica gently pushed him back, "Don't."

Roman's eyes grew cold. "I'll be downstairs."

Angelica went back into the room and sat down on the bed. She knew that things were beginning to get complicated. After all, she did spend the night, and he saw her naked...twice! Angelica shook her head while placing her hair into a ponytail. Whatever *this* was, it was going to stop. She grabbed her phone and went downstairs.

Roman was sitting on the couch waiting for her as she walked down the steps. She stood in front of him while he sat down on the couch looking up at her. "Roman, I'm sorry about all of this...SHIT that I'm putting you through. I'm not in a good place right now. It's not your responsibility to care for me, and I'm sorry that I latched on to you this way. I'm sorry! I hope, in time, that you will forgive me." Angelica grabbed her purse and started for the door.

Roman sat up and grabbed her arm.
Angelica instinctively pulled away! "Angelica!"

Angelica grabbed the doorknob, "I'll catch the bus home. I don't live far. I'll be fine. I need to be by myself for a while. I'll call you soon."

Roman let his hand fall from her arm, "Ok. You know my number."

Angelica smiled, opened the door, and left!

~Three days later...June 12th~

Angelica woke up and looked at the ceiling. "Thank you, God, for letting me waking me up this morning." She sat up, took a couple of deep breaths, and went into the bathroom. As she sat on the toilet, she looked at her tub. As soon as she closed her eyes, she remembered his breath on her neck while they were taking a bath. Angelica slowly opened her eyes and just stared at the tub again.

For the past three days, this happened over and over. She kept reliving that night. Today was the day to seek counsel.

While finishing up in the bathroom, she recalled her parent's concern. Her mom wanted to spend some time with her but respected Angelica's choice to hold off. She needed just a little more time to get mentally stronger before she spent time with her mom. Angelica spoke with her often throughout the day and appreciated the offer to keep the kids a few more weeks. It would be like a vacation away from home for the kids which they absolutely loved! She knew her parents were spoiling them rotten.

Angelica missed them terribly, but they needed this time away just to be kids! She figured they were better off being with their grandparents while she tried to heal. Angelica walked back into the bedroom and turned on the television. She drifted off to sleep and was startled when she heard her cell phone ringing. It was Roman. He had been calling two to four times a day since she left his home. He sent her text messages and left many voicemail messages. Angelica didn't have the nerve to listen to his voice, so she just deleted them all without listening to them. His texts were unavoidable to see, but she didn't respond. She knew that she had to face him soon and put an end to whatever... this was.

While staring at the television screen, she noticed the animated movie Coraline just came on. In the movie, a new family just moved into their new home. Angelica scowled her face. She continued to watch the movers haul the family's belongings out of the moving truck. She smiled and thought about what that might feel like for her and the kids! They could move somewhere else and start anew! Angelica smiled and continued watching Coraline. She admired the little girl's courage, imagination, and tenacity! Her cell phone rang again. Roman flashed on her screen.

She couldn't avoid him forever. Angelica smiled at the thought but knew it was only fair, to be honest. She stared at the screen. Having Roman around made her feel safe, but she didn't have a real friendship to offer. She wanted and needed comfort, understanding, and love. Since her marriage was over, Ian wasn't an option and hadn't been for many years. She knew why she was latching onto Roman. He seemed to be a nice man. Even though she desperately needed what he was giving her, Roman didn't deserve to have someone who couldn't reciprocate. Angelica called him back.

He answered on the first ring, "Angelica?"

She smiled, "Hi. How are you?"

Roman muffled the phone as if he were busy, "I need to speak with you. I'll stop by at 430." He then hung up the phone.

Angelica stared at the phone and shook her head. She looked at the television and stared at Coraline's blue hair. Yes! She needed a change too! She was going to make some changes with herself, her life, and her home! Angelica went downstairs and fixed a bowl of cereal determined to go outside today! After eating, she spoke with the kids and her mom. The kids were doing great and were in FACT being spoiled out of their minds! Today they were going downtown for dinner and movie. Tomorrow they were on their way to Clementon Park! Angelica listened to their excitement and was happy for them! She loved them so much and was determined to get better especially for them.

As soon as they finished talking, she called the therapist that was referred to her from the doctor at the hospital. She scheduled an appointment and thanked God that she took off work for the remainder of the summer! As soon as she began to feel happy about the days of summer, thoughts of the night crept in. She refocused back to Coraline.

Chapter 6 – Lesson: Denial is Real

4:39 pm...

Angelica sat in the living room and watched television. She was feeling pretty good! After watching Coraline and taking a nap earlier, she went out for a long walk, had some soup for dinner, and took a shower. She was startled by a deafening knock on the door. Angelica slowly walked to the door, "Who is it?"

"Roman."

Angelica smiled and hurried her last few steps to the door. She took a deep breath and opened it wide. He was still in his uniform, "Hi."

"Can I come in?"

Angelica noticed that he looked and sounded angry, "Sure." He walked in and stood in the living room. Angelica locked the door, followed him into the living room, and stared at his stance. Was he here for something related to what had happened that night? "Is everything ok?"

Roman stared at her, "Are you here alone? Are your children home?"

Angelica began to worry, "Yes I'm alone. Is everything ok?"

Roman sighed, "You tell me? Are you alright?"

"Yes. What's wrong?"

Roman paced a few steps. "What's wrong is that I was worried about you."

Angelica wrapped her arms around her chest. "I'm sorry. I just needed some time. I called you so..."

Roman stared at her. "Why haven't you answered any of my calls or text messages?"

Angelica stared at him. She could tell that he was extremely upset! "I wanted to apologize for clinging on to you like I was...it wasn't right...I needed some time to..."

"What do you mean," he said forcefully.

Angelica didn't like his tone, "What is wrong with you?"

Roman closed his eyes and walked toward the door. He then turned around and stood in front of Angelica. "I'm sorry." Roman walked closer to Angelica and wrapped his arms around her. Angelica held him close. "I'm so sorry." After a few moments, Angelica tried to take a step back, but Roman didn't release his hold. He looked at her, "Are you ok?"

Angelica looked at him. "Yes. I'm sorry for bringing you into this. I wanted to apologize and to let you know that we...can't..."

"How have you been," Roman asked staring into her eyes.

Angelica noticed that he wasn't letting her go. "I'm getting better."

He looked at her lips and then back to her eyes. "Have you been eating?"

Angelica smiled and tried to ease her way out of the embrace. Roman wouldn't budge. "Roman?"

He smiled. "Is that a yes?"

Angelica laughed and tried to playfully push him away. He still wouldn't budge. "Roman?"

He smiled at her. "What? I'm coming back here at seven to take you to dinner. I'll text you when I'm outside."

Angelica looked into his eyes, "Roman, I do want to go but, I don't think it's a good idea." She tried to step back, and he wouldn't let her, "Roman I'm sorry but..."

Roman held her close and brought his face closer to hers, "Stop saying sorry to me Angelica. I'm your friend, right?"

"Right but I can't give you..."

Roman took a step back, "You can't give me what?"

Angelica looked at the floor, "Roman, I'm not well. I can't give you something that I don't have. I can't be..."

Roman held her in his arms again, "I didn't ask you for anything, did I?"

Angelica liked the way he felt too much, "Roman can you let me go please?" Roman instantly removed his arms from around her. Angelica began to cry, "I can't be your friend right now. What kind of friend could I be to you? I don't have shit to offer anyone right now. I'm too fucking needy, and I can barely leave the house to do anything, I..."

Roman put his arms around her again and just held her. Angelica closed her eyes and held on to him. "This isn't fair to you...I can't be..."

Roman raised her face from his chest, "Angelica, I am a man. I can take care of myself so don't worry about something not being fair to me," he said smiling. Angelica couldn't help but smile with tears still in her eyes. He took his thumb and wiped a tear falling down her eye. They stared at each other for what seemed like minutes. Angelica blushed and turned her head away. "Angelica." She turned her head and looked at him. Roman smiled, "7."

Angelica just finished getting dressed! She put on some makeup and remembered the pep talk her mother gave to her! Yes, she deserved to have a good time with a friend. Her phone rang. It was Ian. "Hello?"

"Hey! How are you doing?"

Angelica frowned, "I'm fine. How are you?"

"I'm ok. I wanted to stop by and talk with you."

"Not tonight. I'll call you," Angelica said trying to end the call.

Ian sighed, "Angelica, we have to talk. Why won't you talk to me?"

"I'll talk to you later."

Ian began to sound desperate, "You keep saying that, but you never call me."

Angelica felt her phone vibrate. She looked at her phone and read Roman's text message, "*I'm outside.*" Angelica heard Ian speaking but wasn't listening, "I'll call you later." She hung up the phone, grabbed her things, and went out the front door.

Roman got out of his truck and stood on the pavement ready to greet Angelica after she locked up. He looked at her walking down the steps to join him, "You look beautiful," he said hugging Angelica.

Angelica frowned at his compliment, "No, you look better than me! I'm going back in to change!" Angelica turned as if she was going back into the house when Roman pulled her close in an embrace. "Roman?!"

"Yes."

Angelica briefly looked away and felt a little uncomfortable being out in public. She tried to take a step back, but Roman wouldn't let her go. "Roman?"

"You ready to eat?"

"Yup," she answered nervously.

Roman laughed, "Ok let's go." He took her hand and walked her to the passenger side of the truck, opened the door, and closed it behind her. Angelica watched him while he walked around the back of the truck and looked at his phone. He placed a call, but she couldn't hear him talking above Sade's Lover Rock. She looked inside of her purse for her lip balm. As she applied the mango moisture, she felt her phone vibrate with a text. Angelica opened her phone and saw a picture that her mother sent showing the kids roller-skating! Angelica chuckled as Roman got in the truck. "What's so funny?"

Angelica put the phone away, "My kids! My mom sent me a picture of them. Everything ok with you?"

Roman smiled, "Of course, why wouldn't it be?"

"You were on the phone. I was just making sure everything was ok."

Roman reached over and grabbed her seatbelt, "Now you DO know that you are in a truck with a policeman. You have to make sure to wear your seatbelt at all times."

Angelica laughed, "Yes sir Officer Roman Xavier Callowhill!" She went to grab the seatbelt and touched his hand. Roman stopped smiling and stared at Angelica. "Roman?"

"Yes."

"You ready?"

"Are you?"

Angelica laughed, "Yup!"

Roman smiled, "You have everything you need?"

Angelica smiled, "Sure do officer," she said with a country accent.

"Oh! You got jokes tonight huh?"

Angelica laughed, "I'm sorry! It's been FOREVER since I last went out!"

Roman gently rubbed her face with the back of his hand, "Don't be sorry."

Angelica felt her face getting warm, and tried to play off her blush, "Alright already! Let's go and eat!"

Roman smiled, put Lover's Rock on repeat and drove down the street.

Angelica listened to the words and felt very nervous. She looked out of the window and heard word for word how she was feeling about Roman. Even though Sade was singing, it was Angelica's thoughts! Why was the song on repeat? "So how was your day?"

Roman laughed, "It was ok. How was yours?"

"It was good! I even went for a long walk!"

"Oh really?"

"Yes, I did! If you had seen me, you would've been so proud!"

Roman smiled, "So you should be really hungry then! What would you like to eat?"

Angelica frowned a bit and laughed, "I don't know. I pretty much assumed we were going for pancakes!"

Roman laughed, "I don't think you're appropriately dressed for IHOP! What would like to eat? Steak...seafood..."

"Yes! Seafood!"

Roman put his hand on top of hers, "Seafood it is."

Angelica looked at his hand on top of hers and smiled. She then looked out the window. "Thank you for doing this."

"For doing what?"

Angelica looked at him, "For doing all of this. Thank you for talking to me, taking me to dinner, caring. Thank you for doing all of this." Angelica began to cry, "I know you are with someone. I just appreciate all of the attention and your time...I don't..."

Angelica stopped talking when Roman quickly pulled over in front of the Art Museum. He put his hazard lights on, put the truck in park, turned and faced her. "Angelica, there will be no crying tonight. Not tonight. You've cried enough." Angelica just stared at him with tears in her eyes. Roman smiled, caressed her face with his hands and wiped her tears with his thumbs. "No tears tonight." Angelica smiled and nodded her head. Roman nodded, released the hazard button, put the truck into drive, signaled, and pulled back into traffic.

Ten minutes later they arrived at McCormick and Schmidt's. "I've never been here before. Have you?"

"Yes."

The Valet opened Angelica's door, and Roman opened his. While he spoke with the valet, Angelica looked at how beautiful Center City looked! Philly truly shined at night! "Are you ready to go in," Roman asked interrupting her thoughts.

"Yes."

Roman took her hand, opened the door, and walked to the podium where the hostess was standing. "Good evening sir. Dinner for two?"

"Yes."

"Right this way sir." The hostess took them to a secluded table by the window. "Is this ok?"

Roman looked at Angelica. She smiled and nodded her head. Roman looked to the hostess, "This is fine. Thank you."

"No problem sir. Tom, your waiter, will be here in a moment. These are your menus for this evening. Enjoy!"

Angelica was so grateful, "Thank you!"

"You're welcome!" Roman looked at Angelica smiling.

Angelica looked at Roman and felt self-conscious.

"Good Evening! My name is Tom, and I will be your server for the evening. Can I start you off with something to drink?"

Roman looked at the waiter, "Yes, can we have two glasses of water please."

"Sure, sparking or..."

"Yes, sparkling. Angelica, would you like a drink?"

Angelica smiled, "Yes! I would love a Pina-Colada!"

Roman and Tom laughed. Tom continued, "Ok ma'am, any preference on the rum?"

Angelica was in unfamiliar territory and just shook her head. Roman took over, "Captain Morgan would be just fine."

The waiter continued, "Great...and for you sir?"

"Just the water. Thank you."

Tom politely nodded, "Perfect, I'll be right back with your drinks."

Roman looked at Angela who was fidgeting in her seat with anxiety. Angelica looked out the window and tried to calm down. Tom appeared again from nowhere and commenced to pouring their Pellegrino. She needed to escape for a moment, "Excuse me, where is the restroom," she asked Tom.

Tom turned around to explain and show her in which direction the restroom was located. Roman then took Angelica's hand, "I'll take you."

Angelica and Tom smiled. Roman rose from his chair and led her to the restroom. "You didn't have to walk me to the restroom Officer Callowhill."

Roman smiled standing near the women's restroom door. "Ms. Kings, I'm just trying to help."

Angelica sneered at the sound of her husband's last name. "I'll be right back."

Roman pulled her close and wrapped his arms around her waist. "What's wrong? What did I say?"

Angelica shook her head. She felt really anxious being so close to him. "Nothing. I just have to go to the bathroom."

Roman nodded his head. "I'll be right here."

Angelica went in, used the bathroom, washed her hands, and looked in the mirror. She looked, good! "You can do this! You can do this!" She took a few napkins, wiped her face, and applied more mango moisture for her lips. Angelica checked her phone and saw that Ian called and left her a voicemail. The kids also sent silly selfies of themselves! Angelica realized that she needed this night! She deserved it! She was a survivor! She could do this! "I can do this!" Angelica laughed, put the phone away, and went out of the restroom.

As soon as she saw Roman, she had to blink a couple of times. From where he was standing, the light glistened over his face. For the first time, she looked at his whole body. He looked..., "Are you ok," Roman asked smiling at her obvious stare.

"Ummm, yes. I'm fine. Thank you." They walked back to the table, and her Pina Colada was waiting for her. "Thank God." Angelica took a couple of sips. "This is really good. I haven't had a drink in who knows how long. Would you like a sip," she asked handing him the glass.

Roman laughed, "No. You enjoy it! What would you like to eat?"

Angelica looked at the menu, "Something with salmon. What would you recommend?"

Roman looked at Angelica. "I'll pick out something for you. Do you like scallops?"

"Yes," she said taking more sips of her drink. "Have you and Monica been here before?"

Roman looked at Angelica, "Yes."

"Does she like it here? I mean it's really nice," asked Angelica sipping more of her drink.

Roman looked at Angelica/ "Why are you asking about Monica?"

Angelica sipped some more, "Why not? She *is* your woman... right? We're friends! You know more than enough about Ian. Why can't we talk about Monica?" Roman's phone rang. Angelica pointed to his phone, "I spoke her up! I bet that's her!" Roman looked at his phone and sent the call to voicemail. "Did I win?"

Roman looked at her sipping her drink. "When did you last have something to eat?"

Angelica looked at her drink, "I had some popcorn earlier why?" Roman didn't say anything. He just took a swig of his water. Angelica put the drink down and looked out of the window. Tom came, and Roman ordered for them while Angelica stared out of the window.

"Angelica."

"Yes."

Roman sighed, "Angelica what's wrong?"

"Nothing, I'm fine. It's a beautiful evening outside."

"Angelica, can you look at me please." Angelica turned her eyes to him. He just stared at her.

Angelica turned her head, "Why do you look at me like that?"

"Like what?"

"You look at me, and then you stare at me like I'm some kind of experiment."

Roman looked at his glass of Pellegrino. "I'm sorry. Does it make you feel uncomfortable?"

"Why do you do it?"

"Because you're beautiful," he said staring again.

Angelica smiled. "Thank you. You don't have to pour on the charm, Roman! I'm not **that** bad."

Roman laughed, "You think you might want some dessert after dinner?"

Angelica laughed too, "Of course! Who knows when I'm going out to dinner with a man again!" Roman stopped laughing, and Angelica could sense his attitude change. "At least YOU have someone special! I, on the other hand, have to cherish these nights!"

Roman took her hand. "You are a special someone, Angelica."

Angelica smiled. "I'm trying to make myself believe that Roman. Not all men are as wonderful as you Roman." He stared at her. "Now there you go! Why are you looking at me like that? You know you are a catch, Roman! I know Monica tells you all the time!" Roman smiled at Angelica, "Ahhhh, and that smile of yours? Please, I know you have women coming at you left and right!"

Tom interrupted their conversation with placing their entrees on the table, "Enjoy!"

Angelica smiled, "Thank you!" She looked at Roman who was still staring. "Especially when you wear that uniform! I know they just throw their numbers at you DAILY!" Angelica closed her eyes, grabbed his hands, and began to pray. "God, thank you for this food, thank you for Roman..."

"Thank you, God, for Angelica! Thank you for allowing us to be together this evening. May you continue to bless us and keep us. Amen." Angelica opened her eyes before Roman and just stared at him. He kept a hold of their hands and looked at her with a look of endearment.

"Amen."

Roman let go of her hands and picked up his silverware. Angelica was blown away!

Chapter 7 – Lesson: After Dinner...There is USUALLY Dessert

Angelica sat in the passenger seat of Roman's truck completely relaxed. Roman stopped playing Sade's Lovers Rock and was playing an unrecognizable song. A man kept singing about what he would do for his woman. Angelica looked out the window. "Who is this singing?"

"Tank. The song is called 'If That's What It Takes.' Do you like it?"

"He's saying a lot...."

Roman looked at Angelica. "I mean if you really love someone, it's like that."

Angelica shrugged her shoulders. "Do you feel that way about Monica?" Roman quickly pulled into a parking lot on West River Drive. "What's wrong? I'm not crying!"

Roman pulled into the parking lot, put the car in park, took his seat belt off, and turned to her. "Angelica, if I felt that way about Monica, I wouldn't have the time of day for you. Period. I wouldn't be anywhere near you like this because I would be with *her*. It would be all about her. I wouldn't have *you* at my house if I felt that way about Monica. I'm not that kind of man."

Angelica frowned her face at him. "Ok. You didn't have to pull over to tell me that."

Roman quickly patted her hand and put his seatbelt back on. He put the truck in gear and drove off. Angelica stared out the window and fell asleep.

~

"Angelica."

Angelica opened her eyes and thought they were still driving. They were at his house! "Why are we at your house?"

Roman unfastened her seatbelt and smiled, "I took you home, but you didn't want to get out of the truck!"

"Stop playing! No, I didn't!"

Roman smiled. "Yes, you did. The neighbors were looking a little suspicious, so I brought you here."

"Are you serious? I'm so sorry! I can catch a cab home."

"It's ok. I'll take you."

"No, it's late, and you have to work in the morning."

"I'll take you. I don't have to work tomorrow anyway."

Angelica smiled, "No! I have monopolized your time enough. I'll catch a cab. We can go inside while I wait, but I'm catching a cab. You do too much!" Angelica quickly got out of the truck before he could say anything about it. Roman walked up to the door and let Angelica in first. Angelica immediately sat on the couch, took her shoes off, and closed her eyes.

"I'll be right back," Roman said going up the stairs. Angelica nodded her head.

What seemed to be minutes later, Angelica opened her eyes to see Roman carrying her upstairs to his bedroom. "Roman, what are you doing?"

"You fell asleep. I tried to wake you up, but you wouldn't get up."

Angelica put her hands over her eyes, "I'm so sorry. You can put me down. I'll go. I'll call a cab now."

"Angelica it's 1:15. It's time for bed." Roman placed her on top of the bed, turned the lights out, and laid down next to her.

Angelica shook her head. "No. This is wrong! I'm not going to do this to you."

"Do what? Angelica, please go back to sleep. I'll take you home in the morning."

"Roman I'm sorry! Please forgive me!"

Roman stayed silent. He pulled her closer to him and placed her head on his chest, "Shhh."

Angelica closed her eyes and fell asleep.

~The Next Morning...

Angelica opened her eyes to bright sunshine. She smiled and looked around the room. Roman was standing in the middle of the floor with a towel wrapped around his waist. He smelled and looked...good. Roman smiled at her obvious stare, "Well good morning to you too!"

"Good morning. I'm so sorry about last night. It must have been the Pina Colada!"

"It's ok."

Angelica got up and went straight into the bathroom. There was a new toothbrush, washcloth, and towel in the bathroom. "Roman, is this for me?"

"Yes."

"Thank you!"

"No problem!"

Angelica showered and brushed her teeth. She put the bra back on and her clothes minus her underwear. She bumped into Roman on the way out of the bathroom. Roman laughed, "I'm not used to sharing my space."

Angelica tried to laugh but stared at his glorious chest, "Yeah, sorry!" Roman put his arms around Angelica, "Roman?"

"Yes."

Angelica looked at his face while her heart started to beat wildly. "Roman."

"Yes," he answered softly.

"I know I sound like a broken record. I'll get ready to go. I know you have things to do! Again, sorry about last night. I appreciate the time you took out of your busy schedule to be with me. Thank you," she said nervously.

"You're welcome. Why is your heart beating so fast?"

"What? No, it's not! I'm fine. Let me get my..." Angelica tried to bypass him and go downstairs, but he wouldn't let her.

"Roman?"

He brought his face closer to hers. "Why do you call my name like that?"

"What do you mean?"

"You know what I mean Angelica. Why is your heart beating so fast? Am I making you uncomfortable."

"Yes."

"Why?"

"I don't know."

Roman took her hands and kissed the back of them. "I'm sorry."

Angelica was so flustered. "Ok. No problem." She went back into the bedroom looking for her purse but couldn't find it. She couldn't find her shoes either. Angelica walked down the hall and the stairs. Roman was in the living room with only a pair of boxer shorts on. Angelica couldn't help but stare.

Roman smiled, "Are you ok?"

Angelica looked away and continued looking for her shoes. "Yes...ummm...I was looking for my purse and shoes." Roman walked over to the closet by the front door and retrieved her belongings. "Thank you."

Roman put her shoes on the floor and her purse on the couch. "No problem." Roman watched her as she opened her purse and looked at her phone. "Would you like something to eat before you go?"

Angelica shook her head, "No thank you. It's 11:35... I feel so bad about last night..." Roman moved closer to her and wrapped his arms around her waist. "Roman."

"Yes," he said smiling.

Angelica looked at Roman square in the eye, "Why are you looking at me like that?"

"Like what?"

"I don't know! You keep..." Roman slowly brought his face to Angelica's, "Roman?"

"Yes."

"Don't."

"Why?"

"I don't know," Angelica said staring in Roman's eyes. He was now smiling at her and holding her extremely close.

"Give me a good reason why I shouldn't."

Angelica stopped smiling, "I need to go."

"No, you don't."

Angelica tried to push him away, "I really should." Roman picked her up and walked up the stairs. "Where are we going?"

"To my room to talk."

Angelica closed her eyes, "Roman this is not right!"

Roman laid her on the bed, "What do you mean?"

"What do you think that I mean? I'm married with three kids! You are in a relationship with another woman! Let me go home...this has gone too far and it's all my fault." Angelica stood up and began to walk out of the room. Roman walked up to her and wrapped his arms around her again, "Roman please this has got to stop!"

"What has got to stop? What is going on Angelica?"

"What do you mean? Why are we here in your bedroom Roman? Why do you look at me like you do? If you are with Monica, why do you hold me like you do? Why are you dressed like that? Why did you let me spend the night last night?"

Roman grabbed her face and kissed her gently. "Now that wasn't so bad, was it?"

Angelica just stared. Roman took her hand and laid her on the bed. Roman laid down next to her on his side. Angelica turned on her side to face him. "Angelica, you are so beautiful."

Angelica smiled, "Thank you, Roman. And you are a very handsome man."

"Thank you." They just laid there in silence staring at one another. Roman moved his body closer and kissed her lips again. This time, he let his lips linger onto hers a little bit longer and heard her moan. He opened his eyes and noticed that hers was still closed. He kissed her again and she kissed him back. "Your lips are so soft."

Angelica laughed, "They are?"

Roman smiled, "Yes." He moved in to kiss her again and this time they became so ensconced in the kiss that she didn't even realize that he was about to get on top of her.

She started moaning and caught herself, "Roman please stop!" she said pushing him away.

Roman immediately stopped and backed away, "Angelica, I'm so sorry! I'll take you home. I'm sorry! Please forgive me."

Angelica looked at Roman's face. He looked torn and ashamed. "Roman, it's ok!"

Roman caressed her face, "I didn't mean to! Please believe me."

"I do. I believe you. It's ok."

"No, it's not. I didn't mean to..."

Angelica hugged him, "Roman...I..."

Roman interrupted her, "Angelica, I know what happened to you. I know that you're still married and that you have three children. I'm not trying to do anything that you're not. Just for the record, I'm feeling the same things that you are feeling for me."

"How do you know what I'm feeling," she said staring at him.

"Your mind and body feel more at ease when you are close to me. Even though I know that you're going through a lot, it doesn't change the fact that I care for you." Roman paused and smiled, "AND...while I was kissing you, were moaning!"

Angelica gasped, "I was not moaning!"

Roman kissed her again and she moaned, "Roman, we can't...," Roman kissed her again and held her very close to his body. Angelica cried, "Roman stop." Roman stopped kissing her lips and kissed her on the forehead.

He looked at her and smiled. "I won't do anything that you aren't ready to do or that you don't want to do. We will move further when and only when you are ready."

Angelica frowned. "I need to leave."

"Why do you need to be away from me?"

Angelica looked at him with tears falling down her face, "Because you are the one who comforts me! The only way I've been able to sleep is to think about you, or to be next to you...and this doesn't help."

She tried to get go to the door but Roman pulled her close to his body onto the bed, "Don't go like this. I'll take you home ok?"

Angelica looked at him. "Thank you."

Roman wiped her eyes with his fingers and kissed her on the cheek. They stared at each other for a while until Angelica kissed him on his lips. She pulled back and looked at him to see his reaction. Roman grabbed her hand and kissed it. They continued kissing heavily. Roman took a deep breath, "How do you feel when I kiss you?"

Angelica smiled, "Like I'm the most beautiful woman on this earth!"

"You are."

Angelica looked down at his beautiful chest, "Are you just trying to have sex with me?"

Roman stared at Angelica, "What? We kissed, and we enjoyed it. I know what you've been through Angelica. I wouldn't do that. Of course, I want you, but I know what's real!"

Angelica reflected on an idea that she had been thinking about for the past few days. She raised her head and looked up at him, "I think I need to ask you something."

Roman looked confused, "What is it?"

Angelica took a deep breath but couldn't help the anxiety taking over, "What happened to me was...I might need you to do something for me...to help me...to get through."

Roman stared at her. "What do you need for me to do?"

"Please don't think I'm crazy!"

"What is it?'

"God can only *really* do this, but you," she said touching his face, "I believe that He sent you to me...to help me. I think I need you to... cleanse me. I know this sounds really desperate because, at this point, I am." Angelica took a deep breath while her hands were shaking. "Roman, I think I need for you to make love to me...so that I can think of you... instead of him. I know you don't love me, and I know that you can't erase what happened to me. But...but... if you can at least give me a beautiful experience, I would have something much better to focus on. My husband is no longer my husband. He has belonged to someone else for a while now while I have been slowly dying."

Roman just stared at her while Angelica trembled with every word, "I know you have done enough for me already! I will forever be in debt to you. If you could just...just...jump start me, I believe that I will be able to deal with this much better than what I am. If you do this for me, I will not act as if I am your woman. I won't turn into some fatal attraction. I promise that things on my part will not get awkward or weird. I will simply fade to black and let you be. And...and if you can't do this, that's ok too." Roman sighed and wiped his face with his hand. Angelica looked at the stressed expression on his face, rose from the bed, and started walking toward the door.

Roman quickly got up and grabbed Angelica. He held her close while standing near the door. He whispered in her ear, "If I do this you must understand that I won't be doing it just for you. You also must realize that things **will** get weird because things will not be the same if we do this."

Angelica nodded her head, "Ok."

"I fixed breakfast for us this morning. How about we go downstairs and eat. That way you can think about what was said in case you want to change your mind. I'll be down in a few minutes."

Angelica nodded and walked down the stairs. Roman stood there and couldn't believe what was happening. Angelica went into the kitchen and opened the oven. There were two plates of eggs, turkey bacon, and toast. She grabbed one, said grace, and began to eat thinking of what she said to

Roman. Angelica was out of her mind! "Oh my God," she said out loud. She stuffed her face, had some juice, and paced the floor thinking about what he was doing upstairs. Angelica was so nervous. She began to think that this was a bad idea. Angelica walked up the stairs with the intention of talking to him about what she asked. She was having second thoughts.

Angelica opened the door and saw that Roman had candles lit around the whole room. He was laying underneath the covers waiting for her. She instantly thought about how she desperately needed this. She needed to feel loved even if it was from a person she met days ago! The little self-esteem that she had left was about to disappear! She started tearing up while she took off her clothes. She got underneath the covers and moved over to where he was. "Roman, I..."

Roman put his finger up to her lips, "We need to be clear about what happens here. There will not be any discussions in this bed." Angelica nodded her head yes. "If at any time you want to stop, just say stop." He looked at Angelica and repositioned his body, "Is there anything that you want to say to me?"

"Yes," Roman started kissing her neck slowly, "I just wanted to let you know that..." Roman moved to the other side of her neck while she continued to speak nervously, "...all of my tests came back negative." Roman kissed her mouth with more passion than she ever imagined. She moaned as he started sucking on her breasts. He stopped and pulled the covers down. Angelica tried to pull them up but Roman gently took them from her and pulled them back down. He raised her right arm and kissed it from her fingertips to her shoulder. He did the same thing to her other arm and both legs!

He kissed and sucked on her toes and then turned her on her stomach. Roman licked behind her knees, sucked, and licked on her thighs and back. She couldn't contain herself, when he turned her on her back again, he kissed her lips, and Angelica wrapped her arms around him. She unleashed her appreciation and kissed him all over his neck and chest. Roman reached underneath his pillow and grabbed a condom. He sat up and let

Angelica see him put it on his rock-hard penis. She couldn't believe that he was that big. She had sex with Ian for so long that in her mind, his size was the only size in existence!

Angelica looked at Roman as he slowly hovered over her body. She felt a little scared and her body tensed up. He put his hands on her face and kissed her until she was fully relaxed. He took hold of himself and Angelica opened her legs. He kept kissing her while he entered her body. "Oh my God!" Roman started moving very slow making sure he kissed all over her neck and face finding his way back to her lips. Angelica moaned louder holding on to his back. Roman grabbed her breast and licked around her nipples. "Roman! What are you doing to me?"

Roman looked at her and smiled while still moving inside of her. He played with her hair and then started to lick and kiss her ear. As he sucked on her ear lobe, she called out to him. Angelica wrapped her arms around his neck.

Roman went deeper inside of her. As Angelica moaned louder, Roman spoke to her, "Are you, my Angel?"

"Yes," Angelica put her hands on the back of his head and kissed him. She moaned with every thrust and had to break away from kissing him when he moved faster. They stared at each other and Roman slowed down. Angelica felt very self-conscious, "Do you like it?" Roman just kept on staring at her and smiled. He picked up the pace and Angelica closed her eyes while Roman buried his head in the corner of her neck kissing and sucking away! "Roman...ohhhh...," she felt herself getting closer, "Roman stop." Roman stopped moving and looked at her. "I can't handle this. You are feeling too good inside me... I can't handle this! It's too much!"

Roman didn't say a word! He kissed her nice and easy and started to back out of her. Angelica pulled him back and started crying. Roman kissed her lips. He took his right hand and toyed with her breast before licking and sucking all over it. When he heard her moaning, he continued pushing inside of her. Angelica moaned louder and louder as she dug her nails into his back trying to hold on for dear life. "Oh, my God!" Her moaning went higher and higher. Roman wrapped his arms underneath her and kissed her while moving in and out of her.

Roman went over to her ear, "Do you like it?"

"Roman!"

"Do you want me to stop?"

"No!"

"I have to."

"Please no."

"I'm about to," he said moaning. He couldn't hold back his moaning and groaning anymore! Roman was about to internally combust if he didn't come.

"Roman!" Angelica screeched while her body, inside and out, quivered!

Roman felt her shaking. He put his hands on her ass and went deep inside of her so that he could come. Angelica whispered, "Take me." She heard him mumbling something underneath his breath. Angelica grabbed his face and kissed all over his neck. As she sucked, he went faster and faster, "Oh God!" Angelica felt herself about to come again! This had never happened to her before, "Roman!"

Roman held onto her ass real tight, "It's coming, baby. Hold on." Angelica kept on moaning. Roman moved deeper and faster causing Angelica to lose her mind! "Angelica, you feel so good, baby! So good!" Angelica smiled and raised her hips off the bed. Roman smiled back at her. He raised his upper body off her chest and grabbed her waist, "You're my Angel baby! You...are...my...Angel!"

Roman slowed down but pressed deeper causing Angelica to groan, "Roman, take it! Take it...please!"

That's all that Roman needed to hear! He laid on top of her and found a space on her neck. He kissed and sucked on that spot, "Angelica!" Roman continued grunting, "Oh!" While he came, he kissed her lips moaning and shaking like crazy.

He slowly stopped moving but continued kissing her lips. "Are you ok?"

"Yes," Angelica said cheesing!

"Are you really ok?"

"Yes," she said running her fingers down his face.

"Good! Now here comes the real question. Did you enjoy what we just did?"

"Yes. Did you?"

"Yes. Any feelings of regret," Roman asked.

"None! What about you?"

"None," he said giving her a kiss on the cheek, "Would you like something to drink?"

"Sure!" Roman laughed and pulled out nice and slow. He kissed her as he grabbed his shorts and got out of bed. Angelica saw a huge scar on his back, "How did you get that scar on your back?"

"I got shot a year ago. I'll meet you in the living room in about ten minutes. Is that cool?"

Angelica smiled, "Yes."

Roman went over to her and kissed her, "You are the most gorgeous woman that I've ever met and, without a doubt in my mind, I absolutely loved being inside of you!" He kissed her again and left outside of the room. Angelica cried tears of joy! She felt renewed, revived! She was brought back to life by her guardian angel.

Chapter 8– Lesson: Be Careful About What You Ask For

Angelica walked down the stairs with her cell phone in hand. While getting dressed in Roman's bedroom, she called her children and spoke to them. They were so glad that they could stay a few more weeks over their grandparent's house. Angelica felt a little bad that she didn't call them earlier, but she lightened up realizing that they weren't even thinking about her. They did miss her, but they were having so much fun that Mom and Dad weren't even thought of! She also talked to her mother briefly before Kendall needed her help with the ice cream. Angelica reached the bottom step thinking of how much she loved her kids. Roman was fully dressed, sitting on the couch looking at her. "Are you ready?"

"Yes."

Roman stood up, walked over to her and kissed her, "I'll be right back. I need to get my wallet." Roman ran up the stairs and grabbed his wallet from the dresser. He looked at the bed and noticed that Angelica made it up just the way he liked. He smiled and left out of the room. Roman went downstairs and saw her in the dining room on the phone. "Ok thank you...bye." She turned around and smiled.

Roman smiled. "Is everything ok?"

"Yes. Are you ok?"

Roman walked up to her and kissed her, "What day will your mom bring the kids back?"

"She's bringing them back next Sunday night."

Roman stood inches away from her. "What would you like to do today?"

"I don't know. I figured that you already had plans. I mean it is YOUR day off."

Roman smiled and kissed her cheek. "Do you want to go out?"

Angelica smiled, "Sure!"

"Good," Roman kissed her forehead and grabbed her hand. "Awe man you know what?"

"What?"

"You left something upstairs in my room."

Angelica frowned and couldn't think of what it was. "Ok, let me go and get it," she said rushing up the stairs. Roman watched her go up the stairs, and when she reached the hallway, he followed her. He reached the doorway and saw her looking all around. He walked in and put his keys and wallet back on the dresser. Roman walked over to her. "Roman, where is it?"

"Where is what?"

"Roman, you said I..."

Roman kissed her before she could even finish her sentence. He pulled away and looked into her eyes. "I want you to stay here until you pick the kids up. Let **me** take care of you until next Sunday."

"What? I don't know. That's too much."

"Too much what?"

Angelica took a deep breath, "Roman I don't..."

Roman picked Angelica up and laid on top of her on the bed, "Angelica, you wanted to get away for a couple of days, right? Why not pack a bag and stay here?"

Angelica smiled, "That does sound good!"

Roman kissed her lips. "Say yes."

Angelica kissed him, "I don't know."

Roman then began to kiss all over her neck while Angelica moaned. "Angelica say yes."

Angelica didn't say a word until he started pulling at her clothing. "Roman, I know I've been saying this all night and morning, but I should go." Roman looked at her and smiled while he completely undressed her. "Are you listening?" Roman took his clothes off and laid on the bed beside her. Angelica stared at his huge erection.

Roman reached under his pillow and grabbed a condom. Angelica watched him slowly place it on. Roman crawled on top of Angelica and kissed her lips gently. She placed her hands on his face and moaned into his mouth. Roman broke the kiss and stared at her. Angelica's eyes began to glisten with tears. Roman slowly placed himself inside of her while staring in her eyes. Angelica wrapped her arms around his back holding him close. Roman kissed her lips while rocking them back and forth.

After about twenty minutes, Angelica couldn't take much more, "Roman...please."

He didn't stop, "What's wrong?" Angelica closed her eyes. Roman kissed her, "What is it? What do you want?" Angelica shook her head. Roman kissed her neck and began to slowly grind his hips into her. Angelica gasped for air as Roman made his way up to her mouth, "You want it?" Angelica looked at him but couldn't say anything. Roman went deeper, and Angelica groaned with desperation, "Now?"

"Yes."

Roman kissed her lips while placing one of her legs over his shoulder. Angelica looked scared and tensed up. Roman stopped moving. He kissed and licked her leg while staring at her waiting for her to relax. As soon as she closed her eyes, Roman kissed her and began to move inside of her making her quail.

"Roman!" Roman looked down at Angelica and kissed her again. Angelica moved her face away from his and screeched as they came together. "Oh my God! Roman what in the world..."

Roman released her leg and kissed her lips keeping himself inside of her, "We need to go and get some of your things from your house. Afterward, I'll make dinner, and we can just relax for the rest of the evening."

Angelica smiled and put her hands up to his face. "I don't know what to say. But I think I'm getting in way over my head with this."

Roman kissed her on her forehead keeping himself inside of her. "How is that?"

Angelica looked away and shook her head. Roman took his finger and moved her face back to his, "How are you getting in way over your head when it's two of us in this?" Angelica looked at him without saying a word. Roman kissed her lips and pulled out of her. Angelica rose quickly and went into the bathroom.

Angelica closed the door and sat on the toilet with tears falling down her face. Angelica was overloaded with emotions. She was violated, her marriage was over, and now Roman. "Get your shit together," she whispered to herself. After she finished up and flushed the toilet, she ran the shower ready to immerse herself in some serenity. Angelica stepped into the shower and began to wash herself feeling better by the minute. As she bent down to wash her feet, she saw Roman standing by the toilet. He just stood there staring at her.

Angelica's heart started to race! He was just standing there naked, "Oh my God." She covered her mouth in astonishment. Was he about to sit on the toilet? She chuckled and opened the shower door, "Do you need to use the bathroom?"

Roman laughed, "Yes I do."

"Ok, I'll get out..."

Roman had walked right in the shower before she closed the glass door. Angelica couldn't help but stare at his beautiful body. His body was impeccable in addition to his length! Roman grabbed his loofah and began to wash his body while looking at Angelica. Angelica leaned against the wall and just stared at him while he washed. After rinsing, he turned to her, "Let me wash your back."

Angelica turned around and let Roman slowly wash her back. After rinsing, he began to kiss all over her back. Angelica's closed her eyes and let the water rinse all her worries down the drain. As he brought his body closer to hers, she could feel him rubbing up against her behind. Roman continued kissing all over the back of her neck while rubbing on her breasts, "Angelica, I want you."

Angelica shook her head no. Roman turned her around, placed her against the wall and looked in her face making sure not touch her, "I want you."

She looked at his naked body and then up to his face. Angelica didn't know what to say.

"I want you, Angelica," Roman said louder.

Angelica sighed and shook her head. "This is too much..." Angelica turned to walk out of the shower, but Roman steadied her back to where he placed her.

Roman smiled, "I want you."

Angelica frowned. "I heard you! I have nothing to give you Roman!"

He put his hand on her face and kissed her, "Angelica, I want YOU." Angelica's tears began again. He put his hands on her breasts and kissed all over her neck. "Angelica, I want you."

Angelica yelled, "Stop saying that! Just stop it! Why are you doing this?! This is so fucked up! I want you too! Now, what? What," she yelled in his face. Roman just stared at her. "What now Roman Xavier Callowhill? What are you going to say now? What trivial shit are you going to say out of your mouth now? How many times are you going to fuck me 'til *you* leave or find someone else?" Roman's face frowned up. "What?! Oh! I get it! This is how it's going to be for the next week? You gonna fuck me until I'm floating on air... making me come two or three times per day? And then what? WHAT?! You'll go back to Monica? What Roman? What the *fuck* do you want me for? We had an understanding..."

Roman tried to put his hand on her face, but she moved it out of her face, "What are you going to do, kiss me and make it all better? Why have you been fucking me like this? Why are you doing this to me... just so....so...you can..."

"Because this is what you should have." Roman tried to grab her hand, but she pushed it away.

"Don't." He tried again, and she didn't do anything. Roman kissed the back of her hand and then kissed her lips. Angelica started to cry again.

Roman looked in her eyes, "Angelica, I want you."

Angelica cried in his face, "I don't have what you want! I don't! I don't have anything! I don't have anything to *give* to you! I don't!"

Roman just stared at her, "If you want me, tell me."

Angelica continued to cry. She looked at the floor, at his feet, anywhere but in his eyes. Roman stepped closer and brought her face to his. Angelica sniffled, "I want you! God forgive me! I do!"

Roman hugged her while she cried into his chest. He pulled back and began to kiss her like he hadn't before. As soon as Angelica began to moan, he stopped kissing her and turned her around facing the wall. Roman took hold of himself, pulled her waist back, and entered her from behind. Angelica's lips were plastered to the tiled shower walls as water from the shower cascaded along her face.

Roman leaned against her back, kissed, and licked all along the back of her neck. "Angelica, I want you!" Angelica couldn't speak. Roman went deeper, "I said I want you, Angelica! I want you!"

"You have me!"

Roman kept going until he felt Angelica begin to shake, "You ready?"

"Yes."

Roman continued kissing on the back of her neck while rubbing her breasts. Angelica yelled for dear life while Roman continued kissing and sucking all over the back of her neck. While she came to her senses, she felt Roman pumping loads of come inside of her! When he stopped, he pulled out of her and turned her around. Roman held her and kissed her until she had to push him away for air. They stared at each other for some time. Roman then grabbed his loofah and washed both of their bodies in silence.

Every moment after that was simply awkward. After the shower, they only talked when needed, and Roman seemed to be on edge. Angelica went downstairs and waited in the living room for them to leave. She vowed to discuss things before they left the house. Once Roman came downstairs, Angelica walked over to him, "Are you upset with me?"

Roman smiled and stepped toward her, "Why do you think that? I'm not upset with you

Angelica. I just don't want you to regret the choice you made. I don't want you to change your mind."

Angelica took his hand and kissed it, "Roman you have been amazing. I don't regret anything. The only thing is that..."

Roman held her close and kissed her lips, "I told you I want you Angelica and you told me that you wanted me. Did you mean that?"

"Yes, I do. Roman, I know that I have plenty of issues, but yes, that's the way I feel."

Roman kissed her, "I didn't wear a condom in the shower Angelica."

Angelica held his hand, "After all of the fucked-up shit that I have been through..."

Roman kissed her again, "I'll...I'll try to be more careful. You have nothing to worry about. We talked about this over dinner. Like I said, I'm tested regularly, and I always wear protection..."

"Except when you have them in the shower right?"

Roman looked at her again and kissed her, "Wrong. It won't happen again."

"If you keep kissing me, we will never leave."

Roman took his keys from his pocket and opened the door for her. As they traveled to her house, Angelica realized that she hadn't talked to Ian. She looked at her phone and noticed five missed calls from him with four voicemail messages. Angelica deleted them without listening. "Everything ok?"

Angelica sighed, "Yes."

"What's wrong?"

"Nothing. I just have to speak with Ian." Roman kept his eyes on the road.

Roman took a deep breath, silently, "I know a good divorce lawyer if you need one. She's really good too."

Angelica looked at him. "Thank you for everything Roman. I really appreciate what you are doing." Roman pulled up in front of her house and parked. "It won't take me long. I'll be right back."

"Ok. I'll just sit on the couch and wait for you downstairs."

Angelica frowned. "You don't want to wait in the car?"

Roman smiled while removing the keys from the ignition. "Do you want me to wait in the car?"

Angelica shook her head. "No. I would rather you come in, but what if Ian comes while you are here?"

Roman shrugged his shoulders. "Then Ian comes!"

They both exited the truck, walked up the stairs, and entered the home. Roman picked up Angelica's mail and handed it to her while closing the door. "Thank You."

Roman wrapped his arms around Angelica and kissed her. "Let's pack these bags."

Angelica laughed! "I don't need that many clothes for one week."

Roman kissed her again. "No, you really don't need to bring anything from this house, let alone clothes," he said rubbing his hands on her behind.

Angelica laughed again, "Roman let me get my things and change my clothes."

Roman stopped smiling. "I'll come upstairs with you to keep you company while you pack ok?"

"You don't need..."

Roman kissed her neck, "I know I don't need to go with you upstairs, but I am. So, let's get this over with." Fifteen minutes later Roman and Angelica walked downstairs with a book-bag and an old suitcase from her college days. "We need to get you some new luggage!"

Angelica laughed. "Hey! It lasted this long! Don't talk about my trusty-dusty luggage! It's not like I've been traveling anywhere anyway! No money wasted!"

Once they reached the bottom of the stairs, Roman put the suitcase down and hugged her. "We will go somewhere soon, and when we do, you will need new luggage!" Roman picked her up and twirled her around in a circle while kissing her neck!

Angelica cracked up laughing! Roman stopped spinning and just held her in the air. He slowly let her back down and kissed her. "Let's go."

When they arrived at Roman's house, Angelica called her mom and the kids! They were in heaven! Over the next few days, they would be going to Ocean City Maryland. Although they couldn't wait to come home, they were having the time of their lives! Angelica was so happy for them! "I love you!"

"We love you to mom! We'll bring you back a T-Shirt!"

"Ok! Be safe and call me tomorrow!"

"We will!"

"Good Night!"

"Night mom," they all yelled in unison!

After putting her things away in the two drawers that Roman gave to her, she walked downstairs and into the dining room. On the way to his house, they picked up Chinese Food to eat for dinner. Roman bought enough food for five people! "I have Chicken and Broccoli, Vegetable Lo Mein, Shrimp Fried Rice and some Egg Rolls!" He walked up to her and held her close while giving her an Eskimo kiss.

Angelica laughed. "Roman, you are such a sweetheart! How are we gonna eat all of this food?" She kissed his lips and looked at him, "I am so hungry right now, I can't even think straight!" She went to pull herself away, but Roman wouldn't let her go. "Why are you looking at me like that?"

Roman looked at her, "I'm looking at you because you're beautiful that's why!"

"Thank you!"

Chapter 9 – Lesson: Try to Keep Your Head Screwed on...While You are Being Screwed!

Roman's smile disappeared. "Please stop thanking me. This is how a real man is supposed to treat his woman. He thinks about her, loves her, takes care of her, and gives her the things that she needs and desires. If he can't afford some of the material things, then at least he strives to get her what he can." Roman kissed her forehead, "I want you to think of me as the closest friend that you have. I don't want you thanking me all of the time."

Angelica frowned her face a bit. "Roman, you don't have to remind me that we are just friends. I know you have other friends and I'm not trying to make this friendship seem...as if it's more than what it is. I know that you ..."

"What?" Angelica looked at him and could see that he was a little upset. "Angelica, I am very aware of what is going on in my life and yours. To be completely honest with you I do *know* other women... which I do see and talk to from time to time. And having sex has **never** been difficult for me..."

Angelica pulled her chair back away from the table cutting him off. "Thanks for the information. I understand. I just wanted to let you know that I don't expect anything from you. I know what this is so you can spare me the details. I know you have women lining up. Can we just eat now?"

Roman pulled her chair back to where it was. "The point I wanted to make is that I'm not in love with any of the women that I associate with. I like them, but that's about it."

Angelica looked uncomfortable. "Can we talk about something else please?"

"Why?"

She looked at the floor, lifted her head up and smiled. "Let's just enjoy our dinner...ok?" She tried moving her chair away, but Roman wouldn't let her.

"No, I want you to listen to me!"

"Ok," Angelica looked at him and tried to hold back her tears.

"Angelica when I want to have sex with a woman, I take her to a hotel or go to her place. I've had this house for about four years, and I have never let a woman step foot in my bedroom. A few have been inside my home, but none have spent the night, or have been in my bedroom...let alone in my bed! My house is my home! My daughter sleeps here when she visits, and sometimes we eat and play in my room! I rarely let women in my home."

Roman put his hand on her face. "But then someone came along...who needed me. I accepted that challenge because I do help those who are in need!" Angelica laughed! "I became her friend. I tried to accommodate her needs, and in doing so, I started to feel for her." Angelica looked up at him with a serious look. "Angelica I know you have issues. I just want to say that," he cleared his throat so that she could hear him loud and clear, "...you won't have them too much longer."

Angelica smiled. "I know that."

"Angelica **I** am your friend right *now*. Soon, I don't know if that will be enough for the both of us." He kissed her gently. "Now we can eat."

~

Roman and Angelica laughed and talked about their individual selves over dinner. They discussed what they liked and disliked about everything under the sun! Stories were shared about their childhood, school years, first loves, and heartbreaks! "Roman, I am full as a tick!"

"I know, me too! Do you want some dessert?"

"I don't think that I have room for anything else! That Chicken and Broccoli was good as I don't know what!"

Roman looked at his watch. "It's too late for us to go out so would you like to watch a movie?"

"What time do you have to get up in the morning?"

"I'm up at 8, and I'm out the door at 8:30."

Angelica stood up. "Let's just go and watch television," she said starting to clear the table.

Roman quickly got up from the table, "No, I'll do it. You just go and relax."

"I'm not letting you clean all this up when you have to get up early tomorrow for work! Let me help you so that it'll be done quicker." She grabbed the Vegetable Lo Mein and walked toward the kitchen. Roman tried to take the food out of her hand, but Angelica ran around the table. Roman laughed while chasing her.

Angelica was laughing so hard. She put the food on the table, "I just want to help you! Stop playing before I pass out!" Roman ran toward her and backed her into a corner kissing her and pressing her body close to him. Angelica put her hands behind his head and opened her legs. Roman moved his lips to her neck where he licked and sucked. "Roman stop," she said as if she was very upset.

Roman stepped back and looked at her, "What's wrong?" Angelica didn't say a word. Roman looked baffled. "What did I do?" Angelica backed away toward the front door. The upsetting look on her face turned to a smile as she ran up the steps laughing. "You know you're in trouble, right?" Angelica ran into the bedroom, turned on the television, and laid on his chaise.

194

About thirty minutes later, Roman walked in the door. "Why did you do that?"

"Do what," she said smiling.

Roman took his shoes off and put them underneath his bed. He took his shirt and sweats off but left his boxers on. He checked the alarm clock and turned the alarm on. Angelica got up off the chaise and laid in the bed. Roman laid next to her, and she put her head on his chest. The Lord of the Rings was on HBO. Angelica was excited because she loved the whole series. Halfway through the movie, Angelica heard Roman snoring! She laughed quietly and turned off the movie.

~Sunday, 1:17 am, June 14th

Angelica opened her eyes. A candle was lit illuminating the room. Roman was licking and kissing on her neck trying to wake her fully. As soon as Angelica moaned, Roman sat up and pulled her panties down. Angelica removed her camisole and looked at his chest all the way down to his pelvis. She put her hands on his chest as if his skin were going to melt if she put too much pressure into her touch. Angelica took her time and kissed his chest.

Roman grabbed her waist and rolled onto his back so that she was on top of him. Angelica nervously looked at him, and he smiled. She kissed on his chest the same as before but then she started to really get into it. She took her sweet time and slowly devoured his neck and all over his pecs. Sounds of pleasure came from his mouth, and she could feel his rock-hard penis poking her while she was on top of him. She turned around and looked at it and then at his face.

He had a blank expression as he caressed her face with his hands. Roman kissed her and grabbed her waist so that he could place her on her back. But his plans were interrupted when Angelica deepened the kiss. She pulled away and took a deep breath with her eyes closed. Roman just looked at her. She opened her eyes and smiled at Roman. Angelica put her right hand on his penis and mounted him! Just sitting there with him inside of her was enough to make her explode without even moving. She opened her eyes and looked at Roman whose eyes were now closed. She put her hands on his chest one at a time making sure that she moved slowly. Angelica started moving, and Roman put his hands on her waist. Roman felt so good inside of her! She had never experienced this level of passion before! She took her hands off of him and felt on her breasts. Roman looked at her, smiled, and rolled his eyes back in his head! Roman then sat up a little bit and sucked on her breasts.

Roman stopped. "You have to get down."

Angelica stopped moving. "Why? You don't like it?"

"Yes I do. I love it! That's the problem." Angelica ignored him and kept moving. Roman sat up all the way, and she wrapped her legs around him. Roman tried to calm down by taking a few breaths. He exhaled forcefully, "I should have taken off today." He looked down to where they were joined and wrapped his arms around her. He put his hands behind her head and kissed the shit out of Angelica. She was so captivated, that she stopped moving and wrapped her arms around him. He slowly leaned forward while holding her which forced her to lay back on the bed. He followed her while repositioning his legs and took control! Angelica wrapped her legs around him so that they were crossed at the ankles and resting on his lower back. Roman looked at her and knew what he wanted to say but was hesitant.

Angelica smiled. "What, you want me to put them down?"

Roman put his hand on her face. "You are amazing!"

"So, you **do** want me to..."

"Yes, I do want you." Roman put his dick deep inside of her making her squeal! "I want you!" He did it again, and Angelica held on tight and continued to moan louder. "I want **all** of you!" He went fast enough so that she could deal with the pressure. Angelica moaned, and he kissed her while moving deeper inside of her but not too deep. He could tell that she hadn't been made love to like this before, so he slowed down a bit.

"Roman, what's wrong, why are you slowing down?"

"I thought that maybe you couldn't take it," he said kissing her on her neck.

"Roman, please don't stop," Angelica begged. "Please." Roman obliged and continued taking her mind and body to heaven. She called his name as she climaxed all over him. Roman now went deeper and harder so that he could put his hunger to end. Angelica held on to him, "Oh God!"

"Is it too much for you," he whispered while kissing behind her ear.

"No!"

"So, you're ok?"

"Mmmm-huh."

"You like it?"

Angelica took a deep breath. "Yes." Roman went deeper, and Angelica loved every bit of it! "Roman why are you doing this to me?"

Roman was about to come and wanted to get deeper. "Put your legs down." Angelica put her legs down. He raised her right leg and let it dangle over his shoulder. Angelica fearfully looked at him while she raised her leg. She shook her head no, and Roman smiled. "Have I hurt you up to this point?"

"No. But you are too big...it's..."

"Just hold on to me and breathe," he softly kissed and licked on her lips while placing her left leg over his shoulder. "I'm gonna take you there, I promise!" Roman started out slow, cursing while his head was turned to the side.

"What's wrong? Roman what's wrong?" Roman didn't answer her and just kept on going, gradually increasing his tempo and depth. "Roman...I...I"

"I what," he said laying over her. Roman looked at her face while her legs were shaking. He kept moving inside of her making sure that her legs stayed up on his shoulders. "Tell me!" Angelica moaned louder, and louder and she knew that she was about to come again. Roman went faster. "Tell me!" Roman kissed her lips, and Angelica went off.

"Roman!" Angelica was getting closer. Roman knew he was about to bust any second. "Roman!" Angelica came calling out his name.

Roman came right along with her. He put her legs down and then collapsed on top of her. Angelica held on to him and rubbed his back. She kissed the side of his face as he laid there motionless. "Roman?"

"Yes."

"Are you ok?"

"No," he said shaking his head in the crook of her neck.

"What's wrong?"

"Everything. I'll be back," he pulled out of her and rolled on his back. He pulled the sheet over his lower body and headed for the bathroom not saying anything to her. Angelica frowned her face and called out to him. Roman didn't answer. He went to the bathroom and slammed the door.

Angelica followed him and stood in the hallway right at the bathroom door. "Roman," she said crying. "Roman, please talk to me...please!" Angelica cried so hard she was about to throw up. She was distraught over Roman being obviously cross with her. She had the same feelings when she was violated! Angelica cried a little bit more and then stopped. Angelica slowly walked back to the bedroom. She wiped her face as she sat on the bed and calmed down. After a few silent minutes, she grabbed her phone and called a cab. Angelica let the tears fall as she put on her clothes and shoes. She placed her clothes back into her bags and went downstairs.

Twenty minutes later, Roman came out of the bathroom and went into the bedroom ready to apologize and explain, but Angelica wasn't there. He put some clothes on and ran downstairs. The front door was open, but the screen door was closed. Angelica was sitting on the porch with her bags. Her purse was on her lap, and the bags were on the porch beside her. Angelica's phone was in her hand while she looked toward the corner.

Roman came out of the house and sat down next to her. Angelica didn't even acknowledge him. "Angelica, I'm so sorry that I didn't answer you upstairs. I was..."

Angelica looked at him, "That's ok Roman. It's ok really. I'm just going to go home. I really and wholeheartedly appreciate everything you have done for me," Angelica said speaking to him in a very mild-mannered way. She smiled and held Roman's hand.

"So, you don't want to know why I behaved like that," Roman asked looking upset.

"Roman, look at me." Roman shook his head looking out at the street. "Look at me!" Roman looked at Angelica hearing the pain in her voice, "I know I'm damaged goods ok? I know that already! I just don't appreciate being reminded of that by someone who I considered to be special. I know I haven't known you that long. You don't owe me anything! I know I was violated. I know my body doesn't look the best, I know I'm still married, I know you're single. I know what's going on! It's ok...I'll be ok."

Angelica smiled, "My life belongs to me! It's mine! I am a grown woman, and I loved fucking you, even though it was pity-fucking! You have given me the best sensual and sexual experience that I ever had! You were better than any other lover and definitely better than the man who I spent ten years married to." She shook her head in disbelief. "I asked for it, right? The dream was going to end anyway. You were trying to help me, and you did! Thank you! I thank you more than what words can say!"

"Angelica, I couldn't...I didn't..." Angelica just looked at him. "I had to leave the room because..." Angelica's cab pulled up his driveway.

"Roman, it's ok. I promise, it's ok, and we can still be friends if you like. It's ok...really. I'll call you. Thanks again." Angelica kissed him on the cheek. She stood up, and Roman held her hand.

"Angelica, come back in the house please."

"No. I'll give you a call tomorrow," she smiled and took a step, but Roman didn't let her hand go.

"Angelica please, I need to speak with you for just a minute." Angelica came closer, and Roman held her close. "I know I hurt your feelings and I'm sorry. I need to discuss some things with you, and I don't want you to go."

"Roman..."

"Please, I *need* you to stay." Angelica's eyes started to water. "I didn't mean to make you cry...please don't cry...please." Angelica looked in his eyes and walked in the house while Roman walked over to the cab. "Here's something for your time."

"No problem," said the cabbie pocketing his twenty-dollar bill. Roman looked up at the sky and then to the cab driving away.

He picked up her bags, walked in the door, and locked up. Angelica was sitting on the couch and looking through her phone. Roman sat down beside her. "Would you like something to drink?"

"Sure."

Roman got up and poured two glasses of apple juice. He drank one down and then poured another wishing it were more than apple juice! He walked back in the living room and handed her the glass. "Angelica, I'm your friend." She looked at him, and he got flustered with what he needed to say to her. "Angelica, I shouldn't have made love to you. I should have told you..."

Angelica got pissed, "You stopped me from leaving, with just a little bit of dignity, to say that?"

Roman pleaded, "Angelica listen, you're not ready for me right now. Your life is not ready for what I have to give to you."

Angelica put the glass down on the table and looked at him. "Thanks for being honest." She sat back on the couch, took her shoes off, and cuddled up with a pillow. "You better get some rest." She laid down on the couch and closed her eyes. Roman got up, turned off the light and walked upstairs. Angelica started crying quietly and held on tight to the pillow. She heard Roman walking back downstairs with a blanket. He draped it over her and started to lay down behind her. "Roman, I think that you should go back upstairs."

"Are you sure?"

"Yes, I'm sure."

Roman looked nervous, "Are you leaving in the morning?"

"Roman, thank you for the blanket!" Angelica ignored his question, wrapped herself up in the blanket, and turned toward the back of the couch. Roman rubbed her back but wouldn't go upstairs. Angelica sat up, "Why are you sitting here?" Roman bent down to kiss her, and Angelica pushed him back. "Roman, stop."

"I just wanted to kiss you."

Angelica cocked her head to the side, "And this is it...we're not going to do this, anymore right?!"

Roman looked in her eyes, "Right."

"Ok." Roman grabbed her faced and kissed her to the point where she felt dizzy. She pushed him back. "Ok!" Roman grabbed her again and kissed her while squeezing her breasts. Angelica pushed him again, "Roman, please. That's it!" He kissed her again and started pulling on her shirt in a frenzy! He stopped kissing her so that he could take her shirt off.

Roman picked her up and walked her up the steps to his bedroom. He quickly laid her on the bed, took off her pants and underwear, pulled his clothes off, and laid in the bed. He opened the small bureau beside his bed, grabbed a condom, and rolled it on in record time. "Angelica..."

"Yes, I know this is the last time we're going to have sex, Roman! You don't have to remind me." Roman entered her body, and Angelica gasped.

Roman shook his head, "FUCK! Would you like to try to take our friendship further?"

Angelica looked at him with a seriously confused face. "What did you say?"

"Would you like to try to take our friendship further," he said kissing her neck.

"That's not fair! How are you going to ask me that while you're kissing me like that?"

Roman stopped. "Yes or no?"

"Are you sure Roman? I have a package deal with three beautiful children whom I love dearly."

Roman smiled. "Would you like to have more children some day?"

"Sure. I think I can handle a couple more, with the right man that is," Angelica said laughing.

"Angelica, yes or no?"

"Yes I would like to try to take our friendship further," she said kissing on his neck.

Roman pushed his cock in deep inside of her! "Two months from now we're going to see if that can happen," he said looking at her. "We're not going to be together like this for two months," he went faster, and Angelica was on Mars!

Angelica started moving her hips and Roman was taken back! "Did you say two months?" Roman lifted her leg and moaned for days, "I said did you say two months?" Angelica slowed down and stopped moving.

"Baby no, please," Roman whined.

She started moving again, "Did you say for two months we won't be together like this?" Angelica wrapped her other leg around his waist while her foot rested on his ass. She moved her hips around and around.

"Angelica stop." Angelica kissed him and kept moving her hips.

"I can't!"

Roman's body began to shudder! "Stay still Angelica!" Angelica smiled and kept moving. "One month," he said panting! "One month...can you do one month?"

Roman put her legs down and laid completely on top of her while rocking them. "I can do one month Roman." Roman put one hand on her face and the other on her hip. He kissed her lips plunging into her until they both came together. Roman rolled over on his back. Angelica simultaneously laid on his chest, and they both fell asleep.

Chapter 10– Lesson: Friends Should Be Dependable!

~Two and half months later, August 23rd~

Angelica was on her way! She was in therapy twice a week: one session for herself and the other session was allotted for her, Ian, and the kids. Ian and Angelica agreed that it would be good for all of them to get counseling for the kid's sake. Kendall was seven, Gavin was ten, and Hailey was twelve. Although they were still fairly young, they were disappointed that their parents were splitting up. The kids were never told about the attack and Angelica wanted it to stay that way!

Ian now lived in the home that they all *used* to live in on Webster Street by himself. Angelica and the kids moved to her deceased grandfather's home on 49th & Hazel Avenue. Ian and Angelica's relationship was amicable. They sat down with an arbitrator and decided to do partial custody of the children. They also decided to split the children's expenses right down the middle. The final divorce decree would be ready in about two weeks.

While the children were adjusting to living in different households, they decided to do a two-week split for the duration of the summer. The kids would spend two weeks with Angelica and then two weeks with Ian until school started. Since it was now mid-July, Angelica felt that it couldn't have been better timing to handle this. In this way, their education wouldn't be affected if they had a really hard time adjusting. Angelica's parents agreed to help her out as much as possible. Her mother agreed that if it were Angelica's turn to have the kids for two weeks, she would take the kids during those particular weekends just to help.

It was now Sunday evening. Angelica drank the rest of her ginger ale, looked at herself in the mirror, and smiled. "Mommy, daddy, is waiting for us," said Kendall pulling her hand.

"Ok baby, let's go!" She grabbed her keys, purse, cell phone, and locked up the house.

"Mom, did you put my bathing suit in my bag," asked Hailey.

"I'm quite sure I did. But if I didn't, I know you have one over your dad's."

"Oh yeah!" Hailey cracked up laughing.

~

About fifteen minutes later, Angelica pulled up to Ian's house.

"Dad, hey, we're here," Hailey said using Angelica's cell phone. Angelica put the car in park. She looked over at the house and saw Ian standing in the doorway waving his hand to her. Angelica waved back. "Bye mom," said Hailey kissing Angelica on the cheek.

"Bye mom," said Gavin and Kendall just waving goodbye.

"Bye!" After grabbing their bags, they ran up the steps and hugged their dad. Angelica put the truck in drive and beeped the horn.

~

Roman was home watching television and waiting patiently for Angelica to come over. Over the past two and a half months, they agreed only to talk on the phone and not to physically see each other. He knew that her divorce would be finalized soon and that they were living in separate houses. Roman and Angelica spoke over the phone at least two or three times a day! He was so proud of her for being so strong in handling her business. Although she rarely talked to him about what happened to her that day, he knew that reliving what happened didn't help.

Roman just got off work and was truly tired. He specifically worked the whole weekend so that he could have Monday and Tuesday off to spend with Angelica. He nodded off for about thirty minutes until he heard a noise at his door. "Hello?" Roman's heart started beating very fast as he got up and walked to the door. He didn't say anything at all! He just opened the door. "Hi, Roman! How are you," she asked smiling beautifully. Roman still didn't say anything to her. He reached for her, gently pulled her inside, closed the door, and locked it. Angelica laughed and put her purse on the couch. "I can't get a hello," she said holding her arms out for a hug.

Roman hugged her tight, "I missed you so much."

Angelica laughed. "I missed you too! Did you eat dinner yet?"

"Yeah, I had a cheese steak and a salad," he said rubbing her back. "Angelica, I know we talked on the phone every day, but I really missed you."

"I missed you too Roman." They hugged again, and he kissed her.

Roman held her close. "Can I have you now?" Angelica playfully squinted her eyes at him as if she weren't sure! "Can you be mine?" Angelica's face turned serious, but she stayed silent. "Angelica, are you ready for me **now**?"

"Yes. I'm ready to be yours," she said confidently.

"Those are some really serious words, Angelica. Are you sure you're ready for me," Roman asked while staring into her eyes.

Angelica laughed. "Yes I'm sure! Plus, you passed the background check with flying colors!"

They both laughed hysterically. Roman took her hand and walked with her up the stairs. He opened the bedroom door, and there were candles lit and red rose petals on the bed. Roman had a bottle of champagne and two glasses on the bureau. He went over to the champagne, popped the cork, and poured some into the Mikasa champagne flukes. He picked them up and turned around to give Angelica her glass. Angelica walked closer to Roman. "What are we toasting to?"

Roman looked in her eyes. "To you and I!"

"To you and I! Cheers!"

"Cheers baby!" Roman drank all his champagne and Angelica did the same!

"That was good," Angelica said.

Roman took his clothes off and just stood there in front of her with only his boxers on. "You see how much I missed you?"

Angelica started laughing at his huge erection!

Roman laughed. "You know what they say? Laugh now, cry later!"

Angelica started backing up as if she were going to leave the room, but Roman grabbed her. "Are you sure about this Angelica. Do you need more time? I can wait if you need more time."

"Are *you* sure Roman?"

"Of course, I'm sure. -You think I'm not?"

"Do you think you're ready to be in a relationship with a woman with three children who are not your own? Do you think that you can deal with the fact that my soon to be ex-husband and I talk on the phone now and then as friends and nothing more?"

Roman kissed her. "Yes, I'm ready for that and a whole lot more! But I want to know if you're ready to be with me."

"Yes, I feel that I am ready."

Roman took her left hand and kissed it. "Are you sure? Before we lay down, are you sure about this? Are you sure about us?"

"I am unsure about some things in my life, but I am sure that I want this. I want more than a

217

friendship. I want to be your special-woman-friend," she said laughing. Roman smiled and kissed her cheek. "But wait one second!"

"What?"

"What about Monica and the others."

"What about them?"

"What do you mean what about them? Is this going to be a monogamous friendship," she said taking off her sundress revealing a black silk negligee.

Roman stared at her up and down. "Yes!" He kissed her lips and picked her up, "Do you want me?"

"Yes." Roman laid her body down on the bed and pulled up her negligee. He licked and sucked on her breasts and kissed all over her stomach. He moved back up to her mouth and pulled her straps down off her shoulders making sure he kissed each one of her shoulders. Angelica put her hand on the back of his neck and guided him back up to her lips.

Roman looked at her. "I missed you so much! I am so happy that you want to be mine."

"Are you?"

"Yes, I am. You're my woman now. I'm going to make up for all those years you wasted...and I'm not referring to your children in any way!" Angelica laughed. "I'm serious. You belong to me now! There is no turning back after tonight."

"What if I change my mind," Angelica said smiling.

"You won't!" Roman pulled off her gown and slowly pushed his boxers down his legs. He laid on top of her and kissed her while putting his hand on his penis preparing for entry!

"Roman?"

"Yes."

"Did you...did you put a condom on?"

Roman smiled, "No."

"Don't you want..."

"No. But if you want me to, I will." Roman laid over top of her waiting.

"I am taking birth control pills," she said smiling.

Roman laughed. "I know baby."

Roman reached over to get into his nightstand, and Angelica pulled him back, "We've taken care of our responsibilities. We have both been repeatedly tested for everything under the sun. I'm serious about us, and I'm ready." She kissed his lips.

Roman kissed her and pushed slowly inside. Angelica closed her eyes and held her mouth wide open. "Can you feel me, baby?"

"Yes!"

"I've been waiting for almost three months just to see you again." Angelica wrapped her legs around him and made sure he could feel her moving with him.

Roman stopped moving and just laid on top of her. Angelica looked at him, "What's wrong?"

"I just need to slow down for a minute."

"Why? Are you ok? Is something wrong?"

Roman looked at her and smiled, "No." He kissed her lips. "Everything is perfect." He put his hands on her hips and moved deeper. Angelica called his name. "Yes."

"Roman, I missed you so much." Roman sucked on her neck and breasts leaving marks behind to remind her who she belonged to. Angelica moaned louder and held on to him. "Roman you feel so good!"

Roman played with her earlobe with his tongue. "Angelica, can I come inside of you?"

Angelica moaned louder and moved her hips more and more. "Roman..."

"Yes," he said.

She put her hands on his face. "Take me please!" He pushed her legs off of his back and grabbed her waist. Roman held on to her and pulled her up so that she was sitting on his lap facing him. He moved to the edge of the bed so that his legs could dangle over the edge of the bed and his feet could touch the floor. Angelica rode him while he held on to her hips moving inside of her as well. He sucked on her breasts and played with her nipples with his tongue. She looked down at his face being smothered by her 36 D's. "What am I going to do with you?"

Roman picked her up again and turned her around so that she was now laying on her back. Roman stood up and held her legs up in the air while watching himself glide in and out of her wet pussy. "You ready for me?"

Angelica shook her head. "No, I want you to come close to me."

Roman put her legs down, slid his arm underneath her, and moved their bodies higher up on the bed while staying connected as one. He then laid down on top of her and met her face to face. "Is this close enough," he said moving very slow. Angelica smiled nodding her head. Roman kissed her lips. "Answer me!"

Angelica laughed. "Oh really?" Roman nodded his head while moving deeper and deeper.

He stared into Angelica's eyes but didn't say a word. She tried to stay focused on his, but her eyes kept closing from his deep penetration.

Roman put his hand on her face, "I'm making love to my angel. Are you ready for me?"

Angelica looked at him. "Yes!" Roman moved faster and deeper! He moved with a type of hunger and desperation that she hadn't experienced before. "Oh shit," Angelica pleaded! She grabbed onto the sheets beneath her and bawled them in her fists. His back was too damp to grasp!

"Are you all mine baby?" Angelica looked at him but couldn't respond. Roman slowed down and circled his hips while moving in and out of her. "Angelica, did you hear me," he asked. When he looked in her watering eyes, he knew! He resumed his fast-pace-stroke to the point where she couldn't even talk. Angelica knew that she came, but it came so fast that all she could do was gasp for air! She had never experienced this type of lovemaking before and was completely dumbfounded!

All she could do was look at the ceiling with her mouth open. Another orgasm was coming around the damn bin, and she was losing it. "Roman..."

Roman slowed down, kissed her lips, and moaned. "It's a lot baby, you still want it?"

"Yes, I want you! I want all of you!" Angelica felt her orgasm building up and then finally letting go as Roman shot his come deep inside of her.

Roman held on to her so tight while coming. He kissed her lips and would not stop moving until it all came out inside of her! Roman rolled over next to her and breathed heavily with his eyes closed thinking about what he just did. He then looked at Angelica who was staring at him. "I noticed that you didn't have a bag with you when you came in the house."

"I left it in the car. I guess I was so excited about seeing you that I forgot to get it!"

Roman kissed her lips. "So, you're staying until Friday?"

"Yeah! Winter's still coming over on Friday, right?"

"Yeah, I'm picking her up after work," he said playing with her hair. "Speaking of work, when are you going back?"

"September the fourteenth. I miss work, but I don't miss work. I know you know what I mean!" Angelica stood up to go to the bathroom.

"Where are you going?"

Angelica looked at him. "Somebody made a mess! I need to clean it up!"

Roman laughed. Angelica went into the bathroom and closed the door. She turned on the water so that she could take a shower. Roman knocked on the bathroom door, and Angelica opened it. "Yes? How can I help you," she asked laughing.

Roman tried to keep a straight face, "I need to talk to you about something."

Angelica walked over to the shower and stepped in. "What's up?" Roman came in the bathroom and just stared at her as she closed her eyes and let the water run across her face. She opened her mouth allowing the water to fall in and out like a waterfall. She grabbed the soap, washcloth and started to wash her body.

Roman looked at the steam coming from the shower and felt the water temperature, "Angelica."

"Yes."

"Baby, why is the water so hot?"

"That's the way I like it." Roman turned down the hot water a little and turned up the cold. "Why did you do that? It has to be hotter than that."

Roman pushed open the shower door, "Why? The water is too hot Angelica! You don't need it that hot!"

Angelica looked at him. "It's not that hot. You're overreacting."

"Ok. How long have you been taking these hot showers? Baby, listen. I understand…"

Angelica shook her head and turned away, "Please."

"Please what? I know why you're doing it, but baby take one day at a time! Try it a little less hot this week. Can you do that for me?" Angelica just stared at him wanting to be upset but feeling like she was going to cry. Roman took off his boxers and got into the shower with her. "Baby, it's too hot for me. Can you turn it down a little?" Angelica turned it down even more for him to enter. He kissed her on the lips, "See you did it for me. I just want you to do that for yourself and me!" Angelica turned toward the shower heads and didn't say anything. She continued washing up, and Roman did the same. Things were awkward and quiet in the shower, so Roman decided to break the tension. He stood close behind her and started washing her back. When he was finished, he turned her around and looked at her. "You want some ice cream?"

Angelica smiled, "Yes." Roman gave her a kiss.

"I'm going down to the kitchen. I'll meet you back in the room and don't turn the hot water back up!" Angelica looked at him and squinted her eyes. "Don't look at me like that woman!" Roman went downstairs to get them some dessert while Angelica finished up and dried off. She walked into the bedroom and looked in one of her drawers for something to wear. Angelica decided to put on a camisole and some pretty panties. She laid on the bed waiting for Roman. Angelica felt like God gave her another chance at happiness with Roman. She knew she was in love with him, but she didn't want to tell him. Angelica felt that it was too soon and the papers for her divorce weren't even signed yet! Waiting until then was best.

"I have a huge bowl of strawberry ice cream, with freshly sliced strawberries and whipped cream," he said holding up the can of whipped cream. He placed the large stainless-steel bowl on the bed and sprayed whipped cream over the ice cream and strawberries.

"This looks so good!" She took a scoop of the ice cream, put a strawberry on it and sprayed some whipped cream on the spoon. "You first," she said putting the spoon up to his mouth.

"No, you eat it first!"

"No, I want you to eat some first! I want to feed you!"

Roman sat down on the bed and kissed her. "That's what I'm talking about!"

Angelica fed him the ice cream and some whipped cream got on the side of his mouth. "Here you have some whipped cream on your cheek." Angelica licked the whipped cream from his cheek and kissed him.

Roman took a spoonful for her to eat. "For my woman!" Angelica opened her mouth, and Roman put the spoon in. As he retrieved it, he picked up the can and sprayed some on her lips. Angelica laughed while he licked and sucked all over her lips. Roman put the can down on top of his dresser next to the bed. He stood up and went over to his main dresser. Roman pulled out a gift box and took it over to where Angelica was sitting. Angelica moved back on the bed with a very confused look on her face. "Angelica, I am so happy that you are here with me. I don't want to say too much, but I will say that I care a lot about you. I care a lot about us and I'm looking forward to having you in my life." He held the box in front of her while she just looked at it.

"Roman..."

"Open it, baby!" Angelica opened the signature Tiffany box. Inside was a platinum Tiffany Petals Key Pendant hanging from a platinum necklace. The key pendant had encrusted round, crystal clear diamonds. Angelica started to cry and just looked at him. "Do you like it?"

"Yes, it's beautiful! But I can't accept this! It's too expensive and...,"

"Turn around." Angelica turned around, and Roman put the platinum necklace around her neck. "The key represents the control and power that you have with overcoming obstacles that come your way." He kissed her on the back of her neck. "The necklace and key also represent me. I'm always close to your heart, and as long as you want me in your life, I'll always be around you! After saying all that...," he said laughing, "...you know what the key represents!" Angelica looked at the necklace and pendant and then turned around to face him.

"Angelica even though we talked every single day on the phone for the past few months, I still didn't know if you were going to come here tonight. I didn't know that you would be ready for us to take that next step. I couldn't see you or touch you for almost three months." Roman brought her closer and held her. "As each day passed by, I realized that I was always thinking about you. Of course, I thought about being with you sexually, but I missed being around you! I missed seeing your pretty face, watching you laugh, and fall asleep. I missed you! I'm a very disciplined and patient man, but these past few months were extremely difficult for me."

He was silent for a minute because he didn't want to stray from what he wanted to say. "Remember last month when I had a really rough day at work? It was around seven or eight o'clock at night, and I told you that I couldn't talk because I was really tired?"

Angelica shook her head yes. "We hadn't talked that whole day. I called you around twelve or so in the afternoon, and you were really short with me. -Like you were mad at me or something! The next day you said the same thing!"

Roman kissed her lips and ran his index finger along the chain. "Then what did you do on that second day of me trying to avoid you? You sent me a message on my phone telling me to go to the door!" Angelica cracked up laughing. "And when I got to the door, I saw a brown shopping bag outside my door with my name on it. You brought me a huge container of spaghetti, a 2-liter Sprite, some Pepperidge Farm Bordeaux Cookies with Vanilla Ice Cream and a note!" Angelica smiled. "You wrote: *I know you're tired! If you're too tired to talk to me, I guess you're too tired to cook so here's dinner! Enjoy!*"

"Then you wrote: *Even though you haven't spoken to me in 2 days, and you have been very short with me on the phone, I still miss you!*" Angelica put her hand on his face and smiled adoring everything about him. "Angelica, I'm in love with you. I know you're ironing out things in your life. This might be too much for you, right now, but I need you to know how I really feel."

Angelica started crying again and looked down. "Roman...," she stopped and took a deep breath.

Roman lowered his head to hers so that they were on the same eye level. "I'm not expecting anything from you, Angelica."

Angelica caressed his face, "Roman, I'm in love with you too! I would be crazy not to! You're my guardian angel, my Roman Knight in shining armor...always rescuing me," she said laughing. Roman pushed her back onto the bed and kissed her. "I wanted to wait until I got the final decree before I told you."

"My angels in love with me huh," he said playing with her hair.

"Completely! So, try not to crumble my heart please."

"Angelica," he said laying back on the bed, "Come here, baby." Angelica did as he requested and kissed him. He looked at the pendant hanging from her neck.

"Roman, you are such a wonderful man! I'm so happy that you are in my life. I really am."

His finger trailed the chain again around her neck. "So, when do I meet the other half of you?"

Angelica laughed. "I don't know. What do you think about Labor Day? Too soon?"

Roman smiled. "That would be perfect. My family's having a barbecue at the Plateau. Some family and friends will be there too."

Angelica playfully nudged Roman. "You know Kendall's birthday is Saturday!"

Roman pinched her butt. "Yeah, what are you all going to do for his birthday?"

"Kendall wanted a magic show with about six of his friends at the house. Ian is supposed to be taking care of magic show part," she said sounding a little dry.

Roman's fingers trailed along her neck, "Why did you say it like that? I'm quite sure he'll pull through for him."

Angelica just looked at Roman not wanting to tell him how she really felt. "You're right. He'll

234

have a good time! Hailey's making his birthday cake, and Gavin is picking out his gift. I'm on party favors, food, decorations, etc." Angelica got real quiet for a minute.

"What's wrong," Roman said rubbing her back.

"Will Winter be there at the barbecue?"

"Yes. Why?"

Angelica shrugged her shoulders like a little kid. "What if she doesn't like me?"

"What?!" Roman laughed, "What if Kendall, Gavin, and Hailey hate **me**?" The both of them laughed. "You know what? I think falling in love was the easy part! Meeting the children and getting **their** blessings can be our biggest challenge. We gotta plan this right baby so don't come to the barbecue wearing something all sexy! I need to be on my best behavior for the kids!"

They laughed and talked till they fell asleep at around three in the morning...only to wake back up at four!

Chapter 11 – Lesson: SOMETIMES...Things Aren't What They Seem

~August 29th – Kendall's Birthday

"Mommy, I don't think the magician is coming. Can you call him," Kendall asked impatiently.

"Baby give him a little more time. He's probably stuck in traffic! Go ahead and finish playing. I'll get the Pin-the-Tail-on-the-Donkey. We can play that until he comes." Kendall walked away gleaming since he loved to play Pin-the-Tail-on-the-Donkey. Angelica was furious!

"Sweetheart, you ok," asked Mrs. Delores.

"Ian was supposed to get the magician. I'll be right back. Can you watch the kids for me, mom?"

"Sure, go!" Angelica went to the house and shuffled upstairs to the bathroom. She was so mad she wanted to cry. When she talked to Ian earlier in the day, he said he had everything covered. Angelica started tearing up a bit but then got herself together.

She did a mental checklist of what she had going on: food, hot dogs, and hamburgers were almost done, the corn was done, the cake was finished, candles, rolls for the dogs and hamburgers, ketchup, mustard, snacks, juice, party bags and favors and his gift. She felt like something was missing. "Shit, ice cream!!" Angelica's cell phone rang. "Hello!"

"Hey, baby! What's wrong?"

"Hey, Roman! I'm so sorry! I'm gonna have to call you back."

"What's wrong?"

She sighed. "How are you? Everything ok at work?"

"Yes. Now, what's going on?"

Angelica took a deep breath. "The magician's not here, and I forgot to buy ice cream for the cake. I'm about to go to the market really quick and make a couple of calls to see what I can do about a magician."

"Angel, look. Just stay right there ok. I'll call you back in five minutes."

"But I really need to go to the market, Roman..."

"Baby trust me. Give me five minutes."

"Ok."

Roman hung up the phone and made a call, "Yeah, you can go ahead on in. She'll be expecting you...Alright man...Peace." Officer Straight looked at Roman and shook his head smiling. Roman called Angelica back, "Hello."

"Yes."

"Baby, the magician is coming to your door right now."

"What? How did you..."

"Baby, I gotta go. I'll call you back ok."

"Ok." Angelica's doorbell rang, and she ran downstairs to answer the door. "Hi!"

"Hello, Ms. Angelica! Officer Callowhill has arranged for me to perform for your son Kendall's birthday party," he said bowing his head speaking with an English accent!

"Why thank you! This way please!" Angelica took him to the back yard, and all the kids started screaming and cheering when they saw the magician wearing the traditional black suit, cape, magic wand, and top hat.

"Attention, please!! Attention, please!! I am Steven the Magnificent, and I'm here to perform for Master Kendall and his party! Is he here?" Everyone yelled and pointed at Kendall who was in awe at the great magician. He had everyone's attention except Angelica. She was looking at everyone else and was so glad that Kendall was enjoying himself. She thought about Roman and started rubbing the key pendant hanging from her neck. Angelica loved Roman so much. He came through for her and her children, and she was so thankful that she had a *real* man in her life. A man who could truly be her friend and partner. Angelica started tearing up a bit as she saw Hailey walking toward her.

"Mom, look! Why are the police here?"

Angelica snapped back to reality and turned around still holding on to her key. Roman opened the side fence and stepped into the back yard.

Angelica was stunned to see him at her house but couldn't tell Hailey to go back to the party because she would get suspicious. She didn't know what she was going to say so she just kept her mouth closed.

"Ms. Bryant. I'm Officer Callowhill. We were just patrolling the area and heard some screaming. Is everything ok?"

Angelica kept her tears at bay, "Yes officer thank you!"

"Hi, Officer Callowhill! I'm Hailey! Thanks for making sure that we were ok!"

"You're welcome Hailey."

Hailey pointed to the grill. "Do you want a hot dog or a hamburger?"

Roman laughed and looked at Angelica. "No, I have to get going."

Hailey continued. "They were screaming because the magician came. You can't stay for a just a little bit," Hailey pleaded.

"No, I'm sorry I can't."

"Awe man! Mom you know Gavin loves police officers! Let me go and get him! Officer Callowhill don't leave yet. Wait one minute," Hailey said running off.

Hailey ran to get Gavin and Angelica looked at Roman. "Thank you so much Roman. You came through for us. Thank you!"

"That's what your man is supposed to do. He's supposed to come through and have your back at all times."

"I wish I could kiss you right now," Angelica wanted him so bad! She loved when she saw him wearing his uniform.

Roman winked his eye, "I wish you could do more than that!"

Hailey ran up to Roman. "Officer Callowhill this is Gavin!"

Roman knelt down so that he could be on his level. "Hello Gavin!"

Gavin was awestruck. "Hi! Are you here to arrest someone?"

Roman laughed. "No, unfortunately not!"

"Awe man!" The dispatcher sounded out a code over his radio. Gavin looked at Roman as if he were a real superhero!

Roman stood up from his crouched position. "Ok family, I gotta go!"

"Can I go with you," asked Gavin.

Angelica looked at him and frowned a bit, "You can't go with him, Gavin. His job can be very dangerous."

Roman put his hand on Gavin's shoulder, "I'll tell you what. The officers are having a barbecue out at the park on Labor Day. Would you like to come?"

"Yeah, we'll be there!" Gavin screamed! Angelica laughed while Gavin and Hailey went back with the other kids.

Angelica winked her eye at Roman. "Very clever officer."

"Here," he handed her a key, "This is to my front door. I have a few gallons of ice cream in the basement freezer. Call me later." Angelica looked as he walked away feeling sad that she couldn't at least give him a kiss.

He turned around and looked at her. "I love you," said Angelica.

"I love you to baby!"

After all the guests had left, Angelica cleaned up while the kids showered and prepared to go over Angelica's mom's house. She finished washing the dishes, cleaning the yard, and putting all the food in storage bags for the kids to take over her mother's. She took a sip of juice, sat down, and looked at the clock. It was 8:16. Her mom called five minutes ago and said that she was ten minutes away. She took another sip and thought about Roman getting off at 8:30. Angelica mustered up some energy and went upstairs to help get the kids ready. She heard the house phone ring and answered, "Hello?"

"Angelica it's Ian. I'm sorry about the magician. I had an emergency and I…"

"I took care of it, but you could have called me just to let me know that you had an emergency,

Ian! Look, if you don't want any drama, don't bring any ok?!"

"Angelica look, I don't want to argue with you."

Angelica laughed, "The kids are upstairs getting ready to go to my mom's for the weekend so if you want to talk to them, that's where they'll be."

"Alright," Ian didn't know what else to say. He felt bad that he was with Michelle the whole time. He made a promise to himself that he would never do that again. "Angelica I'm sorry. I'll call over your mom's tomorrow and speak with them. Again, I'm sorry."

Angelica just hung up the phone without saying goodbye and then heard her front door open.

"Angelica, it's me," yelled her mother.

"Ok! Kendall, Gavin, and Hailey, mom-mom's here!" The kids cheered and ran down the kitchen stairs. Angelica walked down the stairs after them and sat in the kitchen with the kids and her mom.

Mrs. Delores could see that she was tired to the bone. She walked over to her and kissed her on the cheek, "Hey sweetie! The party was great. The kids had a **good** time! I saw that the police came by. What was that about," she said smiling and raising her eyebrows.

"Mom-mom, that was Officer Callowhill. He was checking up on us. He heard the kids yelling and screaming when the magician came," Hailey explained.

"Yeah! He invited us to a barbecue on Labor Day! I can't wait," added Gavin.

"I wanna go too," whined Kendall who was sleepy as ever!

"You will Kendall," said Angelica. "We're all going!"

"Wow, this Officer Callowhill seems to be pretty nice guy huh," said Mom-mom suspiciously.

"Mom-mom, I saw his handcuffs **and** gun! It was so cool," said Gavin with his Ronald McDonald smile.

"That's wonderful. Now, lets' get going so that your mom can finally eat some dinner," she said smiling to Angelica. "Say goodnight to mommy!"

"Good night," they all said giving her a kiss.

"I love you, mommy," said Kendall kissing her cheek.

"I love you too baby," replied Angelica. Hailey and Gavin gave her a hug and walked outside to her mother's car. Angelica walked with her mom and Kendall to the door. "Thanks, mom! Ian might be calling to talk to them sometime tomorrow."

Mrs. Delores looked at her phone, "Is that *your* phone ringing?"

"Yeah give me a minute! I'll meet you outside," she said running to the kitchen to get her cell. Roman's name flashed on the screen of her smart phone. "Hello?"

"Hey baby, how's it going?"

"It's going ok. How was work, you doing ok," she asked walking to the front door.

"Yeah I'm fine. What are you doing?"

"The kids are just leaving. I cleaned up everything and now I'm drinking some juice," she said laughing.

"I'll just come over there then. Is that cool," Roman said taking his sweats off.

"You know what? That sounds great! Hold on one second." Angelica opened the screen door, "Bye! Love you!" She waved goodbye and put the phone up to her face. "Roman, how long will it take for you to get here?"

"I'll be there in fifteen minutes, and we're going out to dinner."

"Ok, I'll be ready. Are you only staying for the night?"

Roman smiled, "I'll stay as long as you like."

Angelica laughed, "I'm not even going to respond to that. I'll be ready when you get here. Should I get dressed up?"

"Surprise me," Roman said running his shower. "I'll be there in fifteen minutes."

"Ok, see you soon. Be careful."

"Alright, bye."

"Bye."

~

Ding-dong!!

"Coming," Angelica walked down the steps in her short, black chiffon halter dress. The halter dress was gathered in the front with a silver leather strap wrapped around her neck. The dress had a low back which she loved. There were two leather straps connected to the one around her neck which fell right along the length of her spine. She put on just a little makeup and some lip gloss with her N. Rodriguez perfume. Her hair was pinned up, and she was so excited to see Roman. She opened the door, "Hey! Right on time! I just have to put on my shoes and grab my bag!" Roman looked at her up and down and walked in the door.

"I'll be back in a second! I just have to get my shoes!" Angelica ran up the stairs and went into her closet to get her sandals. Roman walked behind her up the stairs and into her bedroom. "Roman you look so handsome. Are you double parked? Why'd you come upstairs? I'll only be a minute!"

All he could do was stare at her. She was utterly breathtaking! She looked so vibrant and beautiful. He couldn't say a word. Angelica turned around and saw the look in his eyes. She dropped her shoes on the floor and kissed him. "I missed you so much."

Roman grabbed her close. "You really surprised me tonight with that dress you have on. You look beautiful baby! Do you know of any good delivery places around here?"

Angelica laughed. "We should go!"

"I know, but I need you."

Angelica smiled, "Roman! I know a nice Chinese delivery place about three blocks away!"

"I have a surprise for you," he said kissing her neck and untying her halter dress.

"What is it?"

"I'll show you tomorrow."

"Oh no!! Please tell me!"

Roman took her dress off revealing her black thong and the key pendant around her neck, "I missed you so much."

"I missed you too," she said unbuttoning his shirt while he shuffled his shoes off. She kissed him, he picked her up, and threw her on the bed. Angelica laughed and stared in his eyes. Roman got on his knees, pushed her thong to the side, and started eating her. "Roman stop!"

Roman got up off his knees and went up to her. He could tell that something was wrong the way that she told him to stop. "What's wrong?"

"I'm sorry. Can you just take it slow please?"

"I'll do whatever you want Angelica. Just relax ok. You know I'm not going to hurt you, right?"

"Yes."

"I love you," he said kissing on her neck. He slowly moved all the way down to her pussy. Roman put his hands on her lips and opened them. Angelica breathed deeply. He started licking her straight up and down slowly savoring her. Roman then slightly pushed up on her lips exposing her clitoris and began to lick it gently. Then he just started licking and sucking everything. She could feel his saliva traveling down her ass while he ate her sloppily! Angelica moaned like crazy begging for him.

"Roman, I love you so much!"

"How much do you love me," he said smiling.

"More than I can explain! You can have whatever you want from me! I love you," she looked at him and held his face in her hands while tearing up. Roman stopped making love to her and just laid there looking at her in disbelief. "Roman Xavier Callowhill, I love you more than any woman has ever loved you, for the exception of your mother," she chuckled. "I wish you hadn't asked me that! Now I feel like a complete idiot."

Roman crawled up her body and hovered over her. "Angelica Sofia Bryant, I'm waiting for you. I'm here waiting for you and when you're ready for me, just say the word." Angelica just looked at him. "Do you understand me? I'm waiting for you so that you can be with me. Take your time and do what you need to do because I'm waiting for you, ok?"

"Yes," she said crying.

Roman entered her, "I'm not going anywhere. I'm waiting for you baby," he said moving inside of her. He lifted her leg and gave her what she needed.

Angelica took her leg away from his grasp and put it down, "Roman stop." Roman stopped and pulled out.

"What's wrong?"

Angelica turned around and got on her hands and knees. Roman's eyes widened at her spread from the rear. He pulled up behind her and eased his way inside. Angelica moaned while stuffing her head in the pillow. Roman moaned and talked to her while he made love to her. "I love you so much, baby! Am I hurting you?"

"No."

"Do you like it," he asked smiling.

"Yes...I love it, Roman." They made love for about an hour before they stopped...to order food.

Chapter 12 – Lesson: It is What it is!

~Sunday, 10:02 am

Angelica woke up alone in bed. She thought that Roman was downstairs, so she hopped in the shower. After drying off, she put on a camisole and some house pants. "Roman are you down there?" She could see that he was in the middle of cooking breakfast but, he was in the backyard on the phone. As soon as she opened the screen door, he turned around holding up his index finger. Angelica nodded her head in acknowledgement and closed the screen door behind her. She figured that he was probably on the phone with someone concerning police matters. After she poured herself something to drink in the kitchen, she walked to the front door to see if the mail came. Angelica sighed as she picked the mail up off the floor. Three were utility bills, and one was from her lawyer. Angelica opened the letter and read it.

"Angelica, I have to go," he said walking up behind her. Angelica looked at him with her face frowned up. "I have some things I need to do. I'll be back around four."

"What's going on?"

"It's complicated. I'll call you later on, ok?"

Angelica laughed, "Ok." She walked up the stairs to get her clothes ready for the day.

Roman looked at her walking up the steps and knew she was upset because she didn't even give him a hug or kiss. Roman opened the front door and left out.

~5:19pm

Angelica walked out of the movies with her large jug of cherry coke. She couldn't believe how the movie ended. As soon as she opened her phone, she could see that her mom and Roman called. Angelica called her mom and was reassured that everything was ok. Kendall just called her to say hello. "Mom, can you tell him I'll call him around bedtime?"

"Sure sweetie."

"Did Ian call to speak to them?"

"No, he didn't."

Roman was calling on the other line. "Mom, thank you! I'll talk to you later."

"Ok!"

Angelica answered. "Hello."

"Hey! Are you alright? I've been calling you for about an hour," he said sounding worried.

"I just came out of the movies. I had the phone on vibrate in my purse," she fibbed! "Is everything ok?"

"Yeah, everything is fine. Where are you?"

"I'm at the Bridge on Walnut."

"Are you going somewhere else?"

"No, I'm not."

"Can I meet you at your house then... so we can go to dinner?"

"Ok. I'll be there in about thirty minutes."

"I'll meet you there." Roman put on some nice dress jeans, a Sean John dress shirt, and black leather suede loafers. He put on his Safari cologne, checked his wallet, grabbed his keys, phone, and left out.

Angelica pulled up to her house and saw Roman's truck parked across the street. She acted like she didn't see it and stepped out of her Volvo SUV. The blue jean shorts that she had on were respectfully short. The green halter top that was fitted at the top and flared around the midsection looked gorgeous! Her hair was pinned up, and he could see that she had on lip gloss. She closed the door and dropped her keys in the street. Angelica bent over, picked them up and walked to her front steps while pressing the alarm on her car.

Roman shook his head. Every time he saw her, it was as if he was seeing her for the first time. He hopped out the truck, "Angelica!"

She turned around and smiled. "Hey!"

Roman walked up to her and kissed her. "Good Morning."

Angelica laughed, "Good Morning Roman!"

She started walking up the stairs but Roman still had his hand on her arm. "Come here and give me some love baby." Angelica smiled walked down the steps and quickly kissed him on the lips. "What was that?"

"A kiss," she said laughing.

"I want a real kiss. An Angelica-Kissing-Her-Roman-Kiss!" Angelica got closer to him, wrapped her arms around him and kissed him. She walked up the steps and looked back at him still standing there. "Our reservations aren't' until seven."

"Ok, that's gives me some time to get ready."
Roman walked up the steps behind her and stared
at her while she unlocked the door. "Why are you
looking at me like that?"

"No reason." He couldn't wait until they got
in the house! "Where did you go today?"

"Up to Willow Grove Mall! I brought us
some Cheesecake since it's one of your favorites! I
saw a couple of my friends and then I went to the
movies!" She opened the door, "Where did you go
today?"

"I took care of a couple of things and talked
with a couple of friends." Roman walked in the
house behind Angelica and locked the door.

"Now that doesn't sound as urgent as it did
this morning. What's going on?" Angelica put her
bag on the couch and went in the kitchen.

Roman sat on the couch debating whether
he should lie or tell the truth.

"What's wrong, cat got your tongue!" She
walked back in the living room with grapes in a
large bowl. She popped one in her mouth and sat
down next to him. She took one from the vine and
fed it to him.

"I had to see Monica."

Angelica moved back and looked at him. "Why what's going on?"

"She needed to talk to me about something."

"And why aren't you telling me what that something was about?"

"She wanted to see me one last time. We talked, and that was that."

She put the grapes down and looked at Roman. "So, you leave here with me, to see her because she wants to see you for the last time? It's August Roman, what's up with 'the last time' request? What's going on?"

Roman just looked at her.

"Roman I asked you a question. What's going on?"

"Nothing, I went over there, we talked, and then I left."

Angelica looked at him and shook her head. She walked toward the stairs. "Roman you can show your lying ass out of my house ok!"

"What?!"

"You heard me! You left out of here like a bat out of hell, and now you expect me to believe that you just talked to her and then left?"

"Angelica we just talked and that was it."

"Answer this question for me. What was the emergency?

"What?"

"Why did you leave out of here so quick if you were just going over there to talk? What happened and why did it take so long to TALK?" Roman stayed silent.

"Roman Leave!"

"Why? I didn't do anything!"

"You didn't have sex with her Roman? Why did you have to see her if all you were doing was saying goodbye? You told me it was over in June. It's August Roman," she yelled. Angelica walked up the stairs and went into her bedroom. She laid on the bed and held onto her pillow. Tears fell from her eyes as Angelica looked at her bedroom floor. She stared at her shoes that she was going to put on the night before.

Roman walked into the bedroom. "Angelica, I didn't have sex with her. We talked for a long while, and that was it."

"Can you please leave?"

"Why are you telling me to leave? I'm telling you the truth!"

"Please just go."

259

"No...I'm not leaving," he said confidently.

Angelica sat up. "This is my house, and I want you to leave!" Roman walked over to where she was laying. He kissed her, but she pushed him away before it could go any further. "You don't tell me that you love me and how much you're waiting for me and then abruptly leave without explaining what happened...until five in the evening! And now you tell me it's because of some fucking woman that you had been sleeping with, calls you, and tells you that she wants to see you... because she wants to see you one last time! If you all were only seeing each other for two months, why the fuck is she still lingering on?"

"Because she loves me..."

Angelica shook her head in disbelief. "And you love her too right?"

"It's not like that! She was there for me when I needed some help, and the least I could do was go and see her one more time to say goodbye."

"For you or her? Roman, you know what? It's ok! Just please leave."

"No, I'm not leaving. You don't want me to leave, so stop saying that!"

"Oh...now you just **know** I don't want you to leave huh? That chic got your head all pumped up! Women love you here, there...Roman, I got news for you! We are not getting any younger, so you don't need to play games with me! I don't like being told half-ass truth's, especially involving bullshit! I don't like it or deserve it! I'm not tolerating it from Ian, you, or any other man! I want you to leave!"

"Angelica, look. I went over there..."

"Just save it Roman! I don't even care what happened! All I wanted was for you to be honest with me. If you can't trust that I mean what I say to you, how can you expect me to believe what you're saying to me?"

"I believe you love me, Angelica!"

"So why couldn't you be honest with me about what happened today?"

"I didn't want you to get upset about nothing!"

"Roman, talking about this is just useless at this point." Angelica laid back down and closed her eyes.

"Baby, I'm sorry I wasn't honest with you about putting an end to the relationship I had with

Monica. It was over when I told you, but she was having a hard time letting go. She kept calling me and doing all kinds of unnecessary shit, so I had to go and talk to her this morning so that she could accept the fact that it was really over between us." Angelica didn't say a word, and Roman was getting really scared. "Did you hear me?"

"Yes."

"Do you believe me?"

"If you want me to believe you, I'll believe you," she said with her eyes still closed.

"I want you to believe me because it's the truth!"

"Ok Roman. I believe you."

"Why the sarcasm?"

Angelica sat up and looked at him. "I said I believe you ok. How would you like me to say it to you? You want me to smile, kiss you, and tell you that I believe you and that everything's ok?"

Roman chuckled. "Yes."

Angelica shook her head no, "I'm not doing all that... but I believe you," she said laying back down. Roman walked over to where she was laying. He laid down beside her and kissed her neck. Angelica instantly wanted him. He rolled her over onto her back and kissed her lips. Angelica looked at Roman and didn't say anything. Roman unbuttoned her shorts and started to pull them off, "Roman don't."

"Why not? Why can't I make love to you?"

"Didn't you already have some today?"

Roman looked at her and got up. He stared at her for a moment and then walked downstairs. Angelica didn't move a lick! Roman walked out the house and closed the door. Angelica closed her eyes and started to drift off into la-la land when she heard steps in the hallway. Angelica opened her eyes and turned around. Roman was standing in the doorway. "I didn't have sex with her Angelica. I wouldn't do that shit to you!" Roman crawled on the bed and turned her around on her back. "I wouldn't do that to you, baby! I love you! I've never felt this way about a woman so why would I sabotage it by doing something stupid?"

Roman pulled on her halter top revealing her breasts. Angelica's eyes started watering. "Baby, I want you and not Monica or any other woman. I'm here with you waiting for you. Angelica, you have to trust me when I say that I'm your man and no one else's. I'm not seeing anyone else, and I'm definitely not having sex with anyone else! I want you and only you. When you're ready for me, I'll be that man that you've always wanted!" Roman sucked on her breasts while Angelica tried to push him away. "Angelica stop. Please!"

"Roman, I've heard all this before and I..."

"You haven't heard it from me! I'm not Ian! I'm a **real** fucking man, and I will not lie to you, Angelica!" Roman started to pull her shorts down when she held on to his hand.

"Roman, I understand why you did what you did with the whole Monica situation. I just wished that you just came out and told me. I don't need to hear all the bullshit Roman ok! I've already experienced the bullshit. I'm trying to enjoy being with someone who just wants to enjoy being with me, talking to me, and just have fun with me! I don't want you to feel obligated..."

"Angelica, stop it ok. Just stop," Roman climbed on top of her and kissed her. Angelica felt his rock-hard penis through his jeans! "Baby, I haven't seen you all day!" Angelica just stared at him.

"I missed you." Roman kissed her lips and when he heard her moaning, he stopped and pulled down her shorts and panties. He stared at her freshly waxed world! Roman touched her lips with his fingers and looked at her, "It's so soft and smooth."

"That's what a woman is supposed to do for her man. It's still hair down there, though. I'm not totally bald!" Roman took the halter all the way off, and Angelica stood up. "Now you lay back!" Roman reluctantly laid back while Angelica slowly took off his shirt pants, boxers, and socks. She climbed on top of him and started kissing his lips slowly moving to his neck, chest, and stomach.

She stopped and looked at him. Angelica didn't say anything, and neither did Roman! She took him in her hand, went to the base of his shaft, and grazed his balls! Roman was breathing real heavy while moaning and adjusting his pillow so that he could watch! Angelica licked underneath his balls and then licked and kissed her way back up to the base. She worked her way up to his head and then started sucking away. Roman was in pure heaven! She was sucking his dick so good. It was almost as good as her pussy! He went to look at his dick going in and out of her mouth, but her hair was in the way. Roman pulled her hair aside and held it there so he could see her on the job!

Angelica stopped after about ten minutes and climbed on top so that she could ride him. "Baby, don't stop...do not stop!"

She shook her head no. "That's your punishment for today," she said putting his dick inside of her. Roman closed his eyes because he knew for sure he was in heaven. He couldn't even imagine being inside anyone else like this!

He thought about how she was sucking on his dick and how good it felt. "Angel, you sucked my dick so good baby! Why did you do that?"

"I did it because I love you and I knew you would enjoy it. I didn't want to stop but, I had to," she said rocking her hips. "Surprises were coming out of your dick while I was sucking it."

Roman tightened his grip on her hips. "How did it taste?" He was so turned on! He knew he was going to come any minute if she didn't slow down.

"It was so sweet! I just swallowed it while I was sucking your dick."

"Angel, you gotta slow down baby," he begged.

"No! You feel too good inside of me."

"Baby it's coming. Oh, Shit!"

"Can you come in my mouth?"

"No...you're going to kill me...here it comes..."

"Roman, I'm going to suck it out!"

"No baby!" Angelica hopped off and popped it in her mouth! Come was still coming out of him as she sucked and swallowed. Roman watched and had a pillow in his mouth to muffle his loud screeching. He balled up his fist and hit on the bed while she still sucked on his cock. He opened his eyes and looked at her licking and sucking away. She made sure that she got every drop!

Angelica stopped and looked at him. "Did you like that?"

Roman looked at her and smiled. "Yes, I loved it!"

"Good, now it's time for you to take me to dinner Officer Callowhill!"

He shook his head. "I don't think so! You gotta give me about thirty minutes! You took a lot out of me! I gotta take a quick nap baby!"

"What! You better get up," Angelica said kissing him on his chest!

"No, no, no," he said moving his head to the side laughing.

"I'm going to take a shower and get something to snack on. Would you like something to drink?"

"Yes," he said pulling the sheet over his lower body!

Angelica looked at him while he was on his way to sleep. His eyes were already closed, and he just laid there. By the time she came back up the stairs with his juice and a few cookies, Roman was asleep and snoring! She laughed and closed the bedroom door!

~

September 7th – Labor Day!

"Mommy I can't wait until I see Mr. Roman at the barbecue," said Gavin.

Angelica smiled. "Ok, we'll be there in ten minutes!"

"Mommy, other kids, are goings to be there right," asked Kendall.

"Yeah, of course! They'll be playing baseball, volleyball, dodgeball the whole nine!"

"I can't wait to eat some ribs," laughed Hailey! Angelica laughed along with them while pulling up to the Belmont Plateau and trying to find somewhere to park. "Mom there's a parking spot over there!" Hailey pointed to a parking spot not far from Roman's truck, and Angelica went for it!

She turned off the car and looked at the kids. "Are you all ready?"

"Yes," they all said in unison!

"Ok, the rules! Do not go with anyone unless you ask me!"

"Ok, mom," they replied in their drab tone.

"Last thing! How do I look? Too mommy-ish!"

Hailey laughed, "No! You look pretty mom!"

"Yeah you look good," replied Gavin while Kendall laughed!

"Alright kids, be on your best behavior ok?!"

"Yes, mom!"

Everyone hopped out of the car! While the kids adjusted their clothes and gathered their gear, Angelica looked for the designated barbeque sign that Roman mentioned to her. She found the sign and walked with the kids over toward the group of people.

"Mommy, where is Mr. Roman," Gavin was getting impatient and looked for him through the crowd.

A beautiful woman walked up to Angelica and the kids, "Hello! Welcome to the barbecue! I'm Simone!"

"Hi Simone, I'm Angelica and this Kendall, Gavin, and Hailey my children," she said proudly.

"We're guests of Officer Roman Callowhill," Gavin said in a firm tone.

"Ok! My husband Cyrus and Roman are cousins!" Simone hugged Angelica. "Let me see," she said looking over toward the grilling area. "He's around here somewhere!" She looked at the kids. "Are you all ready for some barbecue?"

"Yes!" They said in unison.

Simone warmly rubbed Angelica's arm sensing her apprehension. Cyrus spoke with Simone about Angelica on the drive from their home in New York to Philadelphia. "Angelica the food is over there on the table. Help yourself to whatever you want."

"Thank you, Simone."

"Mommy let's get some ribs," Hailey said.

Angelica laughed. "I guess I'll be talking to you later!"

Simone laughed, "I'll be here!"

Angelica smiled and walked over toward the food.

~

"Cyrus, that was Angelica," Simone whispered. "She seems really nice!"

Cyrus chuckled. "Don't they all!" Simone hit him playfully on his shoulder. "I'm just joking baby!"

~

Angelica walked with the kids and helped them make their plates. They sat down at a nearby empty table, blessed the food, and started eating. Angelica wasn't hungry, just thirsty. "I'm going to get us something to drink." She walked back over to the food area, grabbed three Capri Sun's, and a Ginger Ale for herself.

Angelica heard Gavin scream, "Mr. Roman!"

She turned around and saw that Roman was at the table with the kids. Angelica smiled and walked back over to the picnic table. "There she is with our juice," Gavin said pointing at her. Roman turned his head and saw Angelica walking toward him wearing blue denim shorts, and a blue and white V-Necked Polo shirt, exposing her diamond key that he bought for her.

"Hey, Mr. Roman! Its' good to see you," Angelica said looking at how handsome he was.

He licked his lips subtly. "I'm glad you all could make it!"

A little girl walked up to Roman, "Daddy, are these the friends that you wanted me to meet?"

Roman looked at Angelica who was smiling at the sight of Winter. "Yes they are! Winter this is Hailey, Gavin, Kendall, and Ms. Angelica, their mother."

"Hi," said Winter smiling at them.

"Winter is such a cool name," Hailey said chuckling. "Were you born during the wintertime?"

"Yup! I sure was! Do y'all want to play volleyball?"

"I do," said Gavin.

All four of them started to walk away, "Be careful," Angelica yelled out. Hailey turned so that her mom could see her and stuck her thumb up in the air. Angelica smiled shaking her head.

"You look gorgeous! Can I have a kiss?"

"Roman!!"

"Alright. I need for you to meet me at my truck over there."

"For what? I can't leave the kids! What kind of mother would I be?"

"You're not leaving them! We're just walking over there for a minute. You'll still be able to see them. My mom will keep an eye on them."

Angelica stepped back and widened her eyes! "Your mom is here," she said holding her chest.

"My mom and my dad are here. I want you to meet them," Roman looked at his watch. "In ten minutes just mosey on over to my truck. Can you do that for me?"

Angelica nodded. "Yes I will."

Roman grabbed her hand and squeezed it before walking away. Angelica ate some of the kid's food since they weren't eating right then. Before she knew it, ten minutes had passed. As she walked toward his truck, Hailey spotted her walking away. "Mommy!" Hailey ran over to where she was walking.

"Yes!"

"I'm having so much fun! Winter is so much fun! Where are you going?"

"Roman wanted to talk to me over there. I'll be right back."

"Ok!" She said running back over to the volleyball net.

Angelica was halfway there and spotted Roman looking at her. She smiled at him and kept on walking until she felt her cell phone vibrating. Angelica stopped walking, pulled the phone from her pocket, and saw that it was Ian. "Hello?"

"Angelica, it's Ian."

Angelica instinctively turned around to look at the kids, "Hey, is everything ok?"

"I need your help with something."

Angelica stared at the kids playing and tried to focus. "Help with what?"

"I know you're bringing the kids over tonight and the agreement was that we have them every other month, but I need you to take them this month."

Angelica shook her head and looked to the sky. "And why is that?"

"I scheduled a trip and I..."

Angelica took a deep breath and began to unconsciously walk toward the kids. "Ian, I won't be able to do that. We made these arrangements with the counselor three weeks ago. I gotta go, I'll see you this evening." She hung up the phone, closed her eyes, took a couple of breaths, and put her phone back into her pocket. Angelica stared at the kids playing while folding her arms across her chest. The kids were having so much fun! Angelica calmed down just from observing the kids having a good time! She totally forgot all about meeting Roman at his truck! She turned around, and he was standing right behind her!

He looked a little angry. "Who was that?"

"Ian."

"What did he want?"

"He said he scheduled some kind of trip which was leading up to me having them this month instead of next month. I'm not doing it!" Roman hugged her and walked with her to his truck. They got in the truck and closed the doors. Angelica sighed. "So, what did you have to tell me?"

Chapter 13 – Lesson: Sometimes Things LOOK Pretty Good...But are They REALLY Good?

Roman took a firm hold of her hands. "Three things and they are all good news. First of all, I missed you so much today." He reached over and kissed her lips.

Angelica moaned and pulled away. "You better stop it before the kids come over and see us," she said laughing.

"Which brings me to the next point. Baby, I know we talked about moving in together, but I have to be honest with you. I can't take this living in two separate houses situation much longer!"

Angelica shook her head no. "I know but we have to give the kids time to adjust. They only know you as my friend. I mean I'm new at being a single parent," she said trying to laugh her fears away.

"Angelica, I'm not trying to rush you in any way. I just want to be with you. I need to be around the kids more so that they can get to know me and the same goes with Winter."

Angelica seriously looked at him. "I just don't want them to get used to you and then..." Angelica took a deep breath. "I understand where you're coming from. It's just that I don't want you to come into their lives if you're unsure about being with me like that! I don't want to hurt them or Winter!"

"Baby I know you're protecting them. I'm not unsure about being with you like that! I'm trying my best not to move too fast with you! I know you're not ready for what I have to give you. I'm waiting for you! But while I'm waiting, we need to be living together. We can live at your house and sell or rent mine. Or we can live at my house and sell or rent yours! Or we can buy a new house, whatever you want to do! I just need to be with you after a long hard day at work. I want to wake up seeing your face laying on my chest. I need to be around you as much as possible. And I want to be a good stepdad to the kids."

Angelica laughed out loud and hugged Roman. "I love you so much Roman!" She kissed him and pulled away smiling. She looked out of his slightly tinted windows and watched the kids playing together. "Winter is beautiful! I hope she likes me. I pray that she doesn't think that I'm some evil woman trying to take her mother's place and take her father away! Why didn't you tell me that your parents were going to be here?"

Roman took Angelica's hands again and stared into her eyes. "Baby. A friend of mine, who is a detective, told me that they're quite sure... that they have the man who assaulted you." Angelica looked at him and covered her mouth as she started to cry hysterically. Roman held her close as she buried her head into his chest. "They said that his M.O. was similar to what he did to you. Even though you can't ID him, one of his victims got a good look at him." Roman held on to her while she cried her heart out. "Baby it's over! It's all over!"

Angelica cried until she couldn't cry anymore. Roman just held her close and rubbed on her back while she calmed down. She wiped her face with tissue that Roman handed over to her and then reached out for him to hug her. Roman smiled, "I love you so much, baby. I told you that everything would be fine, now look!" Angelica laughed. "I **am** your guardian angel! I am here to love you, protect you, and provide you with everything that you may need," he said smiling at her. Angelica looked at him and put her hand on his face and just looked at him.

"I know that look! What do you want to say?"

"Nothing."

"Tell me, please." Angelica still stared at him and shook her head no. "Baby, whatever you have to say, I am ready to hear it!"

"I can't believe you're saying these things to me," she said looking out the window.

"What is it about?"

Angelica shook her head no. "We should be getting back to the barbecue."

"Yeah you're right. It's time for you to meet the fam."

"OH God! Give me strength!"

~

Minutes later, they walked over to the main table to have a bite to eat with his family. Roman held Angelica's hand. "Everybody, this is my very special friend Angelica!" He introduced her to each one of them at the table; there was his mom and dad, his brother Paul and his girlfriend Vivian, his cousin Cyrus with his wife Simone and son Cyrus Jr., along with Cyrus' mom and dad.

"It's nice to meet you," she said for the hundredth time! She looked over at the kids, and they were still playing hard.

Mrs. Sarah Callowhill, his mother, started the questioning while they sat down. "We've heard so much about you! I'm glad we are finally getting the chance to meet you!" Angelica smiled and nervously grasped the key around her neck. "So where do you live?"

Angelica looked at Mrs. Callowhill in the eye. "I have a house in West Philadelphia. On 49th and Hazel."

"That's over by University City right," asked Paul.

Angelica nodded her head, "Yes, it is!"

Mrs. Sarah smiled and ate a few string beans. "And what do you do?"

Angelica looked at her. "I'm a teacher! Well to be more specific, I'm an instructor with the FBI. I work in Center City."

Cyrus looked at her and Roman. He smiled, "Two law enforcers!"

Everybody laughed, and Roman looked at her to make sure she was ok. Angelica smiled at him and took a sip of her water.

"So besides spending all of your time with the kids, and some with Roman, what are some of the things that you enjoy doing," asked Mrs. Callowhill.

Angelica looked at the table and then at her, "Well, of course, I love to clean up," she said playfully. The whole table laughed! "I love working in my garden, roller-skating, working out at the gym, but I really have a passion for singing." Just then the kids came back to the table.

Roman smiled and looked at his family's reaction. "Well, my dear, you're going to have to let us hear something," Mrs. Callowhill crooned putting her hand over Angelica's.

Angelica looked at Roman who was now smiling at her hard. "I don't know! I'm very critical of myself and I..."

Mr. Brandon Callowhill, Roman's dad, pointed his finger at her while shaking his head in disagreement. "Sweetheart! We don't do that kind foolishness here! We would love to hear you sing! Try not to be shy! You ain't' on Apollo!" Everyone laughed except Angelica.

Hailey laughed. "Mom, sing that song that you've been singing in the shower!"

Roman egged her on. "Show 'em what you got!"

Angelica winced, "Ok. The song is called Love is You by Chrisette Michele." She smiled at Hailey and then to Roman. She sang the first verse and chorus with her eyes closed so that she could feel the music and not be distracted by the reactions on their faces. As she closed, she looked down at Roman and smiled. He just looked at her in amazement.

"Damn," said Paul. Everyone laughed out loud, and Angelica laughed right along with them.

Mrs. Callowhill's mouth was wide open, "Angelica..."

Angelica pulled her eyes away from Roman, "Yes ma'am."

"Your voice is simply beautiful! You were wonderful," Mrs. Sarah said smiling from ear to ear.

Simone touched her hand. "Angelica that was beautiful! You really don't have a reason to be shy about that gift at all!" Paul's girlfriend nodded her head in agreement.

"Roman I know she always sings for you," said his father.

Roman looked at the kids and then to Angelica. "She sings different songs, but she never sang that one for me."

"Now she did," laughed his father, "...I never heard that song before, but I know she sang that damn song to the T!"

"Yes she did Brandon," Mrs. Sarah said laughing.

Angelica looked at the kids and looked at Roman closely. "Did you like it?"

"Yes, I did." Roman kissed her on the cheek.

She whispered. "I sang it just for you," she said touching his hand. She looked at the kids again and saw that Kendall was dancing in place.

"Mommy, I have to go to the bathroom."

"Ok," Angelica started to get up.

Roman stood up, "I'll take him. Does Gavin have to go too?"

"I don't know...Mr. Roman, I think that we should run!"

Everybody at the table laughed while Roman and Kendall ran off. Gavin then began running with them, "I have to go too!"

Hailey and Winter looked at Angelica, "Mommy, we have to go too!"

Angelica stood up again, "Ok." She looked at Mrs. Sarah and the rest of the family. "I'll be right back!"

Mrs. Sarah waved her hands. "Go ahead, sweetie! We'll be right here!"

Angelica and the girls walked toward one of the Port-O-Potty's in the park which was not too far away.

Winter looked at Angelica, "Ms. Angelica, how do you like the family?"

Angelica rubbed her back appreciating her thoughtfulness. "They're really nice! I'm having a really good time."

"Good! Hailey's been telling me all about you."

"Oh really," Angelica said looking at Hailey.

Winter twirled in a circle. "Nothing bad...except you and her dad are almost divorced. We talked about a lot of stuff!"

Hailey tapped Angelica's arm, "Yeah! Mom, can I ask you a question?"

"Sure."

"Winter and I saw Mr. Roman looking at you at the table," Hailey said without skipping a beat.

Winter cut in, "Hailey and I just wanted to know if you and my dad were boyfriend and girlfriend."

Angelica stopped walking and just looked at them.

Hailey tapped Winter on the shoulder. "She always does this," she said shaking her head at her mom. "Mom, if you and Mr. Roman are boyfriend and girlfriend, it's ok with us!"

"What?!" Angelica stood there in disbelief at the girls' blatant honesty.

Winter grabbed Angelica's hand. "Ms. Angelica I can tell you are a really nice lady. My dad told me all about you! Plus, Hailey and I are sisters!!" Winter and Hailey hugged each other and laughed. Angelica felt like crying.

"Mom really it's cool with us! Besides, dad has so many girlfriends it's not even funny! Oh! Mom, look, we're going to run over there. We'll be right back!"

Angelica couldn't say a word! She started crying tears of joy right there on the spot as the girls ran off! She shook her head at how they didn't even go to the bathroom!

~

Roman held on to Kendall's hand until he found a lone tree away from where people were gathered. Roman stood on guard until Kendall finished. "Thanks, Mr. Roman," he said while Roman squirted his hands with his pocket sanitizer.

"No problem."

Kendall tapped Roman on the leg. "Do you like my mom?"

Roman laughed. "Yes I do."

Kendall then wrinkled his face! "Did you ever kiss her before," he said looking as if that was a nasty thing to do.

Roman laughed. "Why do you ask?"

"Me, Hailey, and Gavin think that you and mom are girlfriend and boyfriend."

Roman smiled. "What do y'all think about that?"

"Hailey thinks it's cool. Me and Gavin think that you and my mom are just friends but, we wish you were her boyfriend!" Roman smiled even more. "Gavin told all his friends that he couldn't wait to play with you today!"

"Kendall, I am your mom's boyfriend."

"For real," he said with his eyes practically popping out of his head.

Roman laughed. "Yes for real!!"

"High Five RC!!" Roman gave him a high five then Kendall unexpectedly hugged him. "It's ok if you kiss my mom. That's what boyfriends do to their girlfriends right?!"

Roman pointed his finger at Kendall while smiling. "Yes, but only when you're old enough! Does your mom know that you, Hailey, and Gavin talked about this?"

"No! Hailey said that mom had *enough* to deal with. Whatever *that* means...can I tell you a secret?"

"Sure," Roman said while laughing.

Kendall stopped walking and looked sadly at Roman. "My mom cries at night. I mean she's been crying a lot. If I walk to her door, I can see her squeezing her new pillow. She's not real loud, but I can hear her. I know she's not sick or nothin' because I always ask her if she's sick and she says no. Now that you're her boyfriend, you think that you can help her not cry so much at night?"

Roman took a deep breath and knelt down to Kendall's level. "I'll help her. Don't you worry, ok?"

Kendall smiled and nodded his head yes, "Don't tell her that I told you ok?"

"Ok."

~6:49pm

Angelica waived her hand good-bye at Roman's family. "It was nice meeting all of you... thank you!"

Mr. and Mrs. Callowhill stood up and gave Angelica a hug. Mrs. Callowhill hugged her tight. "We'll see you at the next family gathering?"

Angelica looked at Roman who was standing next to her and answered for her. "Yes she will!"

Angelica smiled at him while Kendall walked over to hold Roman's hand. "Mommy, can we ride with RC while he takes Winter home?"

Gavin traveled right behind Kendall and grabbed Roman's other hand. "RC can we ride with you?"

Hailey and Winter walked up and completed the circle. Winter looked at him, "-That way me and Hailey can spend more time together!" Roman looked at Angelica and laughed along with her. The family watched carefully at how they were going to handle being put on the spot.

Angelica shook her head no, "Roman..."

Roman nodded his head yes. "It's ok! I'll take Winter home and bring them back to your house. That way you can do what you need to do while we're gone."

Angelica looked at the kids who were now staring at her with puppy-dog eyes. "Roman, are you sure?"

"Of course!"

Angelica nodded, "Ok!"

All the kids screamed and walked toward his truck with Winter leading the way. Roman gave Angelica his keys while she walked with the kids over to his truck to get them settled. Angelica waved one last time at his family and left with the kids.

Roman looked at Angelica and the kids as they walked to his truck. He then turned to his family. "Thank you," he said giving his parents a hug.

His mom looked at him. "Baby? You sure about jumping into a ready-made family?"

Roman frowned. "Yes. I'm not a kid anymore mom."

"I know, I know! I'm not saying that! I'm just saying that you never let us meet someone so beautiful and sweet as her! I can tell she's special and I know that you've been a bachelor for years!"

"Mom, everything's cool," he said laughing.

Paul patted Roman on the back. "Roman, what she's trying to say is: don't give this one up...for some more butt," said Paul laughing.

"She doesn't have to worry about that," Roman said shaking his head at Paul who was still laughing. Cyrus and his dad looked at Roman and smiled.

Cyrus nodded his head. "Yeah, Paul! She doesn't have to worry about that because he's in love," Cyrus said looking at Simone.

Roman gave Cyrus a brotherly hug. "I love y'all! See ya'!"

Chapter 14 – Lesson: Lies are Sometimes
Used for Good Intentions

As Angelica parked her car on Roman's
street, she could see Roman's truck in his driveway.
She grabbed her purse and couldn't wait to get in
the shower. While turning the car off, she quickly
smelled her underarms! Angelica thought back to
when she pulled up to Ian's house to drop the kids
off minutes ago. Ian walked over to her car and
apologized for asking her to switch months with her
earlier that day. Angelica told him it was ok and
that if he needed her to do something like that, she
needed to be asked *way before* the day of. He
agreed as the kids hurried out of the car. They
shouted out their goodbyes to her as she waved
proudly!

~

Kendall shook Ian's leg, "Daddy! Mr.
Roman is so cool!! We had so much fun and did
you know that they are boyfriend and girlfriend,"
Kendall said.

"Mr. Roman huh," replied Ian trying to keep
his cool.

"Yes, his name is Officer Roman Callowhill. We spent the whole day with him and his family! He is so cool!"

~

Angelica shook her head after reviewing the events of the day. She opened the door and went in her trunk to grab her overnight bag. Roman walked up to her, took the bag out of her hands, and picked her up! Angelica laughed. "I have you all to myself for a whole month! I hope you've been eating right," he said putting her down. Roman held her hand as they walked in the house.

Angelica pulled Roman's arms. "Baby, you know the kids know we're together right?"

Roman laughed and locked the door behind her. "Yeah, Hailey and Winter told me. How do you feel about that?"

"I feel alright, but I do feel...kind of bad... not talking to them earlier about me having male friends."

"Well thank God they like each other. Winter gave Hailey her number and email address so that they can talk! Gavin and Kendall asked if I could take them to a Phillies game. Winter and

Hailey said that they wanted to go to!" Roman kissed her. "What can I say! I'm a loveable guy!"

Angelica pushed him and walked up the stairs so that she could take a shower. Halfway up the stairs, she stopped, and turned to look at Roman who was trailing behind. "What did Winter think about me?"

"Let me put it to you this way! She wants to know when we are moving in together so that you, her, and Hailey can have your ladies' day out with dress up time, going to the mall, and all this other stuff! She asked me if I loved you."

"What? Kendall, Hailey, and Gavin asked me the same thing!"

Roman looked at her. "What did you tell them?"

"I told them yes," said Angelica sitting on the top step.

Roman stood in front of her. "How did they react?"

Angelica put her head in her hands, "They laughed! What did you tell Winter," she asked staring at Roman.

Roman smiled. "She asked me while they were all in the truck! They all heard me when I said that I love you very much! Gavin and Kendall cracked up laughing!"

"What," she said laughing and crying.

Roman sat beside her on the step. "They weren't sad at all! In fact, they were happy as ever." Roman pulled out his phone. "Look!" He showed her a picture of all of them together hugging and saying cheese in a selfie! Angelica looked at Roman and rubbed his face staring at him like she did before. "Tell me," Roman said looking back at her. "Why won't you tell me?"

"Because I..."

"Angelica, I love you! Yesterday I was 90% certain, but now I'm 100% certain that I want you..."

"Roman don't!" She said standing up and going into the bathroom.

"Angelica don't walk away from me," he said getting upset. Angelica still had tears rolling from her eyes. He held on to her arms and lightly squeezed them, "I want to be with you for the rest of my life."

"Why are you saying that to me?" Angelica was so angry, and Roman knew exactly why. "Don't say those types of things to me Roman. You think you mean what you're saying, but you have no idea! Stop trying to move so fast!" She tried to get out of his embrace, but he pulled her back.

"Angelica I'm not Ian ok! I'm not that person, and I'm telling you that...that's where I'm heading! Do you feel the same way about me?" Angelica stared at him and didn't say a word. "Do you feel the same way about me?" Roman just stood there looking at her.

Angelica put her hand on his face like she did so many times before that, "I haven't been surer about anything in my life as much as I am sure...that I want to be with you. You are truly a man's man! I feel honored that you want to be with my children and me! But there's no rush Roman! I'll say no more than that!" Roman kissed her and pushed her against the wall in the bathroom. He walked closer to her and grabbed her waist. "Roman, I have to get in the shower! I'm so sweaty it's a shame!"

"I don't care if you're sweaty!"

"But I do!" Angelica walked past him and started peeling off her clothes as she walked to the shower. Roman just looked at her like he wanted to eat her alive. He watched her run the water in the

shower and took his clothes off as well. He looked
at the silhouette of her body through the shower
door. Angelica paid him no attention and started
washing the barbecue smell out of her hair with the
shampoo that she brought over his house last week.
She turned around and rinsed her hair when she
heard the shower door open. She wiped her eyes
and saw Roman smiling at her butt naked. "Can I
help you?"

Roman nodded his head. "Yes you can."
Angelica finished rinsing her hair while Roman
helped her get the suds out. She grabbed her
washcloth and started washing herself while
Roman lathered up. After washing her body, she
started washing his back. He turned around,
lathered up his cloth and began washing her arms
and neck. Angelica washed his chest and stomach
and looked at his penis. It was throbbing hard, and
she couldn't help but smile. She got on her knees
and washed his legs allowing his penis to rub up
against her. Angelica stood up, put some soap in
her hand, and began stroking his penis. She rubbed
on his balls making sure that she didn't forget about
cleaning underneath them!

Angelica kissed him, "Now you can rinse the front!"

Once he faced the water spraying from the shower head, Angelica turned around and washed the front of her body making sure she paid close attention to the small folds down below. While Roman was still rinsing off, she took the rag and thoroughly cleaned her rear, not wanting him to see her! Roman turned around, and Angelica was covered in suds!

"So, I guess you want to rinse off huh?"

"That would be nice Officer Callowhill!"

Roman moved back and finished washing his self while she was rinsing off her body. She turned around to rinse her back and noticed that he was all lathered up and ready to be rinsed. He walked up beside her. "Can we share?"

Angelica licked her lips, "You can do whatever you want!" Roman kissed her and squeezed her breasts. "Roman that hurts," she whispered.

"I'm sorry baby! I didn't mean to hurt you," he said kissing the breast he squeezed. He then sucked on her breast.

"That hurts too!"

Roman looked at her and smiled. "Well, what can I do that won't hurt you?"

"Give me ten minutes, and I'll show you. I'll meet you in the bedroom!" She kissed his lips and started walking toward the shower door.

"Baby, wait! Can you give me something before you go?"

Angelica kissed him again, and Roman pinned her against the shower wall. He opened her legs and put his penis inside of her. Angelica moaned as she kissed all over his neck face and lips. "Roman, I wanted to do something special for you!"

"This is special," he said enjoying every stroke. He was excited seeing Angelica's body wet with her breasts shaking up and down from his powerful thrusts! He pulled out of her and turned her around. "Bend over!" Angelica did what Roman told her to do and held on to whatever was close by. After about six minutes of him pounding away, she tried to escape. She made it outside of the shower before Roman pulled her back to him. "Where are you going?"

"Nowhere." Roman went to close the shower door, and Angelica grabbed a towel and ran into the bedroom. Roman quickly turned the water

298

off and caught up with her inside his bedroom doorway.

He picked her up and laid her on the bed. "What was the surprise?"

"I brought some whipped cream and caramel that I wanted to try on you!"

Roman laughed. "Oh really."

Angelica smiled and tried to shake her feelings of rejection. She looked at him laughing and felt embarrassed. "That's funny? Ok never mind then."

"What? I was only messing with you baby," Roman said laughing.

Angelica wrapped the towel around her, "Yeah, you're probably bored with all that... at this point," she stated in a defeated voice.

"What does that have to do with anything? I've never experienced it with you?"

"So, I guess that's a yes," she asked pretending to be concerned about the remaining water on her body.

Roman looked at the water drops falling down her neck. "Well, I've had something similar."

"Were you on the receiving end or giving," Angelica asked.

Roman smiled. "Both, why?"

Angelica smiled back at him. "I just wanted to know that's all."

"And are you mad that I did that with someone other than you?"

"No, not at all." Angelica was quiet while Roman rubbed on her arm. She readjusted the towel around her. "I'm going to get something to drink. Do you want some?"

Roman ignored her question. "Baby, I know you said that you hadn't had many sexual partners, but how many have you had oral sex with?"

"Not that many. I'll be right back." Angelica walked out of the room and went downstairs feeling stupid! She didn't mean to react like she did when he said that he had oral sex with others before. It was just that she wanted him to feel like *she* did! She poured some apple juice for herself and drank it looking out the kitchen window into the backyard. She heard steps coming down the stairs, "Shit!"

Angelica tried to look like she was doing something, so she opened the fridge.

Roman tried to break the tension. "It's some ice cream in there if you want some."

Angelica opened the freezer and pulled out the Oreo Cookies and Cream, one of her favorites! "Do you want some?"

"How about we share?"

"Ok." Angelica felt dreadfully self-conscious as she grabbed a big bowl and started scooping the ice cream with the ice cream scooper that Roman handed to her. For some reason, she didn't want to look at him.

"Baby, come here for a minute." Angelica turned and looked at him. For a moment, she pictured him eating another woman's pussy! She then walked over to another chair and sat down.

"I thought that we should move in together by the end of January next year. That gives the kids three months to adjust. What do you think about that?"

"I think that sounds great," she said smiling at him while getting up to finish scooping the ice cream. "I guess now all we have to do is figure out who is going to move and who is going to rent or sell!" She put the lid on the ice cream and put the ice cream back.

Roman walked up to her with his chest bare and his sweats hanging low on his waist exposing his sexy physique. "Baby, you don't sound as excited as I thought you would be."

"I'm excited. I'm just a mother that's all! I'm just thinking of schools and support from our families, insurance, finances..."

"Angelica, if we plan this right, everything will be just fine. And with me making detective in January, our finances..."

"What? You made Detective?!!! Oh, my God!" Angelica jumped into his arms. "Congratulations baby! I knew you would get it! I knew it! I'm so proud of you!" She hugged him again. "You did it! By God's grace, you did it!" Angelica looked at him and kissed him. Roman looked at her with no emotion at all. "Roman, aren't you happy? Why are you looking like that?"

He held on to her close. "Baby what's wrong? Are you having second thoughts about us?"

"No, no! Why are you saying that?"

"So, what is it? Are you turned off because I have more experience in the bed than you?"

Angelica gave him a faint smile. "No, I'm not turned off. I...I didn't mean to react that way toward you. I'm sorry."

Roman caressed her arm. "So how many have you had oral sex with?"

"Not nearly as many as you," she said walking toward her chair to sit down.

Roman grabbed her before she could take a seat. "How many?"

"If you want me to tell you how many, you have to tell me how many!"

"About three or four!"

"Times what? Yeah right! I've only had oral sex with my ex-husband, and as you know, I **rarely** had it with him. I guess his others did it better than I could, or he just preferred them instead! Now would you like to share our ice cream upstairs or here in the kitchen?"

Roman looked at her and smiled. "My angel!"

"Whatever!" Angelica took the bowl and headed for the stairs. Roman took the bowl out of her hand and the spoon from her mouth. He put the bowl on the table and kissed her lips. "Now that we have the living situation in motion, what are your feelings..."

"Roman, one thing at a time. I can't move as fast as the others!" She said sarcastically while smiling at him.

Roman kissed her and sucked on her tongue then let it go. "Your mouth is gonna get you in trouble!"

Angelica took the bowl and spoon and walked toward the stairs. Roman took the bowl and spoon away from her again and pulled her towel off. She walked away and went into the living room. He followed her and pulled her to him. Roman put the towel on the floor. "Lay down." She laid on the towel and Roman stared at her laying there waiting for him. He pulled his sweats off, laid down on top of her, and kissed her until her legs opened. Roman slowly pushed his way inside of her and smiled while looking at her. Angelica looked at him with a faint smile. "Do you want to be with me, Angelica?"

"Yes, I do...more than anything." His face lightened up, and he knew that she was ok.

"Do you want to have a baby with me? Angelica pushed on his chest, and Roman stood still. "What? We talked about this before."

"Yeah, we talked about it! But now you are asking me!"

"What's wrong with that?"

"Nothing's wrong with it Roman! You're...it's too soon!"

Roman started moving inside of her again. "I want us to bring life into this world." He moved deeper inside of her, and Angelica moaned. "You like it, baby?"

"Yes!"

"Can I go deeper?"

"Yes!"

Roman moved deeper. "Put 'em on my back baby!"

Angelica put her legs on his back and interlocked her ankles. "Roman please!"

"You want it already?"

"Yes!"

Roman laid all the way on top of her and sucked on her neck. "I don't care what you did in the past because I'm your future. You hear me!" Angelica looked at him while he moved steadily inside of her. "I never had pussy like this before! Never!" Angelica moaned like never before! Roman listened to her coming and could hear her singing while calling his name! Roman squeezed on her breasts and moved quickly while she moved her hips. Roman kissed her and groaned while Angelica felt him pumping come all inside of her. She thought about what he said about having children and couldn't help but feel a little weary! Roman kissed her lips and couldn't wait to seal the deal!

~2:43...**AM**, Tuesday, September 8th~

A phone was ringing very loud. Angelica woke up and looked for the phone. "Roman your phone is ringing."

"What you say, baby," he said wiping his face with his hand.

"Your phone keeps on ringing." She tried to find it, but with her feeling like she drank a whole bottle of wine by herself, she was of no help.

"I'll get it." Roman got up, put on his sweatpants, grabbed his cell phone, and went downstairs to the kitchen. Angelica laid back down and closed her eyes.

Roman poured himself something to drink while looking at his phone. He looked at the caller ID and was furious! "Hello."

"Roman, it's Monica. I really need to talk with you."

Roman whispered, "Woman are you crazy? What the fuck is wrong with you? It's almost three in the morning, and you want to talk to me?! The last time we talked we had agreed that it was a rap, Monica! Why are you calling me?"

"Roman, don't you miss me? I love you so much! I know you've got to miss me a little bit." Roman didn't say anything. "See I know you miss me! Can you come over?"

"No." Angelica walked down the steps quietly and could hear some of what Monica was saying on the phone since it was quiet in the house and her phone was obviously on shout-mode! Roman was facing the basement door while Angelica crept in the kitchen.

"Why not? I'll do whatever you want me to do! Just come over!" Roman still didn't say anything. "Roman, are you coming baby? Please! I need you! I want you so bad! Please! Just for fifteen minutes. I'll suck it just like I did the last time if you hurry!" Roman shook his head and wiped his face. He couldn't believe that this shit was happening. "Baby you there?"

Angelica snatched the phone from Roman's hand and hung up the phone. She looked at Roman with tears in her eyes. The phone rang again, and this time, Angelica answered it. "Hello."

"Ummm, I think I have the wrong number."

"Is this Monica?"

Monica smirked. "Yes, it is."

"Roman's right here," Angelica handed Roman the phone and put her hands on her hips.

"Hello."

"Oh, why didn't you tell me you had company?"

"Monica look. Like I said before, it's over. I'm committed to someone else now, and I can't mess with you like that anymore."

"You're saying that now, but in a couple of days, you'll be calling me up!"

Roman chuckled. "Whatever! Don't call my house or my cell phone anymore alright?"

"Alright Roman, I won't!"

Roman hung up the phone and looked at Angelica. Angelica stared at him hard. "Before you say anything to me I just want to say that I love you very much. I'm not going to curse you out, and I'm not going to argue with you or debate you on what you and Monica have going on. I am technically still a married woman, so I can't be to upset at you for living your life. I hope you will still let Winter come over sometimes and maybe if you're not too busy, you can take my boys out once and a blue," she said smiling. "Anger doesn't stay with me. It's the pain that lingers on within me. You know... I fell in love again with a good-looking man. Maybe God will give me another chance in experiencing it with someone else. Thank you, Roman, for showing me that I can still pull 'em!" She hugged Roman and kissed him on the lips.

Chapter 15 – Lesson: Even a Saint Sins

Angelica calmly walked up the stairs and started packing up her things. Roman sat down at the kitchen table and dropped his head low. He wet his face in the kitchen sink, dried it off, and walked up the stairs to talk to Angelica. Roman stood in the bedroom doorway while Angelica packed.

"Angelica, I'm sorry about this whole mess. I made a mistake, and I lied to you about it. I went over there that day, and we talked. She begged to suck my dick... and I let her. Afterward, I was sick! I went home and thought about what happened. I called her, and I made sure that she understood that I didn't want to be with her anymore and that I didn't want her calling me anymore. I haven't talked to her since that day!"

Roman walked closer to her so that she could look at him. "I fucked up! I know I fucked up, but my feelings for you are strong to the point where I don't want anyone else but you! We are preparing to unite our family's baby! Why would I tell you what happened that night? We would have never gotten this far if I told you what really happened! Stop packing your stuff! I don't want you to leave. I don't want you to take some time and think about shit! This is it!"

Angelica looked at him smiling. "I'm really going to miss you, Roman." She kissed him and tried to pull away but Roman held on to her.

"You're not going to miss me because I'm not going anywhere!"

"But I am," she said not even looking at him.

Roman turned her so that she could focus on him instead of packing her clothes. "Angelica, I love you so much! Please just look at me!" Angelica looked in his eyes. Tears were falling down his face. "I'm a good man. I just made a terrible decision. Don't throw away what we could have and what we could give our children because of something meaningless! Angelica, I want to spend the rest of my life with you, and I know you believe that! I know..." he said with more tears falling from his eyes, "...that you love me just as much as I love you! Baby, I want to start a new life and family with you!"

Roman kept on. "See... you can't leave because there is too much at stake here! You are the most beautiful woman I have ever seen or been with. You soothe my soul. I think about you constantly from the time I wake up to when I go to bed!" Angelica tried to turn around, but Roman pushed her to the bed and laid on top of her. "I'm going to love you until the day I leave from here. Please don't go!" Angelica turned her head as she cried harder and harder. "Baby don't cry! Shhh," Roman held on to her and kissed her head.

"Why is this happening to me?" She wiped her face with his tee shirt that she had on. "What did I do? Or what didn't I do? Why is it that every man wants to lie and deceive me? I really want to understand because it's getting a little too painful to deal with!"

"Baby, it was me. You are as close to perfect as they come!" Roman kissed her lips and moved to her neck. He took her shirt off and sucked all on her breasts!

"Roman, I don't want to make love to you."

"Yes, you do." Roman tried to keep sucking on her breasts, but Angelica pushed him off.

"No, I don't!" Angelica sat up and tried to get up, but Roman pushed her back down and laid on top of her. He sucked and kissed on her breast making her moan. She tried to push him off, but when she pushed, he sucked harder. He raised up his chest to push his sweats down and Angelica tried to get away. Roman grabbed her while pushing his sweats down. He stepped out of them and laid on top of her. "Roman get up, I don't want to do this," she said crying. Roman tried to open her legs, but she wouldn't let him through. He moved up to her neck and began kissing and sucking on her neck just like she loved! The tension in her legs dissipated and he got through. Roman entered her slowly, and Angelica moaned and cried at the same time.

"I love you, Angelica." Angelica turned her face away. "Look at me!" Roman stared at her really hard. "I love you! I will always love you and be with you no matter what happens between us! I love you! Do you understand?"

"You were with someone else Roman! How would you feel if Ian and I had sex? How would you feel if I sucked his dick not too long ago?" Roman stopped moving and just stared at her. "Yeah, what if I let him eat my pussy and then told you nothing happened! Then later tell you that for three whole fucking hours, he ate my pussy while I sucked his dick AND swallowed his come!" Angelica saw the hurt in his eyes. "The last time I saw him, he begged

313

to fuck me one more time, and I LET him!"
Angelica tried to push him away, but he wouldn't
budge. "Get off of me!" Roman just stared at her
while continuing where he left off. "Didn't you hear
me! Stop!"

"No! I said no Angelica! You are not going
anywhere, and neither am I! You gonna' ride with
me and that's it!"

"I did let him eat my pussy Roman. He
wanted too so bad... so I let him," she said trying to
sound serious. Roman stopped and stared at her!
"I'm just being honest. How does it feel? Does it
hurt?" Roman continued to make love to her. "I'm
going to scratch you!" Roman didn't respond. He
just kept on sucking on her neck. Angelica
scratched the shit out of his back. Roman groaned
but just looked at her. She then took the other hand
and scratched the other side of his back.

Roman could feel the cold air on his back
and knew she broke the skin. He groaned a little
louder and then grabbed her hands. He pinned
each of her arms above her head. Roman moved
deeper inside of her. "Why did you do that to me?"

"Because you hurt me!" Roman tried to kiss her lips, but Angelica kept moving her head from side to side.

"Kiss me," Roman told Angelica.

"Why?"

Roman slowed down. "Because you love me, and you want to be with me and only me for the rest of your life."

Angelica looked at him. "What? Are you fucking on drugs or something? This is NOT going to work at all! You think everything is good because you're fucking me right now?"

Roman stopped moving. "Baby, trust me when I say this to you. I will make you the happiest woman on earth. Now kiss me and show me with your lips how much you love me."

Angelica pointed her finger in his face. "The next time something like this happens Roman...,"

Roman stopped moving. "Angelica, I gave you a 2.5 karat key set-in platinum with a platinum chain just to show you that you have the key to my heart. That wasn't bullshit baby! The next time, I will come harder and harder to show you how much I like, love, and cherish you and what we have. It won't happen again!" Angelica kissed him and held him while Roman moved inside of her. He winced a bit when she put her hands over his scratches.

"Don't ever do that to me again Roman."

Roman looked at her and moved deeper inside while lifting her leg up. "I won't baby. I'm in love with your pussy," he said looking down at his penis moving in and out of her vagina. "I love it!" He picked up the other leg and went even deeper while moaning louder and louder.

"If you keep it up, I'm going to give it to someone else." Roman stopped. "To a man who will make it his top priority to keep her satisfied and happy. You fuck me over, and you will regret it! I will never forgive you, and you won't be able to get me back!"

Roman just looked at her. "You threatening me?" He said increasing his tempo. Angelica made all kinds of noises while she held on to him. "This is my pussy and you ain't never giving it to anyone else!" Angelica could barely hear him since she was practically yelling. She wasn't in pain. In fact, she was in so much pleasure that she was trying not to have another orgasm. So far, she knew she had at least two! "Baby, I'm coming in you." A couple of minutes later Roman moaned louder and louder.

"Kiss me while I come all inside of you!" Angelica held on to his face and kissed him. Roman kissed her again and groaned really loud. "I love you, Angel! I love you!" Angelica kissed him and smiled. Roman kissed her back on the lips. "I meant everything I said, baby! So, get ready!"

~Three weeks later, Tuesday, September 29th @ 4:46 pm~

Angelica walked in her house, took her shoes, and coat off. She put her purse and mail on the table by the door. While looking through the usual utility bills, she came across an envelope with from her lawyer. Her heart was beating incredibly fast as she opened the envelope. She read the jibber jabber and came across the words – Divorce Decree. As she continued to read on, the letter listed all the things that they agreed upon.

While staring at the letter, she thought about how many nights she cried wanting to be loved by him. Her eyes began to water thinking of how much, of herself, that she gave to Ian! She made a promise to herself to never do that again! Angelica took the letter upstairs and ran her shower. Roman said that he would be getting off at eight, so she had some time to wash some clothes and cook something to eat. She thought about calling the kids, but she knew that she would be speaking to them before they went to bed.

She took off all of her clothes as her phone rang. Angelica picked up the phone on her bed. It was Roman. "Hello."

"Hey, baby."

"Hey, what's up? How's it going?"

"I'm getting off early. I'll be over after I pick up some things from the house."

"Roman?"

"Yes."

"The papers came today." Roman was silent except for the beeping noises from his squad car. "Roman, did you hear me?"

"How you feel about that?"

Angelica could hear the tension in his voice. She didn't know if it was from what they were talking about or from whatever he was doing. "I'm good. -Liberated...you know."

"You wanna' celebrate tonight?"

"Sure."

"Alright, I'll make some calls! Just be ready at eight alright?"

"Yes."

"Angelica, I love you."

"-Love you." Angelica hung up the phone and went in the shower. After trying to wash off all the pain from the past years from being with Ian, she went to her room to pick out something to wear. She chose some nice jeans, a t-shirt, and some slides since the weather was still pleasant. While drying her hair, she heard the doorbell ringing. She put on her robe and made sure it was fastened tightly. "Why is he ringing the bell," she said laughing. "Who is it," she sang while running down the steps.

"Angelica, it's Ian."

Angelica got anxious. It was in the evening, and it was Ian's month with the kids! She opened the door. "Ian! What's going on? Are the kids alright?"

Ian looked at her up and down. Angelica looked good! The kids told him how they all go the YMCA more often...now. "Yes. Can I come in to talk to you for a minute?"

"Why?"

"Just for a minute. Please."

"Ok. Wait right here. I'll be right back." Angelica went upstairs and put on a camisole and some night pants. It was 6:18. She had more than enough time to get ready to go out with Roman. She walked down the stairs and went outside on the porch. Ian was sitting in the chair waiting for her to come out. "Ok, so what's' going on?"

Ian stared at her. She looked so refreshed and vibrant! "I know you got the papers today."

Angelica nodded. "Yeah I did!"

Ian chuckled. "So, it's really over huh? All those years... down the toilet."

"Yeah I know."

Ian stared at her. "I'm sorry for all the things I ever did to you." Ian rubbed her arm and moved close to her face. "I'm really sorry. I didn't mean to..."

Angelica questionably looked at his hand on her arm. "Ian, please."

Ian caressed her face with both hands and moved in to kiss her. Angelica shook her head and pulled his hands away. "Ian don't!"

"Why?"

Angelica looked anywhere but at Ian. At that moment, Angelica just so happened to look across the street. Roman was parked right across the street from Angelica's house! He was sitting there on the driver's side staring at them. Although she knew nothing was going on, she still felt uneasy.

Ian kept rambling on and on about nothing. "I just wanted to come by to see how you were doing. I still...and will always love you, Angelica."

Angelica looked at him. "Ian...I'm fine." He was such an asshole! "Are you here because you that I was sad or something?"

Ian smiled. "I just wanted to make sure that you were alright."

Angelica spotted movement across the street within her periphery. Roman got out the truck, grabbed his dress clothes which were on a hanger, and his black duffle bag from the back seat. Apparently, he packed and decided to get dressed over her house! As Ian talked more about nothing, Angelica was lost in his bullshit and looked at Roman walking across the street smiling at her. Ian noticed that she wasn't paying attention and looked over to where she was looking. Angelica stood up as

Roman walked up the steps. Ian confusingly stood up as well.

Roman stared at her and only her as he walked over. "Hey baby!"

"Hey!" Roman kissed her on the lips and stood right next to her. Angelica proceeded with the inevitable introductions. "Ian this is Roman."

Ian walked toward Roman. "Hey Roman. Nice to meet you." Ian offered his hand and looked at Roman as if he had seen him before.

Roman shook his hand smiling. "Ian." He released Ian's weak grip, turned, and faced Angelica so that Ian could still see his face. "Everything ok with the kids?"

"Yeah, everything's good," she said smiling.

"Ok, I'm going upstairs to get dressed." He put his hand on her lower back and softly kissed her neck.

Angelica smiled. "I'll be right up."

Roman smiled at her and looked at Ian, "Ian."

Ian looked at Angelica and then to Roman. "I'll tell the kids you said hello."

Roman nodded at Ian. He then winked at Angelica and walked in the house. Ian had no idea that Roman talked to them just about every night when Angelica talked to them.

Angelica watched Roman put his things down in the living room and walked in the kitchen. "Ian, I really should get going."

Ian stood in front of her. "I guess you *are* ok! Yo' is that the cop from..."

Angelica ushered him toward the steps. "Yes. Ian thanks for being concerned about me but I'm doing ok. Thanks for stopping by."

Ian looked at the necklace and pendant around Angelica's neck. "Ok...I'll let you go." As Ian walked toward his Lexus SUV, he turned and looked at Angelica going into the house. Ian tried not to get mad since he was and had been involved with other women for years. He just always looked at Angelica as *his* property that belonged solely to him. Ian drove off in his car shaking his head in disbelief.

"For heavens' sake!" Angelica mumbled underneath her breath as she walked in the house. Holding a glass of water in his hand, Roman walked toward Angelica. "So, you decided to get dressed over here huh?"

Roman put his glass down on the coffee table and gave her a kiss. "Work was ok. How was your day?"

Angelica laughed. "Everything was fine. I already washed my hair and showered. I just wanted to throw a load in the washer. What time is it?"

"Around 6:45. We have to leave here by 7:30," Roman said walking closer to her.

"7:30 huh?" Angelica kissed his lips. "I'm so glad you're home early." Roman kissed her again pulling her camisole straps down. He started rubbing all on her breasts. He abruptly stopped, took her by the hand, and walked her over to the couch.

"Turn around," he said stopping at the arm of the couch. Angelica turned around and leaned against the arm while Roman pulled her night pants down just enough to achieve the mission. "Why don't you have on any panties?"

"I didn't have time to put any on." Roman leaned to the side to see her face. "Ian came over after I got out of the shower." Roman got on his knees and began eating her pussy from behind. Angelica almost lost her mind! Her knees were getting weak as she tried to put more weight on her upper body. After eating for a couple of minutes, he stood up and made love to her from behind while she bravely held her position over the arm of the couch.

~

Roman opened the passenger side door of his truck for Angelica. Upon stepping in the truck, she couldn't help but notice a bouquet of red roses in the back seat. "I was going to give them to you when I first came out of the truck, but I wanted to surprise you."

"They're beautiful. Thank you." Angelica laid a kiss on his cheek.

"Baby, let's go away for a weekend. Just you and I for a couple of days."

"Really?"

"Yeah! Going out to dinner is nice, but we need to spend some real time together! Like that Akuna-Ma-Ta-Ta from Lion King! No worries for the rest of your day's type of weekend!"

They both cracked up laughing. Angelica rubbed his hand. "I hear you! You know my sister is coming to town this weekend, how's next weekend sound?"

"That would be perfect. Winter is coming over this weekend too so next weekend would really be perfect." Roman started up the truck. "Where do you want to go?"

"I don't know...somewhere not too far, but nice? Hey, I heard the Poconos was nice!"

"Is that where you want to go?"

"Where would you like to go?"

Roman glanced to the right and rear before he pulled out of the parking spot. "Wherever you want to go! I just want to be alone with you!"

"Ok, then that's where we'll go!" Angelica reached over and kissed him on the cheek. "So, you, your cousins, and friends are going to watch the game tomorrow?"

"Yeah and I know you are going out on Friday night. Hey... when you all go out on Friday, don't let me catch you doing things you have no business doing!"

Angelica did a little dance in her seat. "You do know I'm single now! I definitely have to dress the part this weekend!"

Roman drove toward the expressway going downtown. "First of all, you are not single!"

"I damn sure ain't married!"

"Angelica, you are not single!"

"I do have you as a male friend and companion, but I am not married," she said teasing him.

"Like I said! You can word that shit anyway you want to, but you are not single."

"Ok, Mr. Callowhill!" Roman kept his eyes on the road while Angelica looked out of her window

"Angel, when are you going to start singing?"

"I don't know. I haven't even given it much thought."

"Maybe you should look into that and start doing more of what you enjoy doing. You know I play the guitar! Maybe we could make something happen."

"That is such a good idea! I'm going to go through my songs tomorrow and see what happens. Would you really play for me while I sang?"

"Of course I would baby!" Angelica smiled at him and started to tear up. "Get used to this because it's only the beginning!"

~Friday, October 2nd~

That Friday evening after having a beer with his friends and co-workers, Roman went to pick up Winter from her home. He parked outside of Winter's home and called her mother Coleen. She picked up on the first ring, "Hello?"

"Coleen, it's Roman. I'm outside to pick up Winter."

"Ok, I'll send her right out." Five minutes later Coleen opened the door and looked at Roman's truck. She still had feelings for him but knew that it was over between them. She waved her hand and smiled at him. Roman gave a faint smile and waved back until he heard Winter calling for him from inside her house. Roman laughed and got out of the truck to meet her at the curb.

"Daddy!" Winter practically ran down the steps to Roman who was now standing near the passenger door.

Roman gave her a big hug. "How long has it been since I last saw you?" This was his usual line when he picked Winter up for the weekend.

"Daddy, it's only been a week!"

"I know, but you're prettier than you were the last time I saw you," he said kissing her head. He opened her door and closed it behind her. Just then his cell phone began to vibrate. It was a text from Angelica:

Please tell Winter that me and the boys said hi AND Hailey wants her to check her email when she gets a chance! I'm on my way out with my sister and the girls! I'll talk to you tomorrow.

I love you!

Roman laughed and got in the truck. "Winter! Angelica, Kendall, Gavin, and Hailey said Hi. Hailey wants you to check your email when you get a chance."

"Awe man! I forgot to check it yesterday! Dad, we have to hurry up! Hailey and I have a puzzle that we're doing, and we need to get it done by tomorrow," she said buckling her seatbelt.

"So, you and Hailey talk often huh?"

"We talk just 'bout every day. We're sisters! I mean we know that you and Ms. Angelica aren't married, but we act like you are!"

Roman stared at Winter for a few moments. He put his seatbelt on, put the truck in gear, and pulled off down the street. "So how do you feel about Angelica? I want your honest opinion."

"Daddy I really like Ms. Angelica. She's so caring and nice. I really, really like her daddy. It's just that..."

Roman turned onto Ridge Avenue toward the expressway. "What?"

"Please don't say anything... but Hailey told me that her mom cries a lot at night. She said that one night she went in her room and saw her squeezing her big blue pillow. Hailey said she was just lying there sniffling and crying. When Hailey asked her if she was ok, she said that it was her allergies, but Hailey knew that wasn't the truth." Roman now knew why she was crying while holding on to his pillow at night. "Oh, and you know what? Hailey said that her dad is going to try to get their family back together."

Roman smiled at Winter. "Sweetie he probably just said that to her so that..."

Winter put her hand up in the air. "Nope! Hailey said... that he told her... that even though they were divorced, he was going to try to get her back! Hailey loves her dad, but she thinks that you make her mom happier!"

Roman played off his anger. "Well, we'll see who wins her heart!! Right?!"

"That's right!! Callowhill's always win right daddy?" They both laughed as they exited off Ridge Avenue. "Do you think you're going to marry her daddy?"

"How do you feel about that?"

"If you didn't marry her I would be ok with that. But if you DID marry her, I would be the happiest girl in the whole world. Would my mom be upset if I lived with you? Do you think she would let me?"

Roman laughed. "One step at a time!"

"Yeah, you have a lot on your plate too! The ultimate challenge!"

Roman laughed. "How about we go to the market and get some ice cream and ginger ale for ice cream sodas."

"Daddy that's why you're the best!"

~11:43pm

Winter fell asleep in his bed after watching the Disney movie Enchanted. Roman carried her in her room, tucked her in, and kissed her forehead. He closed her door and walked in his bedroom. He picked up his phone and sent Angelica a message.

~

Angelica walked off the dance floor smiling. She found a seat at the bar and sat down while her sister and two of her friends kept on dancing. "Hi," said this tall, handsome man standing next to her.

"Hi!"

The gorgeous man looked at Angelica up and down "What's your name?"

"Angelica. What's yours?"

"Spencer."

Angelica held out her hand to shake his. "It's nice to meet you, Spencer."

Spencer took her hand and kissed it. "It's nice to meet you too." Angelica blushed as she felt her phone vibrating in her purse. She opened it up and read the text from Roman:

I need you to do something for me.

She replied to his text and looked at Spencer. "Are you here with friends?"

~

Roman picked up his phone as he got himself ready for bed. He opened Angelica's text:

Anything!

He laughed while texting her back.

~

Spencer stared at Angelica. "Can I buy you a drink?"

"No. I'm good thanks!" She looked down at her phone and opened Roman's new text:

I want you to sneak in the house, come up in the bedroom, and lock both doors behind you.

"THIS man!"

Spencer laughed, "Everything ok? What...your man wants you to come home?"

"No, not yet!" She typed him another message while laughing.

~

Roman ran his bath water and laid back on the bed watching television. He felt his phone and opened her message:

What if I'm out 'til 4 or 5?

Roman shook his head and replied.

~

Angelica was on her way back to the dance floor when Roman replied:

Can you get here before 2? I need to be inside you before 2!

Angelica laughed, responded, and went to the dance floor.

~

Roman sat in the tub and read her message: *I'll go home, shower, and break in your house all nice and wet...before 2! Don't bother trying to stay up...if you're asleep, I have the most PERFECT way of waking you up!*

Roman laughed and laid back in the tub. He got another text message and opened it. It was from Crystal asking him to call her. Roman deleted the message and laid back in the tub.

Chapter 16– Lesson: Slow Down...When You're Moving Too Fast!

Angelica put her key in Roman's door and opened it slowly. She closed the door back and locked it. Roman left the lamp on in the living room so that she could see her way up the stairs. She turned off the lamp and walked on up to Winter's room. She cracked the door and peeked in on her to see if she was ok. Winter was sound asleep with her cute petite frame!

Angelica closed the door and went into Roman's room. Angelica closed the bedroom door behind her and locked the door. She knew he was sleeping by the way that he was snoring. Hearing him sleep this hard told her that he had a real busy day. As she sat on the edge of the bed taking her sandals off, she felt Roman moving on the bed. He was reaching out for her!

Angelica kicked the other shoe off and laid back in the bed next to him. Roman turned all the way over, looked at her, and smiled. Angelica put her hand on his face and kissed him. She began to undress as he just laid there and watched. While passionately kissing all over his chest, she slowly straddled him without skipping a beat! Roman continued watching and moaning as she moved downward. Anxiously anticipating her wet mouth on his dick, he was hard as ever!

Angelica licked and sucked on his dick so good that he had to tell her to slow down a couple of times. Roman moaned as if he were about to come! He had been waiting so long that he tried his damnedest to hold back! Fifteen minutes later, she got on top of him, and rode him as best as she could. Roman was about to internally combust if he didn't come soon!

"Can you get behind me," she said slowing up. Roman shook his head yes! Angelica got up and positioned herself on her hands and knees right next to where he was laying.

Roman quickly maneuvered his way behind her and eased his way in. While closing his eyes in disbelief at how much he loved her, he bent over and whispered in her ear. "We gonna get in trouble if you wake the baby!"

Angelica looked back at him and arched her eyebrow. "Well, I guess you can't really give it to me then huh?"

"Oh, I can give it...you just have to take it!"

Angelica slowly licked her lips. "I think I'm ready!"

"You sure baby, I don't want to hurt you!"

Angelica reached in between her legs, took hold of his balls, and rubbed them softly. "Show me!"

"Now that's what the fuck I'm talking about," he said while pounding deep inside of her. She did moan, but it wasn't too loud. He kept going faster and faster, then deeper while squeezing her ass apart. Roman then held on to her shoulders by moving his arms underneath her chest and grasping onto her shoulders. He pulled her body back onto his dick while he jammed himself inside of her. Angelica was holding on the best way she could! Roman was fucking her like a madman. "Can I come inside baby?"

"Why are you asking me? Do what you want to me Roman! Do whatever you want!"

Roman pulled out of her and made her lay on her back. He kissed her, reentered her body, and moved slowly. "I want to come inside of you, and I want you to tell me that you want to have my baby."

She laughed. "I don't think I can do that!" Roman pushed harder and harder inside of her. "I'm sorry!"

Roman slowed down. "You don't want to have my baby Angel? Is that it?"

Angelica moaned in between thrusts. "Things are going to change for the worse if that happens, Roman! You know how it gets!"

Roman stopped. "I'm not getting any younger baby! I want us to have a child together. Not right away of course, but I at least want to know if you WANT to or not."

"Roman, I love you. I have three children, and you have one. That makes four children... and you want to have five?"

Roman smiled. "No! I want six, so we're down by two!"

Angelica laughed. "Roman, if our relationship grows to the point where we get married or something like that, then I don't think that having more children will be a problem for me. At that point, I would love to have your child."

Roman started moving inside of her. "Oh, so I would have to marry you first huh?"

"That's the way I would like it!" Angelica moaned and kissed all on his neck. "You taste so good!" Roman loved when she talked to him like that! "Roman you never shot it ON my pussy or in my mouth! I usually just suck it out of your dick," she said moaning seductively in his ear while his body stiffened up. "Can you pull it out and shoot it on my face and in my mouth?"

"Awe shit baby! You want it in your mouth AGAIN?"

"Yes!"

"Ahh shit! Here it comes!" Angelica muffled his mouth by pulling his head in closer so that she could kiss him, but he wouldn't let her. He kept looking down at his dick going in and out of Angelica. As his moaning started to get on the loud side, she grabbed him closer to her and looked at him.

"Roman, can you come in me please?"

"I thought you wanted it in your mouth?"

"Can you do both for me," she asked kissing him.

"Shit!" He laid his body completely on top of hers, wrapped his arms underneath her body, and held on tight. "Why do you want me to come in you,

Angel?" She didn't respond. How could she when he was making love to her just the way she loved it. "If you don't answer me, I'm not going to do it."

"Please! I do want it!"

"Why? Baby tell me! You better tell me quick because it's coming," he said while sucking on her neck.

"I want you to come inside me Roman please," Angelica was seconds away from paradise.

"Here it comes, tell me why! Tell me!" Angelica came right along with him. "Baby, you got what you wanted? You happy?"

Angelica sighed and kissed his lips. "Are you?"

Roman kissed her nose. "I've been happy ever since I met you. I can't wait until we can stop all this sneaking shit!" They both laughed trying not to be as loud as they just were a couple of minutes ago!

Angelica caressed his back. "January will be here before you know it!"

Roman kissed her cheek. "I know. We need to sit down next month and look at our finances so we can make this happen because I refuse to keep sleeping alone. I really miss being with you at night when it's your month to have the kids or whenever Winter is here!" Angelica looked at him and just stared. "I mean how do you feel about that?"

"I miss being with you too."

Roman frowned his face. "Why are you looking so sad? What's wrong?"

"Roman...Never mind. Forget it!"

Roman pulled all the way out of her and laid on his side looking at her while playing in her hair. "Tell me. Please."

Angelica looked away, "I don't want you to think..."

"I'm not going to think anything Angelica! Look at me and tell me," he said kissing her breast.

Angelica looked at him. "I just miss you at night. That's all."

Roman looked at her. "I miss you too but why the sad look? Baby, what's wrong?"

Angelica smiled and moved closer to him. She took a deep breath and looked at him. "I guess I feel embarrassed about admitting to you that I sometimes cry at night when I'm not with you. I spent years of my life sleeping beside a man who broke my heart and who I allowed to weaken my spirit. Now I'm in love with the most beautiful man that I have ever known... and I can't sleep at his side every night, wake up to his touch, his laughter, his snoring!" Angelica laughed while Roman just looked at her with no emotion. "I cry because I spent years giving myself to someone who was undeserving and now that I have someone in my life who is..." She sighed and closed her eyes trying not to let any of her tears get away.

Roman pushed her hair away and raised her head up so that he could see her. "Angelica, I want to be with you just as much as you want to be with me. We just need to get together and start planning."

"I'm not rushing. I'm just telling you how I feel."

"Baby I know you are! It's no reason why we can't make this happen! You want it, I want it, and the kids can't wait to have it!" Angelica smiled. "Angel, let's make this a priority and work on making this happen for our family and us! We're moving at a pace that our family will be able to handle."

"Are you sure you want this Roman? I know I'm a bit fragile, but I *am* capable of taking care of myself and my children if you are not ready for this. There's no pressure or rush!"

"I know what you are capable of and I am ready for you. Sunday night after I take Winter home, we'll sit down and start planning." Roman kissed her lips and smiled. "This will also be the last time that we'll be sneaking around our kids!"

Angelica laughed. "So, you really do love me huh?"

Roman laughed. "Yes I do." He kissed her lips again while playing with her nipples. "We'll also be discussing the expiration date of when you will be officially off of the pill!" Angelica laughed while he sucked on her breasts.

"I'm extremely fertile Roman! Be careful with what you ask for!"

"I'm glad you're fertile! Maybe we can knock out two at once!"

Angelica pushed him away. "Two at once! I'm trying to be with you, and you're trying to kill me!"

Roman cracked up laughing. The both of them couldn't stop laughing as if they were drunk! "I want at least two more babies! That's not too bad!"

"Yes, it is! Two more times of getting fat, looking undesirable, not being able to make love to you the way I would like, and as often as I would like...it's going to be torture."

Roman looked at her seriously. "You won't get fat, and you will never be undesirable in my eyes... and making love while your pregnant will be fun!"

"Yeah, that's what they all say," she said sarcastically.

"Angel, I will..."

Angelica inched her body away from him. "Roman, let's wait until that time comes. Stop moving so fast! Don't say..."

Roman repositioned her body so that he was now hovering over top of her body. "Don't try to tell me what I can say to the woman who I love more than anything! I want us to add more on to our family! I want this Angelica! I realize just how much you love me even to consider having more children with me! I'm your guardian angel remember? Let me do my job!" He passionately kissed her lips and made love to her one more time before they both fell off to sleep!

~5:15am

Angelica looked at Roman who was snoring out of this world. She wrote a quick note on a piece of paper from his drawer, got dressed, and left out of the house making sure to lock up behind her. She got home in fifteen minutes! Angelica ran up the stairs and sat her ass on the toilet!!!

~10:39 am

Angelica woke up to her phone ringing astronomically loud! She reached across her pillows and grabbed the phone. "Hello," she said in her sexiest and groggiest voice.

"Angelica it's Ian. Is this a bad time?"

"No, what's going on? Is everything ok?"

"Yeah, everything is fine."

Angelica stretched, and Ian pictured her elegant body stretching like she always used to do before she got out of bed. "Ian?"

"Yes."

Angelica laughed a bit. "Did you need to speak to me about something?"

"Can we have dinner sometime? Just you and me."

"What's going on Ian?"

Ian took a deep breath and felt like he was on center stage about to give his greatest speech. "I really need to sit down with you and talk to you about the kids, our marriage, and the divorce."

Angelica shook her head. He was such an asshole! "I have an even better idea. When you drop the kids off in two weeks at my house, we can talk in the kitchen while they get settled."

"That sounds great. I'd like that very much."

Angelica couldn't help but notice a change in the way he was talking to her. "Ian are you ok?"

"Yeah, why?"

"I don't know. You sound a little strange that's all."

"I'm just...a little bit more aware of things. That's all!"

"I must admit you do sound peaceful! Can you tell the kids I said hi and that I'll talk to them at bedtime?"

"Ok Sofie."

Angelica frowned up her face. "Ok Ian! What's with all the Sofie! You haven't called me that in years! What's really going on?"

Ian laughed. "When was the last time I called you Sofie?"

"When Kendall was born."

Ian laughed. "I said: Sofie we did it again!"

"You sure did." Angelica felt a little uncomfortable speaking to him. "Ian I have to get ready to go. I'll talk to you in a couple of weeks."

"Ok then!"

"Bye!" Angelica hung up the phone and laid in the bed for a minute thinking about Ian calling her Sofie. He would always call her that when he told her that he loved her or when something special was happening. Her phone rang again, "Hello."

"Why did you leave without saying goodbye," Roman asked her in a pissed-off tone.

Angelica sighed. "Roman, I left because I didn't want it to be awkward for Winter to wake up and see me there in your bed! What's wrong with that?"

Roman calmed down. "Baby, I'm sorry. I was just a little worried when I woke up and didn't see you next to me. I looked throughout the house, and I thought that maybe something happened to you."

"I left a note on your dresser, Roman. I wouldn't just leave without saying anything!"

Roman looked on his dresser and read the note:

Roman, call me when you get a chance! I love you
~Angelica.

"I was just worried that's all. I'm sorry," he said. "What are you doing today?"

"I have a couple of errands that I have to do before three, why what's up?"

"Well, I thought that I could take two, out of my three lovely ladies out to dinner and then to see a movie."

"When?"

"How's eight o'clock?"

Angelica smiled and stretched again, "That sounds great. You want me to come over your place or..."

"I'll call you when I'm on my way to pick you up."

"Ok...see you later on."

"Alright, baby. Hey, did you eat yet?"

"No, I'm about to go downstairs and get me a bowl of Frosted Cheerios!"

Roman laughed. "Now you know that's my cereal!"

"Yeah I bought a couple of boxes while I was at the Acme the other day."

"So, you're teasing this morning huh?"

Angelica looked at the time on her phone, "You know what? I better go! Me and Linda are supposed to get our hair done at the same time and then go out to lunch with my mom. I'll call you later on."

"Alright have fun!"

"You too! Tell Winter I said hi! I love you!"

"I love you too!

Angelica quickly showered and went to pick up Linda from her mother's house. It only took her twenty minutes to get to 23rd Street near Fairmount. She parked on the already crowded street and ran to her mom's house. Angelica opened the door. "Hello!"

"There she is! The new Miss Bryant!" Linda gave her a hug. "I had so much fun last night! We partied hard girl! I remember you told me that you were heading out but where did you go?"

Their mother walked in the living room from the kitchen. "Morning ladies!"

"Morning, mom!" Angelica gave their mother a hug and a kiss.

"You girls want a muffin and some juice before you head out?"

"I'd love one mom," Angelica said thinking of how she always loved her mother's homemade blueberry muffins.

Linda shoved Angelica. "Angelica, don't even try it! Where did you go last night?"

Angelica batted her eye lids. "Out!"

Mrs. Bryant broke it down for Linda. "In other words, Linda, she went to see Roman!"

"Oh!! The NEW heartbreaker!"

Angelica pointed her finger at Linda. "Don't start Linda!"

Linda put her hands on her hips. "It's not my fault that I warned you about Ian's wandering eye!"

"Ian is not the issue here! Roman is nothing like Ian!"

Linda smirked. "Let me be the judge of that! When can I meet him?"

Angelica smiled. "Not on this trip! You're leaving tomorrow morning!"

Linda cocked her head to the side. "Well how about today? After we eat lunch with mom?"

Angelica shook her head, "I don't think so. His daughter, Winter, is over for the weekend."

Mrs. Bryant smiled. "Winter and Hailey have gotten so close! They are like sisters!"

Angelica smiled. "I know mom! They call each other and send emails!"

Linda looked at Angelica. "Things sound like they're getting pretty serious!"

Angelica smiled. "I love Roman very much. He is all I ever wanted in a man, AND he loves my kids! Do you know that Ian neglected to get a magician for Kendall's birthday party! Roman knew about how I felt about Ian coming through for his birthday, so he reserved a magician for the party just in case! He even came to the party while he was working just to make sure everything went ok!"

Mrs. Bryant nodded her head in agreement. "He is good to Angelica! I've seen how he talks to her and how he treats her! He reminds me of your father! He's very protective yet passionate about Angelica and the kids," Mrs. Bryant said to Linda.

Linda raised one of her eyebrows. "I've heard the stories. I just need to meet him. After the incident, Angelica you need to be weary of men right now. They will try and ease their way in and try to take control while you are vulnerable!"

Angelica put her hand up to Linda's face. "Stop it ok! Roman is not like that all! Now let's go and get our hair done so we can pick mom back up and eat!" Linda went upstairs to grab her purse when Angelica's phone rang. It was Roman. "Hello."

"Hi, Ms. Angelica," said Winter whispering!

"Hi, Winter! How are you?"

"I'm fine. We're out at the mall. My dad thinks I'm calling my mom, but I just wanted to ask you something."

"Sure, what is it?" Angelica walked in the kitchen so that she could get her muffin.

"I talked to Hailey this morning. She wanted to know if you could pick her up so that all four of us can go to dinner and to the movies. She already asked her dad, and he said that it was ok."

Angelica laughed. "Let me square all of this away with Hailey and her dad. After I speak to them, I'll call you right back."

"Ok," Winter said getting excited.

"Can I speak to your dad?"

Winter laughed. "Yes!" She called out, "Here daddy!"

Roman purposefully gave Winter some space when she talked to her mom. Since they were in the toy store, he didn't go too far. "What's wrong," Roman said walking up to Winter in the toy store.

Winter smiled. "She wants to speak to you."

"Hello," Romans voice was real dry, "Hello?"

Angelica heard the disdain in his voice, "Roman, it's Angelica!"

Roman started laughing and looked at Winter. "What in the world is going on? Winter, I thought you were calling your mother!" Winter laughed in the background while Roman squinted his eyes at her playfully! He continued on the phone. "What's up baby!"

"Roman, Winter wanted to know if Hailey could come along with us to the movies. Apparently, they talked this morning and planned it all out! Hailey even asked her dad already!"

"What!" Roman cracked up laughing, "They are a something else. Well, it's up to you baby because it's definitely fine with me." Angelica could hear Winter applauding and cheering in the background.

Angelica laughed. "I'll call Ian and Hailey to make sure we're on the same sheet of music."

"Baby, call me back and let me know."

"Alright, I will. Bye!"

"Bye." Roman looked at Winter. "I can't believe you tricked me!" He picked her up and gave her a kiss on the cheek.

"Ms. Angelica is so sweet dad! I think she would be a good step-mom!"

"You think so?"

"I know so daddy! Mr. and Mrs. Roman Callowhill!" Roman tickled her and made her laugh uncontrollably. After he stopped, Winter got her breath and looked up at her dad. "Daddy do you really love her?"

"Yes, I do. How do you feel about that?"

"Daddy, please! I'm not going to fall apart! I know you love me!"

Roman looked at her in disbelief and just shook his head, "Winter...," he said stooping down to her level, "I love Angelica a whole lot. But it is extremely important that you understand something. The love I have for her will never get in the way of the love that I have for you. You came from me, and I will always love you no matter what you do, where you go..."

"I know dad! I love you too," Winter hugged him so tight! "I wish we can all be a family one day. You, Ms. Angelica, Hailey, Gavin, Kendall and maybe another little sister or brother..."

Roman kissed her cheek. "One day at a time baby! One day at a time."

~

Angelica called Ian. "Hi Ian, it's Angelica."

"Hey, how's it going?"

Angelica's face looked as if she smelled something fishy in the air. "Everything's good! I'm calling because Hailey wanted to go out with us to dinner and a movie."

Ian smiled. "I told Hailey that it was ok with me for her to go with you all and spend the night."

"Thanks, Ian. I'll be by there at 7:30 to pick her up."

"Ok, I'll let Hailey know. I can come and pick her up tomorrow. Just call me and let me know what time."

Angelica smiled to herself admiring Ian's new attitude. "Ok, I'll do that." She hung up the phone and shook her head while calling Roman.

"Hey babe, what's up?"

"Everything's set. I told Ian that we would be there at 7:30 to pick Hailey up. If that's too early, I can..."

Roman shook his head. "No, that's perfect. So, you'll be here around when?"

"Around seven if that's ok with you?"

Roman played like he had an attitude. "I wanted you here with me this morning!" Angelica laughed! "I'm not playing. You have some making up to do. I was very upset! You know after we talked last night, I just knew I would be waking up to your beautiful face, but I didn't! Was that all talk?"

"No," she said still laughing.

"Well, I guess we'll see tonight at the slumber party."

"What!" Angelica was still laughing.

"Yeah, that's the latest! Winter said they had been planning this for about a week! The plan was for them to set up in the living room, but WE have to stay upstairs. I told Winter that they could go on the third floor instead of in the living room and we would be on the second floor in my room."

"What! Did you say that to her Roman?!"

Roman laughed. "Angel, Hailey and Winter know that we sleep in the same bed baby! No, they haven't seen us but just think about it. When you're over here at night, and they're about to go to bed at Ian's, they know that we are together. They can put two and two together baby! So, there is no need for you to bring your pajama's! I've got something right here for you to wear."

"Oh yeah?"

"Yup!"

Angelica shook her head, "I'll be there at 7!"

"I love you!"

"I love you too Roman, bye!"

Chapter 17 – Lesson: Never Give 100 Percent of Yourself to ANY ONE...You'll have Nothing Left for Yourself!

~6:38 pm

Linda, Angelica, and their mother sat at the kitchen table just reminiscing about the good old days. Linda hugged Angelica. "I was so upset when mom told me what happened. I'm sorry I wasn't here."

"Linda please! You live in Florida and have a husband and two kids of your own! We talked just about every other night. That was good enough for me!"

Linda slammed her fist on the table. "I just can't believe that Ian left the fucking door unlocked!"

"Linda, please," her mother replied. "It's over, the man has been caught, Ian and Angelica aren't married, and most importantly Angelica is fine!"

Linda shook her head, "I know mom."

Angelica was fuming mad! She stood up from where she was sitting. "I'm going to get ready to go and pick-up Hailey. I'll call you all later on."

Angelica grabbed her purse, hugged her mom, and left out the door.

~

After Angelica left, Mrs. Bryant let Linda have it! "Linda, why did you have to bring up the fact that she got raped?"

"Mom, I just wanted to apologize!"

"Yeah and then you talked about Ian leaving the door open! Sometimes you can be so insensitive. That's probably why she didn't want to tell you herself in the first place!" Mrs. Bryant left her in the room alone, went up to her bedroom, and closed the door behind her.

~

Angelica started crying on the way to pick Hailey up from Ian's. She loved her sister, but at the same time, she couldn't stand her! Angelica told her mom not to tell Linda about what happened, but she did anyway! While wiping her eyes, she made a left onto the parkway heading back to West Philly. She hated thinking about what happened that night and most of all she hated knowing that other people knew about it! Fifteen minutes later Roman called her cell phone. Angelica was at the corner of Ian's block. "Hello."

Roman could hear the sadness in her tone. "Baby what's wrong?"

Angelica sighed. "Nothing why?"

"You sound like you've been crying! What's going on?" Roman was getting upset.

"My sister just doesn't think sometimes before she says things. She didn't say anything bad it's just the fact that she mentioned... that day...that's all!"

"Why the fuck would she do that?"

"I don't know. Linda wanted to apologize for not being here. Then she said how she couldn't believe that Ian left the door unlocked."

"That's your sister and I never met her but baby that's some bullshit! *Now* I understand why you didn't want to tell her in the first place!"

Angelica wiped her eyes. "I know."

"Don't even worry about it. Your sister's leaving tomorrow...right?"

"Yeah," Angelica replied pulling up to Ian's house. She double-parked and put her hazard lights on.

"Good! Where are you now? I can't wait to see you!"

"I'm outside of Ian's." Angelica was so into her conversation with Roman that she didn't see Ian walking up to the car.

"Sofie?" Angelica looked at the passenger side window, and Ian was looking at her smiling.

Roman heard Ian calling Angelica by her middle name. "Baby, you alright?"

Angelica stared at Ian. "Yeah, I'll call you when I'm on my way," and hung up with Roman without saying goodbye.

Ian looked at Angelica's hair and noticed she made some changes to her hair color. "Your hair looks really nice."

"Thanks, Ian. Is Hailey ready to go?"

"Yeah, she'll be right out in a minute! How's your family?"

"They're good! How's your family?"

"They're fine. My mom told me to tell you to call her when you get a chance."

Angelica started to worry. "Really? What's going on?"

Ian continued to stare at her. "I don't know. My mom called me yesterday and told me. For some reason, she has always talked to you first, then me!"

Angelica laughed. "Please tell her that I'll call her tomorrow morning."

"I will." He said smiling into her eyes.

Angelica looked at him up and down. "Ian, what's gotten into you? I mean what's going on?"

"What? I'm just smiling!"

"I know, but you're smiling at ME!"

Ian leaned more into the passenger side window. "What, I never smiled at you before?"

"No. I'm not saying that! I know what it is. You've met someone special! I'm happy for you!"

"I guess you can say that. I lost her... then found her again." He kept staring at her as if he were trying to send her a mental message or something.

"Mommy!"

Angelica looked at Hailey running down the steps. "Hey sweetheart! You ready?"

"Yes!" Hailey gave her dad a hug, "I love you, Daddy. See you tomorrow!"

Ian laughed. "I love you too! Angelica just call me when you want me to pick her up."

"Ok, Ian!" Hailey opened the door to the backseat since Ian was still hanging onto the passenger side door.

"Angelica?"

"Yes," she said looking at him.

"Please don't forget to call my mom."

"I won't!"

"Bye, dad," Hailey yelled out loud! Ian backed away from the car and waved his hand goodbye! Angelica put the car in drive, turned off the hazards, and drove off. "Mom, I can't wait to see Winter! Where are we going?"

"Why don't you call Roman and let him know we're on our way."

Angelica pressed his name from her contacts and waited for him to answer, and then handed Hailey the phone. "Hello?"

"Hi RC! It's Hailey! We're like...mom how far are we from his house?"

Angelica laughed. "Five minutes!"

Hailey continued on. "We're five minutes away RC! Where are we going?"

Roman shook his head smiling. "It's a surprise! How are you doing?"

"Good! I've missed you AND Winter! So have the boys...they talk about you all the time! Tell Winter, I'm on my way! Bye!"

Roman laughed his head off! Hailey was so damn funny! She always said what she had to say and that was that!

Angelica paralleled parked on the street. As soon as she turned the car off, Hailey was out the door! She spotted Winter waiting on the front porch! Angelica just stood there with the driver's side door open looking at Hailey and Winter hugging each other! Angelica wanted to cry so bad. She hoped and prayed that everything was going to work out because the kids were really attached. Roman came to the door looking for Angelica. Tears started rolling down her eyes as she smiled at him. He walked over to her in his Black Nike Sweat Suit. "What's with the tears?"

"I'm scared Roman. I don't want to hurt our kids!"

"We're not going to hurt our kids, and I'm not going to hurt you! I know we've talked about a lot lately. We're only going to do what we feel we can handle! One day at a time!"

"I know! It's just that I've never been this happy before...with any man."

Roman hugged her and kissed her lips, "Good, because I have never wanted any woman more than I want you!"

Angelica laughed. "You already have me!" She said kissing him on his lips. Angelica pulled away from him so that she could close the door. She locked the car and turned to him so that they could walk across the street together.

Roman held her from behind, "I don't have you yet, but I will soon!" He hugged her tight making sure that her ass leaned against him.

Angelica nodded her head. "We better get ready to go."

"Go where? Me and Winter cooked dinner for you and Hailey!"

Angelica turned around and smiled. "Are you serious? You are amazing!"

Roman held her hand and walked across the street with Angelica. "Dessert will be after the movie if that's ok with you and the girls."

"Being with you is dessert for me!"

"Ok, Ms. Angelica Hallmark!"

Angelica laughed. "I'm serious! I hope you CAN give me something sweet to eat this evening!"

Roman kissed her neck. "That won't be a problem!" When they walked in the door, Roman pulled her to the side and kissed the hell out of her!

"Roman," Angelica said talking through the kiss. Roman opened his eyes and closed them. He kept kissing her and held on to her. Angelica moaned, and Roman kept on going! Winter and Hailey ran down the stairs and saw them kissing. Roman kept on going but eased up a bit on the intensity.

"Hailey look! Daddy and AB are kissing!" Hailey and Winter laughed as Roman pulled away slowly. "Daddy?"

"Yes," he said still looking at Angelica.

"That's the first time I saw you kiss AB."

"Me too," Hailey said laughing. Angelica laughed, and Roman turned toward Winter and Hailey.

Winter elbowed Hailey. "Daddy, tell AB that you love her!"

"Angelica, I love you," Roman said staring at Angelica. Winter and Hailey applauded.

Hailey elbowed Winter. "Mom, now you tell RC that you love him."

Angelica smiled, "Roman I love you!"

"Now you may kiss the bride," yelled Winter and Hailey! Roman held her close and dipped her forward while kissing her! Winter and Hailey cheered and clapped while they kissed. As Roman picked her up and twirled her around, Winter and Hailey ran back up the stairs.

Roman looked at Angelica. "It's crazy, right?"

"Yes!" They both laughed.

"Angel," Roman held her close and kissed her neck. "I have something I want to show you." He took her hand and walked her in the kitchen. "Wait right here for a minute. I forgot to get something." Roman ran upstairs and came back down. "Ok! He pressed the warm button on the stove and opened the basement door. Angelica walked down the stairs in the basement, and Roman followed.

"What am I looking for," she said passing the laundry room. She stopped at an open doorway. Inside the room, her eyes fixated on the microphone, his guitar, and a brand-new couch. He had been building a small studio in his basement! Angelica walked into the room and looked at the speakers, computer, amplifier, and its acoustic setup. She put her fingers on the microphone and started tearing up. "Why are you doing this?"

Roman walked in the studio. "Do you like it? I know it's not big and definitely not state of the art equipment, but..."

"What? Roman what you did was the most selfless thing anyone could do! You built a studio for us!"

"I built it for you!" Angelica ran up to him and hugged him.

"How can I ever show you how much I appreciate you?"

"You...," he said touching her breasts, "...can show me by making love to me right now."

Angelica anxiously looked at him. "Roman, the girls are upstairs!"

Roman held her close and played in her hair. "I told them I was showing you the new studio."

"They knew you were making it?"

"Yes!" Roman locked the door and kissed her lips and neck as he backed her up to the couch. Angelica pulled her shorts and panties down. She slowly pulled off her shirt and bra, then laid on the couch. Roman pulled his pants down and climbed on top of her. He was so excited that he rammed inside of her. Angelica instinctively grabbed on to his arm. "Did I hurt you?"

"No, you're just big that's all!"

Roman looked worried. "Did I put it in too fast?"

"Just a little but I'm ok."

"I'm sorry baby! I just missed you that's all!"

"Baby, it's ok! I love you!" Angelica kissed him. "Make love to me!"

Roman felt bad and sighed. "I'm not trying to hurt you..."

"Roman make love to me now please!" Roman went deeper, and Angelica moaned louder and louder!

"Let me hear you, baby!" Roman raised her leg and fucked the shit out of her! Angelica sounded just like a woman getting fucked in a porno!

"Oh God! Roman fuck me!" He crossed her legs and put them over his right shoulder. Angelica went off!

"Take it, baby! Take it! I love you so fucking much!" He put her legs down and laid on top of her. He stopped moving and just stared at her with a weird look on his face. "Do you still love him?"

"What," Angelica said panting.

Roman looked really uncomfortable. "Ian. Do you still love him?"

"What? Why are you asking about him while we are making love?" Roman was silent as he turned his head to the side. Angelica shook her head. "I care for him as a friend and because he is the father of my children...probably just as much as you love Winter's mom."

Roman disgustingly frowned his face. "I don't love her mother!"

"And I am no longer in love with Ian. I care about him...I have love for him as the father of our children Roman...that's it!" Angelica sat up a bit. "Why are you asking about Ian? What's going on?"

Roman whispered. "Angelica, I don't want you to yank my chain! I want you so bad! I'm not trying to hear in a couple of months that you're considering getting back with him for the kids or whatever! I'm not trying to hear that shit!"

Angelica kissed him. "You have me, Roman."

"No, I don't! You're my woman not my wife!" Angelica didn't say anything. Roman kissed her lips. "I'm not trying to hear that bullshit,

Angelica!" He moved slow and deep inside of her. Angelica started moaning and telling Roman not to stop. "I'm not trying to hear that you're going to leave me, Angel!"

"I would never do that to you, Roman! Never!"

"I love you, Angel! I swear on my life I do!"

"I love you too Roman!"

Roman kissed her. "Marry me then!"

Angelica laughed. "I just got divorced!" Roman stopped, and they both laughed like crazy! Angelica pulled him forward so that he could keep making love to her. She sucked on his chest and kissed his lips. "Can you come in me?"

"If you marry me?"

Angelica sucked on his neck. "I'll marry you if you come in me!"

Roman's eyes rolled back in his head. "When?"

"Mmmmm, now!"

Roman looked at her. "No, when will you marry me?"

"I'll tell you when you come in me! Roman please."

Roman couldn't hold out any longer anyway. "Here it comes!"

"Roman please give it to me!"

Roman came all inside of her while Angelica hummed through her orgasm! Roman breathed heavily. "When? When are you going to marry me?"

Angelica grazed her hand along his hairy chest. "In order for me to marry you, I need to be proposed to...then MAYBE I'll marry you ONE day!"

Roman kissed all over her breasts and then her lips. "Have it your way then!" Roman backed out of her. Angelica stood up and bent over to get her clothes. Roman looked at her wetness as she bent over and wanted some more. She stepped in her underwear and began pulling them up. "What are you doing?"

"Getting dressed, we have to get ready to eat!"

He laughed, "I don't think so! You mean to tell me you bent over like that in front of me and now we're going upstairs? Naww!"

"Yes, we are! We have to go!"

Roman bent her over the arm of the couch and widened her stance. "Spread 'em!"

"Oh God! I've been waiting for this for so long!"

"Well, I'm about to give it to you right now!" Roman went to work on Angelica for about twenty more minutes. Angelica came about two more times before Roman shot it all on her ass and back! He took off his shirt off and wiped the cum off of her back and in between her legs. "Damn!"

Angelica laughed. "It was a lot huh?"

"Yeah." Roman balled the shirt up and threw it on the floor. Angelica put her shorts on and then her shirt. She fixed her hair and stood straight up. Roman smiled and put his hands in her hair. "The color looks really nice on you. Did you do that for me?"

"Yes!" Angelica kissed him and looked down at his flaccid, lengthy, friend. "I guess he's had enough huh?"

"Yeah for now!"

~

After eating Roast Beef, Mashed Potatoes, Peas, and rolls, all four of them went to the movies on Delaware Avenue. Following the movies, they went to the market close to Roman's home. They needed to get caramel, more whipped cream, and cherries for the sundae's that they were going to make. While in the market, Winter would hold Angelica's hand down one aisle, and Hailey would hold Roman's! There was so much good energy flowing between the four of them!

As they exited the market, the girls walked ahead of Roman and Angelica laughing and enjoying each other's company! Roman and Angelica walked hand in hand closely behind them! Everything went sour when Angelica heard a woman walking up behind them in the parking lot calling Roman's name. Everyone turned around and looked at the woman who appeared to be smiling, but Angelica could feel that something was going on.

Roman looked at the kids. "Winter and Hailey, the door is open! Go ahead inside and turn on the radio. We'll be right there," commanded Roman. The woman caught up with Roman and Angelica. She stayed silent until the kids got in the truck. Angelica looked at Roman, and he stared back at Angelica.

The woman looked at him impatiently and broke the silence. "Hey Roman! What's going on?"

Roman turned to Angelica and walked up close to her. "Go in the truck with the kids!"

Angelica's head was cocked to the side. "What?"

Roman reassuringly put his hands on her arms. "Baby, just go. Let me handle this."

Angelica was fuming. "What the hell is going on Roman?"

Roman kept his cool. "Nothing...is going on! Trust me! Nothing is going on! Let me handle this."

Angelica walked to the truck, got inside, and watched what was going on from the passenger window.

Monica looked at Angelica in Roman's truck and smiled as if to say, 'and what?'. She focused her eyes back to Roman and looked at him up and down. "Roman, it's lovely seeing you here. How have you been?"

Roman was about to explode, but Monica couldn't tell. "Monica, let me see your phone."

Monica started to get loud. "Why? What does my phone have to do with this?"

Roman smiled. "Calm down. Turn your phone off."

Monica did as she was told and smiled at him. "Why did you tell me to turn it off?"

Only after viewing that Monica's phone was turned off did Roman speak. He took a step toward her and stared at her. Roman spoke softly. "Monica, when you saw me in the store with another woman and children, you should have never said anything to me! I told you before that we are done. I told you that we could be friends, but you know what? Fuck you! -You trying to hurt my family?"

Monica looked scared. "I don't want to hurt you. I want to be with you!"

Roman stared into Monica's eyes making her shiver. "I don't ever... want to see you again." Roman started walking away from her.

"Roman, I'm sorry," Monica pleaded.

He turned around and looked at her. Roman slowly walked up to her again and smiled. "I just said that I never want to see you again...and here you are again *making* me look at you! Leave me the **FUCK** alone, and I mean it." He looked at her phone again. It was off. Roman whispered, "The next time I won't be so nice."

Roman walked away and took a couple of big breaths. He got in the truck and put the key in the ignition. Hailey and Winter were busy singing songs from the radio. Angelica looked out the window at the woman who was now getting in her Mercedes Benz. She was a beautiful young woman with a beautiful body. Angelica figured she was in her late 20's or early 30's and instantly felt intimidated. She wanted to cry so bad, but the kids were in the back, so she just held on.

Roman was mad as hell! He told Angelica this was a done deal! More bullshit! "Baby, you alright?"

Angelica looked at him and then turned her head back to the window. Roman mumbled some words to himself and pulled off toward his house. Roman and Angelica stayed silent the whole way to his house. As soon as Roman pulled up in the driveway, Winter and Hailey jumped out of the car and ran up to the house with the bags. Roman got out, and Angelica followed in the rear. "Mom what's wrong, it's sundae time!"

"I know baby. I'm just a little tired that's all."

Winter walked over to Angelica. "We can make you some tea with lemon. That will make you feel better!" Roman opened the door.

Angelica smiled at her beautiful self. "You're right! I'll have a cup of tea!" Winter and Hailey ran in the house with the goodies while Roman stood by the door. Angelica looked at him and didn't know whether to cry or slap him in the face!

Roman closed the door so that they could talk on the porch. "Angelica I'm really sorry about what happened but let me assure you that..."

Angelica felt sick. "Roman, don't. Please don't. I don't want any more reassurances or promises. I don't want to talk about us moving in, having children, or getting married. I don't want to say anything or hear anything from you right now. Please."

Roman put his hand on her arm. "You can't do this. You have to talk to me!"

"Roman, PLEASE!!!!"

"What? Angelica, that woman will never be anywhere near me than where she was today! I will never be with any other woman Angelica! You are the only..."

"Roman, please! We've been through this before! What's next, she's pregnant with your child! What's next? Huh! What's next?"

"Angel..."

"Don't fuckin' Angel me Roman! Just be honest! Just tell me that you still have feelings for her! Be honest with me...please. Please...I'm begging you! Just be fair," she said crying.

Roman swallowed the lumps building in his throat from the anguish in her voice. He knew she was hurting! "Angel, I told her that I didn't want to be near her or even see her...ever! I have not talked to her or any other woman since we last had this type of discussion."

Angelica looked at the ground. "I don't believe you, Roman."

"Yes, you do! You believe me because you love me almost as much as I love you!"

"What the fuck does my love have to do with you and that woman Roman? You said I wouldn't be hearing about her anymore!"

"I didn't know that she was going to be at the fucking market, Angelica! How could I have known that? How can I control that?" Roman grabbed her. "This bullshit with this woman is nothing! It's nothing! Trust me baby! I want you and no one else! I've been putting my all into our relationship and our family. I have been the one patiently waiting for you to want to move forward.

Why would I want to ruin that? I want this baby! I want this more than anything! You've got to believe me!"

"Roman," she said crying and whispering. "I don't have it in me now to fight! I'm all burned out! I don't have the energy!"

"Let me carry it baby... you don't have to do a damn thing! Just be with me and let me handle all that you can't!" Angelica put her head down and looked away from his face. "Look at me!" Angelica looked at him with loads of tears in her eyes. "I will not fail you!"

"Roman..."

"What?"

"I've never asked you to promise me anything."

"I know you haven't!"

"I want you to promise me that you will do everything that you said you would! Promise me that you won't fail! Promise me that you won't bring another woman before me... that you will never give up on us becoming a family and becoming one. If you mean what you have been saying to me, you..."

Roman smiled with glassy eyes. "I promise! I promise on my life, Angelica! I promise," he said kissing all over her face and lips. Angelica collapsed in his arms and felt lightheaded. "Baby what's wrong?"

"I...I don't feel too good." Roman picked her up, took her upstairs, and laid her in the bed.

"Baby what's wrong?" Roman started to get worried. "Angel what is it?"

"Nothing, I just feel a little dizzy that's all." Roman laid beside her and held her in his arms. "I wouldn't want to be anywhere else but right here in your arms."

Roman kissed her on her head. "Good because this is where you'll always be!"

Chapter 18– Lesson: There are Three Sides to a Story: What One Says, What the Other Says...and the Truth.

~Thanksgiving, November 26th~

Roman made arrangements for the both of their families to have Thanksgiving at his house. He was picking up Winter, Hailey, Gavin, and Kendall at seven. Dinner was at eight and everything was ready except for Angelica.

It was her holiday to work, and she couldn't get out of it. She pulled up to her house at 7:45. She planned on picking up the kids at 8, but Roman said he would pick them up from her mother's house since she had to work. Angelica ran a bath and tried to relax before getting dressed for dinner over Roman's. He invited his parents, her parents and a few of his cousins to dinner. As she laid in the tub, she started drifting off to deep-relaxation-land until the phone rang. "Hello."

"Hey, baby! How's it coming," Roman asked cheerfully.

"I'm good. I'll be leaving out in about twenty minutes or so."

Roman frowned. "Ok, you feeling alright?"

"Yes, what about you?"

"I'm good just waiting for you!"

Angelica smiled, "Ok, I'll see you soon."

"I'll come and get you. That way you won't have to drive," he was so excited! Angelica had never seen him so jovial!

"Roman, don't bother! You've done enough today. I'll be there soon."

"I'm on my way! Bye!" Angelica sighed, quickly washed, and got out of the tub. She picked out a nice sweater and a pair of jeans since she didn't feel like getting all dressed up. Ten minutes later while Angelica did her hair, she heard someone at the door. She walked down the steps and smiled looking at Roman walking through the door. "Hey!" Roman closed the door behind him and locked it. He kissed her lips and hugged her like he hadn't seen her in a long time. "I missed you today! We need to get away again like we did in September!"

Angelica laughed. "We will! But let's eat first!"

"Ok, I get your drift! Wait you didn't even give me a hug!"

"I'm sorry!" Angelica hugged him, and Roman kissed her slowly backing her up against the wall in the living room. "Roman, we need to leave."

"I worked a double yesterday so that I could have off today. I haven't made love to you since Tuesday!"

Angelica kissed him and sat him down on the couch. She unzipped his pants. "Just a little bit, right?"

Roman laughed. "If that's the way you want it."

~An hour later~

Roman and Angelica walked in the door of Roman's house, and everyone cheered! "Sorry, everybody," Angelica said walking in the dining room saying her hello's, giving hugs, and kisses around the table. Roman hung up their coats and joined them in the dining room.

"Roman, you want to say the prayer," asked Roman's dad.

Roman stood before his family. "No dad. You can go ahead and bless the food, but before you do, I just want to say a couple of things." Roman turned toward the family, took a deep breath, and smiled. "I want to thank all of you for being here tonight. There is nothing more important than family! I love each and every one of you, and I thank God that he has allowed me to experience this...level of unconditional love. I would also like to add one more thing."

Roman turned his body and faced Angelica. He took her left hand, kissed it, and held on tight. Angelica looked at him and smiled. "Angelica, I feel like I've known you for years. You've been through an awful lot this past year, and I have been there with you every step of the way! We enjoy doing lots of things together... but most importantly we genuinely enjoy making each other happy! We love each other and each other's children as if there isn't a difference between mine or yours! You KNOW I would do anything for you! AND what chokes me up, even more, is the fact that," Roman paused to clear his throat. "I KNOW you would do anything for me!" Roman stayed silent for a few seconds as tears fell from his eyes.

Angelica became worried. She slowly stood up and wiped the tears from his eyes. "You ok," she whispered.

Roman grabbed both of her hands, "Angelica, I love Winter, Hailey, Gavin, Kendall...and, of course, you!" Roman let go of her hands and confidently moved his chair out of the way. He stared at Angelica as he knelt down on his knees. Everyone stared in awe as the kids chuckled. "My Angel! I want to spend the rest of my days being with you and loving you! Will you marry me and live the rest of your life with me?"
Angelica cried and took a brief look at everyone around the table. They were all smiling from ear-to-ear! Angelica was so scared! She looked down at Roman and kept on crying.

Roman stood up and held her. Angelica held on to him for dear life. She cried into his chest like she did so many times while shaking her head no. Roman put his hands on her face and raised her head up to him. "Don't do this! Angelica, I love you. I want *you...all of you!* Angelica, will you marry me?"

Angelica just stared at him.

Roman caressed her face and kissed her lips while tears began to fall from his own eyes. "I love you! Let me show you! Give me a chance...please."

Angelica looked at him and didn't utter a word. No one in the room moved or said a word. It was as if they were all stuck in time. They couldn't believe what was happening.

Roman's hands started shaking. "Do you love me," he whispered.

Angelica looked at him. "Yes."

Roman sniffled and smiled. "Do you want me?"

Angelica bowed her head, "Yes."

Roman picked her head up. "Angelica, I want you and there is nothing that can change that. Be with me! Marry me!" Angelica lowered her head again and Roman lifted it up. "Complete me Angelica! Show me how much you love me... let's live the rest of our lives together."

Angelica smiled and put her hand on his face. She looked in his fearful, teary eyes, and kissed him. "Roman...I will marry you."

Roman kissed Angelica in front of the family while they all cheered! Angelica wiped his eyes while he nervously pulled the ring box out of his pocket. Cyrus laughed and shouted out, "Man...now you *know* you are supposed to put it on her finger while you are on your knees, man!"

Roman smiled at Angelica. "I know but I want to be close to her when she sees it." Angelica held on to his waist while he opened the Tiffany Jewelry Box.

"Roman!" She looked at him. "Baby," she said crying. "Roman!" Angelica started shaking her head, no, and Roman knew what she was about to say.

Everyone looked at them and at how Roman and Angelica were interacting in their own little world. Roman took the ring out of the box. "Baby, I know you're not materialistic, but it's a symbol of how much I love you and how much I want us to be a family." Roman put the Jean Schlumberger's signature ring on her finger. The engagement ring was set in platinum with a round diamond center stone. There were pave diamonds all along the sides of the ring. The most captivating part of the ring was how a strip of platinum set with pave diamonds, surrounded the round stone in an infinity shape. "That's me right there always protecting you," he said pointing to the infinity shaped platinum band of diamonds. "And these," he said while pointing to the other diamonds, "are all of our kids and kid's kids!" Everybody cracked up laughing. Roman and Angelica kept staring at one another. Roman kept his eyes on her while speaking to his father. "Dad, please bless this food!"

As his dad blessed the food, everyone had their heads bowed and eyes closed. Angelica opened her eyes to peek at Roman. To her surprise, he was already looking at her! They didn't say anything to one another. They just stared at one another while listening to Roman's dad. "Amen," everyone said simultaneously!

Winter, Hailey, Gavin, and Kendall ran over to Roman and Angelica. Roman and Angelica took them in the living room while everyone fixed their plates. Kendall started first. "Mommy, RC gave me, and Gavin rings too!" He said holding out his pinky ring with Gavin.

Winter laughed. "Yeah, and he bought me and Hailey necklaces with a ring hanging on it," said Winter showing Angelica her necklace.

"Mommy, are you happy," asked Gavin, "...because I am!"

"I'm happy too," Angelica said kissing Gavin on the forehead.

All the other kids repeated. "I'm happy too!" Roman laughed while Kendall and Gavin hugged him from his left and right!

Winter walked closer to Angelica. "AB, can I call you Mom-Mom now," Winter said looking at Angelica's new ring.

Angelica opened her arms to her. "Of course you can!"

Winter hugged her. "I love you Mom-Mom! Now you have two daughters!"

Angelica cried. "I love you too Winter! Yes I do! You guys are the best you know that?"

Kendall jumped up and down. "We're are the Kings and the Callowhills," shouted Kendall!

Everybody in the house cracked up laughing! Roman and Angelica sat down on the couch while the boys ran into the kitchen to eat. Hailey and Winter stood in front of them as if they had more to say. Hailey winked her eye at Winter, "Winter I'll be right there!"

"Oh...ok!" Winter winked back at Hailey and ran off to the kitchen with the boys.

Hailey moved Roman's arm so that she could sit on his lap. Simone tapped Cyrus and the others so that they could listen to what Hailey had to say since she was the oldest. "RC, I know you love my mom a lot. I just wanted to say that on behalf of me and the gang, we love you too! We love how you spend time with us, how you talk and listen to us, and how you don't treat us like step kids. You treat us like we're **your** kids! We love you Pop-Pop!" Hailey kissed Roman on the cheek and hugged her mom. "Time to eat!" Hailey ran into the kitchen to where Angelica's mom fixed their plates. Angelica laid her head onto Roman's shoulder while rubbing his chest. Roman raised her head and kissed her lips. Angelica's stomach started growling, and they cracked up laughing!

Roman kissed her lips again, "C'mon baby let's eat!"

~

A week later Angelica and Roman decided to live in his home instead of buying another one right away. They agreed to keep her home for now! Not buying a new home right away would allow them to save more money and to plan efficiently. The children were with Ian since this was his month and Winter was coming over the week after next. Angelica got off from work early and went straight to Roman's. She pulled up the driveway and saw

Roman's truck. She opened the door and took off her coat and shoes. "Roman?"

"Yeah."

Angelica's heart started to beat so fast that she could hear it in her ears. She started to run upstairs. "Roman are you ok?" She went into the bedroom, and Roman was spread out on the bed underneath the covers. She touched his forehead, but he wasn't warm or sweating. "Baby, what's wrong?"

"I don't know. I've been throwing up all day. I can't keep anything down."

Angelica went to the bathroom and grabbed a thermometer and some Tylenol. She sat down at his side and took his temp. He didn't have a fever. She went downstairs and grabbed a can of Ginger-Ale from the fridge. After pouring it into a cup, she took it upstairs and gave it to him to drink.

Roman frowned and shook his head no. "I'm going to throw it up!"

Angelica smiled! His reply remined him of how the kids would react when they became ill. "No, you won't! Drink it. It'll help your stomach."

He shook his head as if he were a child. "I hate throwing up."

Angelica rubbed his back and tried to soothe him. "Baby, take this so you can feel better." Roman took a few gulps and laid back down. Angelica took her shoes off and laid down next to him in the bed. She continued to rub his back until he went to sleep. Angelica went downstairs, made Roman some chicken noodle soup, toast, Gatorade, water, and Ginger Ale. She brought it upstairs on a tray and put it on the dresser in his room. While smiling at his peaceful state, she laid down on the chaise to watch television. About forty-five minutes later, Roman woke up to see Angelica sitting in the chaise watching a movie. She saw his face rising from the bed and went over to him. "How do you feel?"

"I feel a little better."

"Good," she got up and grabbed the tray. "I put the soup back on the stove while you slept. But here's some Gatorade, Ginger-Ale, and water. I also made you some toast."

Angelica started to walk to the door when Roman pulled her back. "Wait!"

"What's wrong?"

"Baby, I can't eat."

"Why?"

"I'm going to get sick again."

"Roman, I'll be right back. Just let me get the soup ok?" Roman just laid his head back down on the pillow. Angelica went downstairs and used the huge ladle to scoop out some soup into his bowl. When she arrived in the room, Roman slowly sat up in the bed and frowned his face at the smell of the soup. Angelica laughed a little, "Roman, I don't believe you! What's wrong?"

He adamantly shook his head. "I can't eat that! I'm telling you, I'm gonna be sick!"

Angelica laughed! She realized that this was the first time she witnessed him being sick. "Just taste a little bit! Take a few sips, and we'll wait a couple of minutes to see what happens." Roman sipped on the broth and sat back. Angelica kissed his hand and put the tray off to the side of the bed.

"Awe Shit!" Roman hopped out of bed and ran to the bathroom. Angelica followed him and watched him throw up clear fluid into the toilet. She grabbed a washcloth, wet it, and wiped his face while he flushed the toilet.

"Are you done, or do you have some more coming?"

"I think I'm done."

"Come and get in the bed and drink some Ginger Ale or Gatorade. I don't want you to get dehydrated."

"I don't want to eat or drink anything!"

"Roman if you don't drink, I'm going to have to take you to the hospital." Roman took a sip of the clear Gatorade and laid back down. "Your job called the house phone earlier while you were asleep. I told them that you still weren't doing well. They're not expecting you to come in tomorrow and I won't be going to work tomorrow either."

"Why?"

"What? Baby, you're sick! I need to take care of you!" Roman smiled at her. Angelica wiped his face and kissed his forehead.

"Naw, you go ahead and go to work tomorrow. I'll be alright. I just need some rest that's all."

"No! Now you just relax. Even though you're throwing up, I know you're hungry. I can make some Jell-O just in case you can't hold the soup down. What do you think?"

Roman touched her leg. "I wish I had the energy to eat something else!"

"Man, if you don't stop, I might just have to take advantage of you!"

Roman tried to laugh. "I don't even think I have enough juice in me."

Angelica hugged him, "Roman, please! I'm not even thinking about your dick right now. I just want you to get better. You know what?" Angelica paused for a minute and looked at Roman. "Speaking of sex, I need to call my doctor tomorrow and see if he can call in another refill for my pills. I know he thinks I'm crazy, but between your house and mine..."

Roman took a sip of Gatorade and looked at Angelica. "I thought you had them filled already."

"I did, but then I misplaced them during the move. I thought I had the pills in one of my drawers one day and the next day I didn't!"

Roman took another sip. "So, when was the last time you took any?"

Angelica didn't answer. "I think that I'll get that depo shot instead of the pill."

Roman sat up. "What's with the depo shot?"

"It's a shot that you get every so often for birth control. I've never had it. I've always took pills, but I think..."

Roman interrupted her. "I don't know about that babe. I think we should just stick with the pill. What about all those side effects!"

Angelica laughed. "I'm going to take a shower!"

"Alright."

Angelica went to the bathroom and ran her water. She took her work clothes off and stepped in the shower. Angelica sang a song that she wrote when she fell in love with Roman. Writing it down was something that she needed to do. Every time she sang the song, she changed it up a little according to how she was feeling. Roman heard her beautiful voice and closed his eyes. He knew she was singing about him and even though he was weak, he felt so good knowing that she was there to take care of him.

Roman envisioned her naked body in the shower while listening to her faint angelic voice. He opened his eyes, took a couple of swigs of Gatorade, and got out of the bed. Roman was on his way to the 3rd-floor bathroom so that he could pee, but he stopped in the 2nd-floor bathroom doorway. Angelica was in the shower washing her hair and singing.

Roman began to get really excited! He watched as she washed her breasts and moved downward to her stomach. She then began to wash in between her folds down below making sure that she thoroughly cleaned herself. As she moved the cloth to her ass and cleaned it, he bit his bottom lip, and rubbed on his penis.

Roman took his shirt and pants off right there in the hallway and walked in the shower with Angelica. She wiped the suds from her eyes and looked at him. "Roman, you should be in bed baby."

"I need you."

Angelica laughed. "Ok, let's wash up and get out so you can get some rest." When she turned around to grab the shower gel from the caddy, Roman pulled her close to him instead and kissed her. Angelica kissed his neck. "Roman don't, you really need to get in the bed."

"I need to be inside you."

"Let's go in the bedroom then so you can lay down baby!" Roman widened her stance by stepping in between her legs. He grabbed his dick and put it inside of her. Angelica tried to push him away, but he stood his ground. Angelica raised one of her legs and wrapped it around his waist. He took hold of it and held it while he dug deep inside her. "I want you right here."

"But you're sick!" She said holding his arms, "Let's go in the bedroom." Angelica slowly pushed him back. She washed his body and let him rinse his self while she stepped out of the shower. She didn't put on a towel or anything. She just walked away dripping wet!

Roman quickly turned off the water and wrapped a towel around his waist. When he walked in the room, Angelica was stretched out on the bed and still very wet! She sat up with her legs opened and looked at Roman. "Come here and stick the thermometer in my mouth so I can see if you have a temperature!"

Roman walked over to the bed and Angelica moved quickly to his waist. She put him in her hands and sucked on his dick while he stood up. Roman moaned and held onto her head while she made love to him with her mouth. "Angel...my baby...I love you so much...Suck it!"

Angelica stopped. "Lay down!" Roman laid on his back while Angelica grabbed his cock and guided it into her pussy. Roman cursed and held on to her breasts. She rode him for about fifteen minutes until he picked her up and flipped her on all fours!

Roman spread her ass and entered her slowly. "You know you're about to get pregnant, right?"

"It's going to take a while before that happens! I'm fertile, but I've been on the pill for years!"

Roman laid his body on her back and sucked on the back of her neck while gently squeezing her nipples. "Yeah alright! You can think that all you want, but I know!"

"You know what?" Angelica arched her back and pushed back on his dick making him curse. "You've been taking my pills haven't' you?"

"They are **our** pills, and they're keeping **my** kids at bey!" Roman kept on moving inside her while sucking on her neck.

Angelica laughed. "Roman, you gotta slow down!"

Roman stopped. "Baby, we talked about this! I love you. You love me, and I'm not getting any younger!" Angelica laughed and shook her head. "Besides, as much as we make love, you should be pregnant by the end of the year!"

"Roman, let's wait until after we get married like we said."

Roman started moving faster. "YOU said that shit, not me!" Angelica squeezed onto a nearby pillow as she tried to deal with him pounding inside of her as if he were digging a whole! "You gonna' have my baby?"

"One day, but..."

Roman raised up off of her back and held on to her waist making sure that he didn't skip a beat. "You gonna' have my baby, yes or no?"

"Yes, Roman yes. Whatever you want!"

"That's more like it! I want you to marry me on New Year's Eve Angelica!" Angelica smiled but didn't say anything. "You hear me?"

"We can't get married yet."

Roman stopped moving. "Marry me on New Year's Eve. We won't tell anyone about it. We'll have a bigger wedding and all of that just like we originally planned later on. I want you to marry me on New Year's Eve."

Angelica ignored his request and reason, "Roman, I love you so much! Please don't stop!"

Roman started moving again making Angelica go crazy! He pressed on, "Tell me."

Angelica shook her head no, "Let's wait." Roman instantly pulled out of her and laid her on her back. Angelica slowly opened her legs while Roman stared at her while on his knees. She looked at his beautiful body! He was rock hard with come oozing from his penis like honey. Roman looked down at what Angelica was staring. She shook her head no again. "It's too soon!"

Roman, just stared. "Tell me yes!"

Angelica licked her lips. "I want you." Roman frowned up his face as if he didn't understand what she was saying. She grabbed her breast with one hand while putting the index finger from her other hand in her mouth. Roman just stared at her. "I want you." Angelica's finger found its way to her lips...down below. As she played with herself, Roman knelt down and joined in the fun with his mouth. Angelica removed her finger and held on to his head.

Roman rose from between her thighs and entered her once again. "Be my wife on New Year's Eve." Roman moved deeper and deeper getting closer to eruption.

Angelica moaned and let out her loudest cry, "NO! It's too soon!" Roman circled his hips, and she lost it! "OH God!"

He smiled. "Be my wife next month!"

Angelica yelled, "NO!"

Roman smiled and slowly raised each one of her legs over each of his shoulders. He then lowered his upper body so that he was inches from her face. He then kissed her lips softly and began to move slowly inside of her. He whispered, "Who...the fuck... are you yelling at?" He grabbed her ass with both hands while Angelica groaned! He picked up the pace just a little bit. He kissed her lips. "If you don't answer me, I'm changing the number from 2 to 4."

Angelica pushed on his chest. "What?! No! Stop...we are not having 4 more kids!"

Roman slowed down but moved deeper. "If you...make me wait...you will have to make up for that wasted time! Now," he said moving faster, "...what'll it be?" Angelica tried to catch her breath but couldn't say anything. "Marry me next month...or be barefoot and pregnant for the next 3 or 4 years!" Roman knew she was close! He began sucking on her neck and whispered. "What'll it be?"

Angelica yelled, "Yes! Oh God, I love you!" Angelica cried while climaxing. Roman continued steadily making love to her but, was in awe at how beautiful she looked when he made her come. Roman closed his eyes thanking God for Angelica. He mentally asked God to bless her, his new family, and her womb so that they could have more children. He proceeded to increase his pace at a frantic rate. Angelica practically screamed with every stroke! Sweat poured from his forehead as he roared while coming inside of her!

Roman lowered her legs, collapsed on top of her body, and kissed her lips. "I've been waiting all of my life..." he paused for a minute and turned his head to the side. Angelica turned his face back around so that she could see him. "All those dreams you ever had about the type of husband you've always wanted. You know what I'm talking about?!"

Angelica nodded her head. "Yes."

Roman looked at her with glistened eyes, "I'm right here! You're gonna' be Mrs. Roman Xavier Callowhill."

~ New Year's Eve! ~

The Kings and Callowhill children were
being watched by Cyrus and Simone in NY. They
were going to stay there for the weekend while
Roman and Angelica got married, unbeknownst to
them! Roman's parents and Angelica's parents were
the only ones who would attend the wedding. They
obtained their marriage license and were to be
married at St. Crispina Catholic Church.

Roman dressed at his house with his mom
and dad while Angelica dressed at her house with
her parents. Roman arranged for a black limo to
pick Angelica and her parents up from her house at
8 p.m. On the way to the church, Angelica looked
down at her off white, silk gown. Since they were
still having a bigger ceremony for the family next
year, she thought that an evening gown would be
fitting. The dress had a beaded halter neckline. The
beaded neckline continued around her neck, down
along the side seam of her dress to her lower back
which was completely open. The gown fell past her
ankles but with her heels on, the length was perfect.
As she looked out of the window, she thought of

when she and Ian got dressed up and went to City Hall to exchange vows. Now she was going to have two wedding ceremonies. Angelica smiled at the thought of marrying the man of her dreams twice!

~

Roman sat in the limo looking at his mom and dad holding each other's hand. The both of them were looking out of the window in different directions, but they still stayed connected through their touch. He smiled and thought of him and Angelica doing the same thing with their children when it was time for them to get married. Roman's dad looked at him smiling. "You ready for this?"

Roman nodded his head. "I'm ready."

Roman's mother smiled, "Roman, Angelica is a beautiful woman! She loves you so much!" She paused for a minute. "When you asked to marry her on Thanksgiving, I talked with her later that evening. I congratulated her on the engagement, and do you know what she told me?" Roman's dad smiled because she only told her husband what Angelica said that night.

"What," Roman asked while looking a little bit weary.

Roman's dad nodded at his mother, and she continued. "She said Mrs. Callowhill, I've been dreaming of him all my life and I am so thankful that God heard me! That's when I kissed her cheek, hugged her, and welcomed her to the family. Roman, I know that she loves you and **WILL** be with you no matter what!"

Roman's mouth trembled slightly. "Mom, I love her so much."

Roman's dad took his hand. "Son, it's hard being a new husband and a stepfather, but if you and Angelica work together, talk to each other, and make sure to spend time with one another, everything will work out fine!"

~

Fifteen minutes later, Angelica's limo pulled up to the church. There was a light on by the main entrance to the chapel. Angelica's dad stayed silent as he secured her ankle length coat around her. He opened the door and allowed her mother to exit first. Her mom gathered the bottom of Angelica's dress before she took a step out of the limo. Her mother smiled. "C'mon baby!"

Angelica took a deep breath and stepped out of the limo. The both of them flanked her left and right as they walked in silence to the church. When Angelica and her parents entered the chapel, they went to a nearby room off to the right to take off their coats and to freshen up. Angelica's phone rang and her mother immediately picked it up. "Hello...ok...thank you, bye. Angelica when the usher knocks on the door, it's time."

"Ok ma." Angelica looked in the mirror and put more lip gloss on. She looked at her ring and smiled. She hadn't seen Roman all day, and she missed him.

Knock, Knock!

Angelica jumped at the sound of the knock. She thought she would have a few more moments to gather herself. "Angelica it's time sweetheart!" Her mom handed her a bouquet of cream roses that was waiting for her in the room. Angelica just stared at them.

Angelica's dad saw her trepidation and took her hand as she began to cry. "I love Roman so much, daddy! I just...I just don't want to go through the pain again...I don't want to go through that again!"

Angelica's dad smiled. "Then make this the last time! Love him without end! Be with him until there is no more time! Now go...and show Roman what he's been waiting for!" Angelica hugged and kissed her dad. Her mother wiped her tears and kissed her cheek.

~

Roman stood at the altar with his father dressed in a black Armani classic tuxedo with a white shirt and black bow tie. He looked at the door waiting for Angelica's mother to walk down the aisle. The usher opened the door, and his heart began to beat like crazy. Angelica's mom entered the sanctuary. Everyone looked at her as she ambled down the aisle. Roman and Angelica didn't want any music playing during the ceremony. They just wanted silence.

~

The usher looked at Angelica. "You look beautiful!"

Angelica smiled. "Thank you!" Angelica's dad held her close in agreement.

The Usher peeked in the sanctuary and saw that her mom was seated in the designated pew. She closed the door. "Are you ready?"

Angelica looked at her shoes and decided to take them off. Her dad laughed and helped her to remove the heels. "Better?"

Angelica laughed and hugged on her dad's arm. "Yes!"

The Usher opened the door wide. Angelica and her dad walked through the doorway very slow. She had never done this before and was extremely nervous. Roman stared at her as she walked slowly. Angelica smiled, but Roman didn't smile at all. She felt a little worried until her dad squeezed her hand in reassurance. Angelica finally reached the altar. Unexpectedly, her dad turned toward her, and kissed both of her cheeks. He grabbed Roman's hand and pulled him into an embrace. Her dad took his hand and placed Angelica's hand in his. Mr. Bryant then walked over to where his wife was seated and kissed her lips.

Roman wanted to hold both of her hands, so he handed the bouquet of flowers to his mother. He held her hands and looked at her up and down. Roman slightly shook his head and smiled before looking into her eyes. Angelica rubbed her thumbs along the back of his hands and returned the stare. After the Reverend had spoken to them about marriage and unconditional love, they exchanged their vows. The reverend then turned to Angelica. Angelica instantly looked at Roman. The reverend wasn't supposed to be looking at her! This wasn't a part of the plan...the rehearsed plan! The reverend smiled. "Angelica before I pronounce you man and wife, Roman has requested to vow something to you."

Angelica looked at Roman with a surprised look on her face. Roman smiled with all of his being. "I know you're looking at me like that because you probably wanted to say something with me, but I don't want you to talk. I just want you to listen to me. *This* is *our* special day, Angelica. A day that is shared between you, me, God, and our parents. Angelica, I'm making a promise to you that I will always be there for you and our children. It doesn't matter what happens in our lives, Angelica. I will **never** leave you! I will always be your husband. You will always be the only woman for me. I love you, and I will love you forever." Angelica whimpered out loud! She couldn't help it! Roman put his hand on her cheek.

The Reverend nodded. "Now with the power vested in me, I now pronounce you husband and wife. Roman, you may now kiss your Angel."

Roman held her in his arms and ran his fingers along her face. "Can I kiss you, my beautiful Angel," Roman asked while tears cascaded down his cheeks from his eyes.

"Yes."

Roman took his time and kissed her forehead and then both sides of her cheeks. Adoringly he looked at her and smiled. He slowly wiped her eyes and gently caressed her face with both hands. Roman stepped closer. "Can I have you forever?"

Angelica smiled. "Yes."

Roman closed his eyes and gently kissed her lips. When he pulled his lips away, Angelica opened her eyes and smiled. "I love you Angelica Sofia Callowhill."

"And I love you Roman Xavier Callowhill!"

Roman held onto her waist and kissed her again. Angelica felt his body shuddering and broke their kiss. Roman's eyes were filled with tears. Angelica caressed his face and wiped the tears from his eyes. He grabbed her close and hugged her while his tears fell onto the crook of her neck.

After Roman and Angelica comforted themselves, their parents walked up to the altar, and hugged them both. Roman's mother tapped Roman on the shoulder. "Roman what time is it?"

He looked at his watch. "It's 10:39."

Roman's father laughed. "Well, y'all better get going!"

"Yeah, get out of here," Angelica's mother added!

Roman looked at Angelica. "Baby, let's go!" He took her hand and hurried to the back of the church. They went into the side room to get Angelica's coat, and Roman kissed her like never before!

"Roman, I want you so bad!"

"I want you too," he said putting his hand up her dress.

Angelica laughed. "Come on so we can go home!"

They hopped into the limo and made it home in fifteen minutes. Roman grabbed her hand, and they ran to the front door. Roman had kissed her before he opened the door. "How do you feel Mrs. Callowhill?"

"I'll feel even better when I get inside." Roman opened the door, picked her up, and carried her over the threshold while she cracked up laughing! He pushed the door closed with his foot and started walking toward the stairs. "WAIT!"

"What?"

Angelica stared at the door. "You have to lock the door."

Roman put her down and locked the door. "You don't have to worry about anyone hurting you...ever! Do you understand me!" Roman kissed her, picked her up and took her upstairs to his bedroom. He laid her on the bed and looked at her. Roman sat down next to her and began running his hands through her hair in awe of how beautiful she looked.

"Roman, I need to tell you something."

Roman softly whispered. "What is it."

Angelica took a deep breath and let it out, "When I got raped..."

Roman's face completely frowned up. "Baby, let's not talk about this on our wedding night."

"I wouldn't, but I need to say this to you now."

"Ok."

Angelica sat up and looked at him. "When I was raped, I didn't tell the police everything that the rapist did."

Roman frowned his face. "Well, what did you leave out?"

Angelica took a deep breath. "The rapist told me that if he wanted me to stop...I had to have an orgasm."

Roman looked disgusted. "What?!"

Angelica heaved with tears. "He told me that he needed me to come and if I didn't he was going to do it to me all night."

Roman stared at her. "Did you come?"

Angelica covered her eyes. "Yes I did."

Roman shook his head and held her hand. "I know you told me that he didn't physically hurt you but what is upsetting you now?"

"Roman, I had never experienced someone making me feel that way before. Ian never did the things that he did that night."

Roman sighed really loud. "So, what are you saying?" Angelica didn't say anything. "So, what are you saying," Roman yelled.

"He was making love to me Roman. The way he moved inside of me, the way he held and kissed on my body, I knew he was making love to me!"

"I can't believe this shit!"

"I'm telling you the truth!"

Chapter 19– Lesson: Unconditional Love is the Only Kind of Love

Roman looked the other way and started walking out of the bedroom when Angelica grabbed him. "Angelica, what the fuck is going on? Are you telling me that you're in love with the man who fucking raped you?"

"NO! I want you to understand that even though I didn't want it to happen...I never had a man make me feel like that until I made love to you! You have surpassed all of my expectations of how a man is supposed to make a woman feel." Roman just looked at her while she continued. "The man who blindfolded me while he sucked and kissed all over my body, made me see that I deserve better! I mean he was a fucking rapist," she said yelling, "...and he made love to me better than the man who I knew for most of my fucking life!"

"Angelica so what's the fucking purpose of you telling me this on our wedding night?" Angelica just stared at him crying. "Huh? I just married you...and you found that *THIS* is the right time to talk about this shit?"

417

"Was it you?" She muttered underneath her breath.

"What! What the fuck is wrong with you Angelica?" Roman walked down the steps, and Angelica grabbed him by the arm. "Angelica don't touch me!"

"Please, Roman please!"

"Please, what," Roman yelled making Angelica tremble inside.

"The way you make love to me, it's the same, Roman!"

Roman couldn't look at her. "Angelica this is fucking crazy! You need some fucking help!"

Angelica looked at him crying hysterically. She stopped crying after a few moments. After taking a few deep breaths, she had a blank stare on her face. "You're right." She walked up the steps, took off her dress in the bedroom and changed clothes. Angelica looked in her drawer, folded up a few outfits, and put them under her arm so that she could take them with her. When she walked down the stairs, Roman was on the couch with his head in his hands.

He looked up at her and frowned to see that she had changed her clothes and had a few changes of clothes in her hand. "What's going on?"

"I shouldn't have married you. I do need help, and I'm sorry. I'm sorry for letting you down and for asking you what I did." Angelica went in the kitchen to get a plastic bag.

Roman stood up. "So where are you going?"

"Roman I said I'm sorry. I'm more than ashamed of myself right now. I need to leave. This is all my fault."

Roman walked over to her. "Baby, you're my wife! I love you, and I'm here for you."

Angelica looked at him and frowned her face. "What did you say?"

"I said you're my wife and I love you."

Angelica shook her head. "And then you said I'm here for you!"

"I am," Roman yelled with his hands in the air.

Angelica looked at him and cried some more. "Roman. I have to go!"

"Why?"

"That's the same thing he said to me," she yelled.

Roman held her close. "Baby don't cry! We'll get through this."

Angelica pulled away. "I have to leave. We can get the marriage annulled at a later date."

"What? NO!" Roman walked behind her and grabbed her hard. "Angelica what the fuck are you talking about?"

Angelica just stared at him crying. "I don't know what the fuck is going on, but I KNOW it's you! I couldn't see you, but I smelled you, I felt you!"

Roman looked at the ceiling. "Angel please!"

"Tell me, Roman! If it wasn't you, swear to God on your children that it wasn't you!"

Roman shook his head. "Angelica!"

"So, it's a fucking coincidence that your left leg trembles like crazy when you come...just like the man's did? Your love for sucking all over my body, the way you eat my pussy, the way you suck on my breasts, are all those things just coincidences Roman? If it is, God help me!"

Roman looked at her and held her hands. "Angel, please! That day is behind us! Let's just enjoy our wedding night and know that I'm going to take care of you." He held her tight, kissed her, and took the clothes out of her hands.

Angelica caught him off guard, pushed him aside, and headed for the door. She grabbed her purse and opened the door. Roman ran behind her and forcefully turned her around. "Angelica stop!" Roman shoved her on the couch, closed the door, and affixed the lock. He turned around and realized what he just did. Angelica was scared! She couldn't believe that he pushed her like he did! Angelica balled herself up in the corner of the couch and cried. Roman walked toward her. "Baby, I didn't mean to..."

"Don't touch me!"

"Baby..." Roman touched her, and she pushed his arm away. "I'm sorry baby. I didn't mean to do that. I just don't want you to leave!" He turned to Angelica and put his hand on her face. "I told you that I wouldn't hurt you and I meant that!" Angelica looked at him and stared. Roman sat down next to her and held her while kissing her head. Angelica sat there and put her head on his chest. A few minutes went by, and Roman turned her around so that she could see his face.

"Angelica out of all the men that you have been with, how many did you actually know?" Angelica didn't say anything. She just looked at him. "You know why you're not answering? You're not answering because *you* know... that out of all the men that kissed you and explored your body, you didn't really know *any* of them. Including your weak ass ex-husband." Angelica just stared at him.

Roman caressed her face with his hands. "That man... who did what he did... enabled us to be here! It was fucked up...I know... but we are here now! We are a family, and we love each other! If you want to hate what happened to you, do that!" Angelica couldn't speak. She just looked at him crying profusely. "Angelica, I will **never** leave you! We will always be together no matter what!"

"What are you saying?"

"I'm saying that I love you! I'm saying the same thing I told you at the altar! Nothing has changed!"

"What are you telling me, Roman," she yelled!

"I'm saying that I'm your man, I'm your husband, I'm your friend! I'm here for you!"

Angelica closed her eyes and held her head in her hands. "It was you, wasn't it?" Roman picked her up and took her upstairs while she cried like a baby. He laid her on the bed and then took all his clothes off. Roman then undressed Angelica. He positioned his head in between her legs and ate her pussy until she cried out loud coming all over his tongue!

Roman moved up to her face. "Happy New Year's Mrs. Callowhill! I love you, Angelica," he said putting his dick inside of her. Roman stopped once he was fully inside of her and looked at her. He took hold of each arm and kissed them. He then interlocked each one of his hands with hers and extended her arms above her head. Angelica stared back with tears in her eyes. Roman kissed her. "Do you hate me, Angel?" Angelica didn't say anything. Roman moved inside of her more and asked her again. "Do you hate me?"

"No."

Roman looked at her. "Are you lying to me?" He moved deeper inside of her and she gasped for air. "Are you lying to me?"

"No Roman."

Roman licked and sucked on her neck. "You still love me, Angelica?"

"Why did you do that to me?"

"Do what baby? I married you because I love you! You need to feel me!" He moved faster and deeper paying attention to how her body was shivering once again.

"Roman, I can't take anymore!"

"Why? You're coming too fast?" Angelica stayed silent while Roman continued making love to her. "Feel me, baby! Feel what I've been keeping inside for such a long...long...time...Hold on..." He put her legs over his shoulders and began making love to each and every cell in her body! Every time he moved an inch, she could feel him telling her how much he loved her. "Forgive me, God! I love her so much. I love her so fucking much," he whispered. Angelica put her hands on his face and kissed him. "Forgive me for loving you so much Angelica!" Angelica kissed him again. "It's coming, baby!"

Roman stared at her with tears in his eyes. "Do you love me? You still wanna have my baby?"

Angelica kissed him while he got closer to coming. He moaned louder and louder cursing as he got closer. Angelica held on to his face, Roman went deeper and deeper. "Angel here it comes! You wanna have my baby? Answer me," he said practically yelling!

Angelica sobbed. "I'm having your baby already."

Roman dumped all inside of her and cried. "Oh my God! Oh, my God!" Roman continued praising God and kissing Angelica. "The first, last, and the only woman in my life. Angel, I love you!" Roman collapsed on top of her and buried his head in the pillow crying. Angelica kissed his neck and held on to him so tight that she was crying herself. He raised his head and kissed her lips while he continued crying. Neither one of them said a word. They just tried to console one another. Roman looked at her. "When did you find out," he said pulling out of her and rubbing her stomach.

"Two weeks ago."

"Why didn't you tell me," he asked fearfully.

"I planned on telling you tonight... and I did."

Roman looked into Angelica's eyes. "Angel, you have made my dreams come true." He continued staring into her eyes as he silently tried to explain some things to her. Angelica put her hand on his neck and just stared into his eyes.

She sniffled a couple of times while shaking her head. "Roman?"

"Yes."

Angelica kissed him. "Talk to me."

Roman closed his eyes, cleared his throat, and looked at her. "I met you a few years ago when I bought the house next door on Webster Street. I met you, talked to you briefly, and I knew I wanted you. I didn't know you were married until days later." Angelica looked at him carefully. "While fixing up the house, I could hear how the both of you would argue all the time!"

Roman paused for a moment and started to lay beside her, but Angelica pulled him back on top of her. "Finish!"

"One day, I was working on the house, and I heard Ian fucking you! I got so upset until I heard him saying Stacy!" Angelica shook her head and turned her head to the side. Roman changed the subject. "Angelica, I don't care how many times I say it! I love you and I always will. I will never hurt you!"

"So, is this ...."

"You met my parents and family Angel. I fell in love when I met you."

"But was it..." Roman wouldn't let her finish her sentence. He didn't want to hear her ask the question.

"Baby..." Roman rolled over on his back and pulled her on top of him. "Remember in February when Ian slapped you in the face and made your nose bleed?" Angelica's eyes watered as she shook her head. "What happened?" Angelica realized where he was going. "He left out the house...and then what happened," he said rubbing her thigh. "He came home that next day...early in the morning. Tell me what happened baby," Roman started sucking on her breasts.

Angelica sighed. "He came in the house all beat up. His nose, leg, and arm was broken. He said that he was jumped by four guys."

"Four guys my ass! I fucked that pussy up for hitting you! And then what? You forgave him...didn't you? He smacked the shit out of you and made your nose bleed. You knew that shit was foul! You shouldn't have even let that pussy in the house after that, but you forgave him, right?"

Angelica shook her head and looked at the ceiling. Roman kissed her and held her close. "Do you still want me?" Angelica didn't say anything. She just looked at him and turned her head so that she could look at something else other than him. "Is that a no? Is that it?" Angelica remained silent and kept her eyes fixed on the wall. "Angelica?"

"Yes."

"Do you still want me," he said with his voice cracking at the end.

"Roman..."

"Angelica, I fell in love with you! There is no one else and will never be anyone else. I bet my life on it!"

"Tell me," she yelled!

"I know it was wrong, but that man made you feel like the most desired woman in the world. He made you feel things that you've NEVER felt before! He gave you your confidence back! He stripped your self-esteem... so that it could be rebuilt! He even made you realize your self-worth! Even though it was an extreme measure... he brought you back to life... from being treated like you WERE dead from your own fucking husband!" Angelica just stared at him. "Let me show you something." He got out of bed and went in his closet.

She heard him messing around with his safe. He walked out and handed her some paperwork. "Read this." Angelica looked at the documents and saw that it was his will and life insurance policies. As she read his will, she couldn't believe the things he wrote about her. Angelica looked at the insurance papers and saw her name, Winter, and his parents' names as the beneficiaries of his policy. What she couldn't believe was how the documents were dated from June 2008!

"Do you believe that the love that I have for you is real now! I updated all that in June of this past year, Angelica! I never felt this way about any woman. As much as I loved Winter's mother, that was nothing in comparison to the way that I love you! Angelica, as God as my witness, I love you more than anything!"

Angelica didn't know what to say. She just stared at the ceiling. Roman laid down behind her and held her close. "I don't know what to say or how to feel." Roman rubbed on her thighs again and just laid there. Angelica could feel him hardening on her ass. Roman didn't move or say anything. He just stood still. "Roman?"

"Yes."

"Are you asleep?"

"No," he answered breathing heavily.

"What are you doing?"

Roman sighed. "Thinking."

"About what?"

"About you...About us." Angelica closed her eyes and then felt his hand rub on her stomach. She heard him let out a sigh and felt his body getting closer to hers. "Are we having a baby or are you going to get an abortion?"

Angelica turned around and faced him with tears in her eyes. "What? Why would you say something like that to me?"

"Just tell me?!" Roman was getting upset by the minute even though he knew he didn't have the right to be.

She yelled in his face! "Don't you ever say anything like that to me ok? Don't you ever say anything like that to me ever!"

For some reason, Roman just snapped! He took his hands off her. "That's why you didn't tell me right away because you *WERE* going to have an abortion! Right? Right?"

"Roman, I didn't tell you because I wanted to make sure that I didn't miscarry for one. Two, I wanted to wait for our wedding night, which *IS* tonight, so stop yelling at me and acting like a complete asshole!" Angelica sat up and walked out of the room.

"Angelica wait!" He yelled. Angelica kept on walking toward the third-floor stairs. "Wait, I said!"

Angelica stopped and turned around. "Who the fuck are you talking to like that? I am not your fucking dog, so don't be giving me fucking commands! You know... you have a lot of fucking nerve talking to me and saying the shit that you're saying to me!" She got up in his face and pointed her finger at his eye without touching him. "I've done nothing except love you!" Angelica walked away, and he grabbed her arm. "What... you gonna hit me now? Now that you fucked me, played with my fucking head, knocked me up, and married me...now you're going to show your true side?"

Roman squeezed her arm. Angelica yelled in his face! "Go ahead Roman, hit me! That's what you really want to do...isn't it? Isn't it?!" Roman let her arm go and just stood there. Although she was furious, Angelica began to cry. "When I was away from you at night, I would cry because I wanted to be next to you! I wanted to hear you breathing, I wanted to see you while you snored, I wanted to feel you next to me. I would cry Roman because I wasn't WITH you! I knew this shit was too good to be true! Now I'm carrying your child, and after everything, you're accusing *ME* of wanting to kill the life within me? How can you fuckin' live with yourself," she screamed. She ran up the stairs crying like crazy leaving him standing there. Angelica went in one of the bedrooms and slammed the door.

Roman walked down the stairs and into the second-floor bathroom. While taking a long shower, he tried to calm himself down. He knew he was wrong for asking Angelica if she was going to have an abortion. In remembering the first time that they had dinner in center city, she shared so much with him about her life. He recalled how devastated Angelica was when she told him about the miscarriage she had after Kendall was born. She shared her doubts about being able to conceive again. Over time, Roman assured her that he knew they were destined to have a child. Roman remembered her crying one day. She asked him if he still wanted to be with her if she couldn't have any more children. As he washed his hair, he recalled telling her that there was nothing that would make him *NOT* want to be with her. He was so ashamed of himself! Roman rinsed his hair and finished washing so that he could talk to her.

Roman went into his bedroom, put on some night pants, and got his self together. He walked up the stairs and knocked on the door. "Angelica, can I come in?" After she didn't respond, he knocked again. "Angelica, can I talk to you?" Roman turned the doorknob and entered the room. Angelica was stretched out on the bed underneath the covers sniffling. Roman laid down on the bed next to her, "I'm sorry Angel. I'm sorry for everything that I've done to you. If you leave me, I will have to accept that."

Angelica turned to him. "Can you hold me please!" Roman put his arms around her.

"I'm sorry baby! I didn't mean what I said."

"Roman, just hold me please."

Roman held her and kissed her, "I need to talk to you."

Angelica sat up and looked at him. "Roman, I love you, our children, and the baby that's inside of me. Right now, I just want you to hold me! I just ... I just want my husband to hold me...just hold me please," she pleaded crying her eyes out.

Roman quickly embraced her. "Shhh! I'm right here baby. I'm not going anywhere. I'm sorry! I'm so fucking sorry."

"Just hold me, please. I just need to feel you holding me." Roman held her close, and Angelica snuggled up in his chest. After what seemed like hours, Angelica was finally asleep in Romans' arms. Roman couldn't sleep. He loved Angelica with all of his being and knew that she loved him just as much. Roman put his hand on Angelica's stomach and smiled. She was having their baby after all that she had been through. Roman picked her up, carried her downstairs to the second floor, and laid her in their bed.

Once Angelica's body hit the cold sheets, she opened her eyes. Roman was hovering over her smiling. "I love you, Angelica. You are everything I ever wanted. You are all that I will ever want!" Angelica began tearing up. "No more tears," he said wiping her eyes. "No more talk about that night baby! It's not good for you to keep reliving something that has no hold over us! No more talk about how or what if's because NONE of that matters anymore! We will spend the rest of our lives being together and enjoying it every step of the way...the good with the bad! I don't care about the circumstances that led you to want me...as fucked up as they are. I don't care!"

Angelica started wailing, and Roman calmed her down. "Angelica listen to me very carefully because we will not talk about this again. We are going to lay it to rest here and now ok?" Angelica nodded and just listened. "Angelica, what happened that night, happened for a reason. Whether you or I like it or not, we both know... that it is because of that night that we are here. Do you understand that?" Angelica shook her head yes. "Because of that night, you took a stand for yourself and left Ian. Because of that night, you fell in love and married a man who loves you more than life. Because of that night, you are bringing another...new life into this world... with that man. Because of that night, you have changed the lives of our four children...uniting them in a way that they never thought was possible. Do you understand?"

"Yes."

Roman took a deep breath. "That night...was a *NECESSARY* sacrifice for you to get to this point...with me...with us! That is how I see that night. That night...made you and me! It doesn't matter how you look at it or what details you add to it! That night was the beginning of *YOUR NEW* life. It was the beginning of *US!*" Roman held Angelica's face and stared hard into her eyes with tears falling down his cheeks. "Some sacrifices are necessary baby! They are hard! God knows! *BUT THEY ARE NECESSARY!*" Angelica nodded her head. Roman kissed her lips and held her close while they cried together. "I will always, always love you! Always!"

~

~February 5th, 2010, Friday evening

"Mommy today is Daddy's birthday," Kendall yelled as he fiddled with the picture he made for Ian at school.

Angelica kept driving. "I know! I know you all are going to have so much fun!"

Kendall continued. "He's taking us out to Dave and Busters and then we're going to the movies with him and Lila!"

Gavin smiled. "Yeah, I hope she doesn't ask me a thousand questions this time!"

Angelica laughed. "Be nice Gavin. If your dad is taking her out with you guys, he must like her a lot! I'm not saying that you have to like her, just take it easy!"

Gavin put his hands up in air! It was just another gesture that he adopted from Roman, "Alright!"

Angelica pulled up to Ian's house, put the car in park, and turned on the hazards. Surprisingly, Ian was standing at the door waiting for them. The kids jumped out of the car, as usual, grabbing their book bags and other knick-knacks. Angelica opened the door enough for her just to step out of the car to look at Ian. "Am I late?"

"No, you're good!"

"Ok! Happy Birthday!" She didn't hear his response because the kids bum-rushed her with hugs and kisses saying their goodbyes. "Remember what I said, Gavin!" Gavin winked at Angelica, and she just shook her head at her growing young man!

Angelica turned to get back in the car when Ian started walking down the front steps. She waited to make sure that the kids got in ok before she pulled off when she saw Ian running toward the car. "Angelica wait!"

She turned the car off and opened her door. "What's wrong?"

"Nothing's wrong. I wanted to know if I could talk to you for a minute."

"Sure, what's up?"

"I mean...can I talk to you in the house."

Angelica looked at him. "Ian I really need to get going."

"Fifteen minutes of your time. Please."

"Ok." Angelica kept the hazards on, grabbed her purse, and walked out of the car. Ian closed it behind her, and she walked in the house. Ian had rearranged the furniture, hung up a few of his paintings, and had some jazz music playing. The house looked great and smelled like sweet mango. She sat on the couch and looked at him. "So, what's going on?"

Ian looked at her up and down. "How are you?"

"I'm fine. Actually, I'm great how are you?"

"Good. I know you told me that Roman proposed to you and I know that you're getting married later this year."

"Yeah, we are. Is this about you and Lila?"

Ian smiled. "No. it's about you and me."

Angelica shook her head. "I don't understand."

Ian sat down next to her. "It's simple. I think that we need to really put all things aside and try to mend our marriage back together."

Angelica stood up. "Ian. We're divorced. Our marriage is over and has been over for some time now. What are you talking about?"

Ian stood up in front of her, "Angelica, I honestly thought that I wanted to be single again. I thought that this was the life that I was missing out on, but it isn't! It took me a long time to see that you were always the woman for me. I am so sorry that I neglected you, your feelings, and your desires while I was your husband. I disrespected you, I treated you horribly, and I didn't love you the way that you deserved. I apologize for everything that I have ever done to you, and didn't do for you, while we were together."

Angelica looked at him. "Thank you, Ian! I appreciate the apology." Angelica turned to walk toward the door, but Ian stood in her way of leaving.

Ian hugged her. "I will always love you!"

Angelica smiled and grabbed her bag that was still on the couch. She heard her phone ringing and answered. "Hello."

"Hey, baby. Everything ok?"

"Yes, I'm on my way home. How was work?"

Roman grimaced. "It was kind of rough today baby. What do you want to do for dinner?" Ian's face got a little wry. He purposefully cleared his throat aloud, and Angelica angrily look at Ian. Roman heard it. "Where you at?"

Ian took her hand trying to kiss it, but Angelica pulled it back. "I'm dropping the kids off at Ian's."

Roman didn't hear the kids in the background. He got real quiet for a minute. "So what's going on? Everything alright?"

"Yeah, Ian and I were just talking. I'm on my way out the door now."

Ian smiled. "Alright Sofie. I'll talk to you this weekend. Hailey said that she'll call you, later on, tonight," Ian said making sure that he was loud enough for Roman to hear. Angelica looked at him like she wanted to smack him.

Roman heard what Ian had said and was laughing on the other end. "Alright, babe. I'm on my way to the house. I'll see you when you get home."

"Ok, I love you."

Roman smiled. "I love you to baby!" Roman hung up the phone and kept on driving toward the house.

Angelica turned to Ian. "What was that all about?"

Ian looked as if he didn't know what she was talking about. "What?"

"Bye Ian," Angelica started walking toward the door when Ian pulled her back, gave her a hug, and tried to kiss her on her neck. Angelica pushed him back. "Ian, don't disrespect me like that! I already have a man, and you have a woman! What we had is over. We're just friends, and that's it! That's all it will ever be!"

"You'll be mine again Sofie!"

"Cut the bullshit, Ian!" Angelica left out of the house and headed home.

~

    As Angelica pulled up behind Roman's truck in the driveway, she thought about what she wanted to eat for dinner. She bundled up, got out of the car, and walked to the house. "Hello?!" Angelica closed the door behind her and turned the lock.

    "Hey baby, I'm upstairs."

    "What are we going to eat? I was hoping we could eat Chinese," Angelica hung up her coat in the closet and walked upstairs. "I am so hungry! I could eat a whole cow for real!" As she approached the doorway to their bedroom, she saw Roman sitting in the bed with a huge piece of gauze on his thigh. Angelica immediately clenched her stomach. "Roman what happened?"

    "Baby, come here."

    Angelica began to cry. "What happened to you?"

    "Angel, come here." Angelica continued crying and walked over to him. "It went in and out. It's not a big deal. I didn't want you to worry. I didn't want you to get upset." Roman kissed her. "I told you I had a rough day today," he said smiling.

"Roman, I have to know if something happens to you! You have to tell me so that I can be there with you. I don't care if it went in and out! You need to tell me!"

"Ok." Angelica got closer to him and hugged him adoringly. "So, what are we going to eat," Roman asked as he wiped her eyes.

"How about a steak, baked potato, and some salad."

"I thought you wanted some Chinese?"

"No, I'm making dinner tonight," she said kissing him on his head. "So, do you want onions, mushrooms, peppers, the whole nine on your steak?" Roman held her hand and kissed it. "I'll take that as a yes! Your baked potato...will that be loaded as well?" Roman held her other hand and kissed it! "Ok, I'm going to get in the shower really quick and then I'll cook. Do you need anything?"

Roman shook his head. "Take your time. I'm going to take a nap." Angelica kissed Roman on the lips and took out some clothes to wear after she took a shower. Roman watched her while she got her things together. She walked out of the room, went to the bathroom, and closed the door. While Roman laid there almost halfway to sleep, he heard her cell phone ringing in her purse. He went into her bag and grabbed her phone. The caller ID showed Ian's House. Roman thought about answering but decided not to. He sent it to voicemail and was going to tell Angelica when she got out of the shower that the kids called her. Then her phone vibrated two times. She had a voicemail message and a text from Ian's house. Roman opened the text:

Angelica,

I meant what I said about still being in love with you. I'll do ANYTHING to get you back and to reunite our family. Please call me so that we can talk some more, or we could go out to dinner. I love you so much, Sofie! P.S. I couldn't help myself...I missed kissing you so much ;)!

Ian

Roman closed his eyes and took a deep breath. He was about to explode! Roman inhaled a few more times and replied to Ian's text message.

~

"Daddy, your phone, is ringing," yelled Kendall.

"Thank you," Ian walked in the living room and looked at his phone. He opened the message from Angelica:

Ian,

I'm coming over to talk. I'll be outside in 15 minutes.

Ian looked at the time and ran upstairs to change his shirt and wash his face.

~

Angelica walked in the bedroom after her shower to find the bed empty. "Roman! You downstairs?"

Chapter 20 – Lesson: Remember to Follow Your
Instincts...

Roman pulled up to Ian's street in
Angelica's car, parked the car at the corner, and
walked up to the house. Ian was standing at the
door waiting for Angelica. He looked like he had
seen a ghost when Roman stood there at the bottom
of the stairs. Roman had on a black, thick down vest
with a black hoodie underneath, black baggy
sweatpants, and black Tim's. Ian, who didn't have
on a coat thinking that Angelica would be coming in
the house, grabbed his coat, put it on, and walked
down the steps. "Roman?"

Roman stared at him and tried to reign in
his rage. "Ian, look...I love Angelica, and I love the
children that you and her have together. I want us
to be able to get along since I'm their stepfather,
but I'm going to tell you straight up. I know my
place. I know my role. You...need to stay in your
place."

Ian became enraged. "What? What the fuck
are you talking about?"

Roman laughed and stepped a little closer
looking evil as hell! "Ok. Imma be real quick about

this. It's over between you and Angelica. Don't be sending her fucking messages about how much you love her...and all that fucking bullshit."

Ian tried to get an up on the conversation! He wanted to show that he was in full control. "Roman look..."

Roman stepped closer. "I'm *TALKING* to you for the kid's sake. I won't do what should be done...but just know that you need to stay in your fucking place."

Ian looked at him up and down. "What the fuck are you talking about?! You don't need to do me or *MY* family any fucking favors! Who the fuck do you think you are showing up at my fucking door?"

Roman had an evil looking smirk on his face. "Don't fucking call my *wife*... or talk to my *wife* about anything outside of the kids," Roman said quietly while staring him straight in the eye.

"I'll do whatever the fuck I want," Ian said laughing. "Angelica ain't your fucking wife! That's mine right there...ALL day!"

Roman kept staring at him. He looked to his left and right and stepped up in Ian's face. "Send my wife another out of pocket message and Imma knock your fucking head off."

Ian backed up a bit. "Or what," he asked laughing trying hard to hide his fear.

Roman stared right in his face and sucked his teeth. He then turned and walked away toward Angelica's car. Roman could hear Ian mumbling some nonsense while he walked down the street, but he didn't pay him any attention. He opened the car door and heard his cell phone ringing. "Hello."

"Roman, where are you," Angelica asked sounding very worried.

"I had to step out for a minute. I'm on my way back. Did you need something while I'm out?"

"Roman, you shouldn't be out driving around, doing anything," she said getting upset. "You need to be at home in the bed," she said yelling.

"I'm on my way home right now. Is dinner ready?"

"You'll see when you get here!" Angelica hung up the phone so quick that Roman knew she was mad! He drove home and pulled up the driveway ten minutes later. While unlocking the door, he could smell peppers and onions cooking inside.

Roman opened the door and walked in the kitchen. Angelica wasn't in there, and neither was dinner. He could smell that she cooked, but the kitchen was clean. She had already washed the dishes that she used to cook. Roman walked up the steps and could see that the bedroom door was closed. As he walked closer to the door, he started to get excited. He opened the door and looked at Angelica laying on the bed with a black silk nightgown. She raised her right eyebrow. "How do you feel?"

"A lot better now that I'm at home with you."

"I have your dinner warming in the oven." She got off the bed and walked to the bedroom doorway. Roman pulled her close to him and put his hand on her stomach.

"I missed you so much today," Roman kissed her lips and walked her back over to the bed so that they could lay down. "Who are you looking so beautiful for?"

"My man!"

"Oh! Do you think that he makes love to you better than me?"

Angelica shook her head. "No one has ever made love to me the way that you do Roman...except..."

"What? Except who?"

Angelica laughed, "There was this guy...when I was in college!"

"Yeah ok," he said laughing. "How's my baby doing," he asked kissing her stomach.

"The baby's fine. Are you still going to the appointment with me next Thursday?"

"Yeah at 6:30 right?"

"Yes," Angelica kissed his lips. "So, we're really going to have five kids huh?"

"No! Six," Roman adjusted his pillow while Angelica laughed.

"Roman, where did you go?"

"I had to take care of something really quick. So..." Roman said rubbing her belly, "...if it's a girl, I want her name to be Sofia."

Angelica smiled. "Sofia is very cute! How about Xavia for her middle name?"

Roman looked at her and kissed her. "Sofia Xavia Callowhill or Brandon Xavier Callowhill!"

Angelica rubbed his arm and looked at his leg, "Roman, what if I..."

"Baby, don't! Everything will be fine!

~Friday, March 12th

Angelica who was now a few weeks away from being four months pregnant looked forward to getting off work at three instead of five! Even though she had a miscarriage years ago, her OB/GYN Dr. Bernstein didn't want to take any chances. They agreed that a reduced work schedule would help to eliminate unnecessary stress. As she packed her things getting ready to go home to take a nap, she looked in her locker and grabbed some peanut butter crackers for the road. She heard her phone ring. "Hello."

"Hey Angelica, it's Ian."

"Hey."

"I wanted to know if I could speak to you this afternoon at the house. My mom is going to watch the kids for us while we talk."

"Ummm, ok. What's this about?"

"I just need to talk to you about a few things that's all.'"

"Ok, I'll be there in a half."

"Ok." Angelica had a weird feeling but went ahead and drove over to the house. She called Roman to let him know what was going on, but he didn't answer his phone. She left him a message and drove over to Ian's. Angelica tried not to worry, so she turned up the radio and sang along with Eric Benet's Chocolate Legs. She couldn't wait to get home! It was date night, and they were going out for dinner and a movie. Angelica pulled up to Ian's and parked on the street. She got out of the car and walked up to Ian's house. Angelica checked her phone before ringing the bell. Roman hadn't called her back or left her a text message. She tried to call him again, but he didn't answer. Angelica left another voicemail and text message. She then rang the doorbell. Ian opened the door. "Hey, come on in." Angelica walked in the house, and Ian took her coat. "Have a seat in the dining room."

"So, Ian what's going on?" Angelica sat down feeling weird.

Ian slowly sat down across from her and smiled. "The kids tell me that you're pregnant."

Angelica heard the tone of his voice and felt her hands trembling. It's been a long time since she heard that tone! She became infuriated since she was now a Callowhill! "Yes, I am."

Ian yelled! "So, when were you going to tell me?"

Angelica laughed. "Ian, I don't owe you any explanations about anything!" Angelica got up from the table, grabbed her coat, purse, and headed for the door.

"Angelica," Ian yelled!

She turned around ready to curse him out. As soon as she turned her head, Ian punched the shit out of her face! Angelica fell to the floor! When she tried to get up, Ian laughed! "What the fuck were you thinking?" He kicked her in the stomach! "-You trying to make a fool out of me? It's' bad enough y'all are fucking living together!"

Ian's phone started to ring, and he instinctively turned to look at the phone. Angelica mustered up enough energy to kick him in the groin – much thanks to Roman's self-defense moves he taught her months ago. Ian yelled and collapsed to the floor! Angelica grabbed her purse and hurried out of the house holding her stomach. Ian tried to get up to catch her but couldn't. "You fucking bitch!

I hope you lose the fucking baby you fucking stupid ass whore!"

Angelica got in her car and pulled off crying. She was so hysterical that she had to pull over on Cobbs Creek in route to Roman's house. She called Roman, and he finally picked up. "Hey baby! Sorry, I missed your call." He heard her crying on the other end. "Angel what's wrong?"

"Roman, I'm on Cobbs Creek Parkway... at the BP gas station," she said shaking like crazy. "I need to go to the hospital."

Angelica heard the sirens going off in his car, "I'll be there in ten minutes baby, hold on ok. I'm on my way."

"Romannnn...." Angelica was crying hysterically. "Please...oh God..."

"Angel," Roman was trying to stay calm. Just when he was about to start asking questions, Angelica hung up the phone. She held on to her stomach trying not think about the pain in her abdomen. She knew her crotch was wet, but she didn't want to find out if it was blood or not. Angelica closed her eyes and tried to calm down. She couldn't believe what Ian did to her! In about ten minutes, she heard police sirens and opened her eyes. A black Caprice Classic pulled up along the side of her car. Roman wore a tan winter coat, white shirt, and tan slacks since he was now a detective. He ran up to the car, and Detective Straight hopped out as well. Angelica slowly opened her car door. It was freezing cold outside, but she couldn't feel the frigid air. Roman looked at her face. Ian punched her so hard that her left eye was practically shut. The left side of her face was red and swollen. He noticed that she was holding on to her stomach as well.

Officer Straight looked at Angelica and Roman. He could tell from the look on Roman's face, that he was going to explode. "Roman, let's take her to Lankenau."

Roman totally ignored him. "Baby, who did this to you?"

She looked up at Roman, "I tried to call you..."

"Who did this," Roman yelled.

Angelica felt ashamed and lowered her head while weeping. "Ian!"

Roman looked at Straight. "Take her to the hospital. I'll be back!"

Angelica yelled. "Roman don't go...the baby!"

"What's wrong?"

Angelica started to break down. "He kicked me in the stomach and I..."

Roman picked her up and placed her in the back of the Caprice while he held her close. Straight locked up the Volvo and told the gas attendant to leave the vehicle where it was while flashing his badge. Angelica continued crying in his chest while Roman held her tight. "It's going to be alright baby! I'm right here!" Straight got in the car, turned on the siren, and drove fast as hell to Lankenau Hospital.

After Roman flashed the hospital his badge in the ER, they quickly took Angelica back in the Triage area. Roman called Dr. Bernstein on his cell and told him what happened. Luckily, he lived a few blocks from where the hospital was located. After doing all types of blood tests and ultrasounds, Dr. Bernstein and the ER doctor came to speak with Roman. Straight was outside of the hospital talking to their captain about what had happened. Roman looked at Dr. Bernstein and the ER doc trying hard like hell to keep his tears at bay.

"Roman," said Dr. Bernstein. "Angelica is doing great! We've sedated her so that she can get some rest. Everything is ok with her eye. It's obviously swollen, but she can see just fine. From what I can see, and the results of the tests, everything anatomically is functional. Her ribs are bruised, but nothing is broken."

The ER physician shook his head in agreement. "We've also had pictures taken of her face and abdomen. Officer Kilpatrick took her statement and is waiting for you down the hall there."

Roman lowered his head, closed his eyes, and rubbed his temples with both hands. "Dr. Bernstein, how is the baby?"

Dr. Bernstein put his right hand on Roman's left shoulder. "The baby is doing just fine. The fluid that came out was urine and not amniotic fluid. I want her to stay until Sunday so that I can keep a close eye on her to monitor them." Roman grabbed Dr. Bernstein and hugged him. "She's going to be fine."

Roman pulled away, nodded his head at the doc's, and went to Kilpatrick. Kilpatrick stood in the hall and nodded at Roman. "Callowhill, I'm sorry about what happened to your wife. We went to his house, but we couldn't locate him. We got a couple of cars going to his mothers to pick him up. Your wife said that he told her... that his mom was watching the kids while they talked."

"Thanks, Kil." Roman hugged him and walked toward the exit.

Straight was standing there by the car, "Roman, you ready? I talked to the captain. He said to call him on Monday," said Straight.

"Thanks, man. I need you to take me back to her car so I can drive it home. Then I need you to drop me off at my truck so I can pick up the kids."

"I'm following you. You know how we roll." Roman gave him a brief nod. After dropping off Angelica's car at their house, he went over to Ian's parents' home to pick up the kids. Ian's mother knew what was going on and didn't put up a fuss when Roman gathered the kids up.

Gavin was so excited. "Pop-pop! What's going on? The cops were at grand mom's earlier," asked Gavin.

Roman smiled. "Gav, we really got to go, son," he said trying not to tear up at how much he could see Angelica in Gavin's eyes.

Kendall ran downstairs. "Pop-pop!" Kendall ran into Roman's arms. "Are we going home?"

Roman couldn't help but laugh. "Yes."

Both boys yelled, "Yayyyy!!"

"Where's Hailey," Roman looked around from where he was standing.

Hailey ran down the steps and saw Roman dressed in the clothes that he usually wears to work. "What's up Pop's," she said hugging Roman. "Mom's working late?"

"I have a surprise for you all, so we better get ready to go! The door is open!" All the kids screamed and ran outside. "It was nice meeting you Mrs. Kings."

"Likewise. Please keep me posted. If there is anything I can do, please call me. Hailey has my telephone number."

"Thank you." Roman left out of the house and walked up to his truck to make sure the kids were in their seat belts. He then walked over to Straight. "I'm going to pick up Winter and take them all to my mom's for the night. I need a squad at my parents in case he tries to take them."

Straight nodded his head. "I hear you, I'll tell the cap."

As Straight pulled off, Roman walked over to his truck, opened the driver's side door, and looked inside. "-Seatbelts on, right?"

"Yessss," they all said in unison laughing.

"Good. We're leaving in five minutes!" The kids cheered as Roman walked to the back of the truck. He pulled out his cell phone, took a couple of deep breaths, and called his cousin Cyrus.

~

Angelica opened her eyes and put her hand on her lower back. She felt so stiff. She took her time in stretching and noticed that Roman was sleeping on the couch not too far from her bed. "Roman."

Roman opened his eyes wide as if she startled him. He walked over to the bed and sat down right beside her so that he could hug her. "I love you."

Angelica smiled. "I love you too! I'm so sorry!"

Roman held her hand. "Don't! Let's not talk about it. I don't want you to get upset. How do you feel?"

"Stiff, but I'm ok. How's the baby?"

"The baby's fine. Dr. Bernstein wants to keep you until Monday just to be on the safe side."

Angelica began to cry. "You think I'm going to lose the baby?"

"No! Baby, everything is going to be just fine," he said rubbing her stomach. "That baby has two very strong parents! Our children are fighters

461

baby! We're gonna make it!" Roman kissed her on the neck and continued to rub her stomach.

Angelica looked in his eyes. "Where is Ian?"

Roman's face hardened. "They haven't found him yet, and I just told you not to talk about it," he said seriously.

"Roman," Angelica whispered. "Don't do anything that would jeopardize our family. I need you!"

He gazed into her eyes. "Baby, you know that I love you and our children, so I'm not going to lie to you. You will never see...or hear from him again." Angelica sat up and frowned at Roman. Roman looked at her face and smiled. "I'm not going to be any more specific than that."

Angelica shook her head in disbelief. "What? Tell me what happened."

"What did I just say to you, Angelica." He caught himself getting upset and calmed down. "It's over. There is no need to talk about him or what happened...anymore." Roman kissed her lips and played in her hair. "Now, lay back down so you can get some more rest."

"Where are the kids?"

"At my mom's. Paul's taking them roller-skating and to the movies later on." Roman kissed her on her neck. "You still love me?"

Angelica smiled. "I'll never stop loving you! You're my guardian angel!"

Chapter 21 – Lesson: You'll Know When You've Had Enough!!!

May 22nd - (Angelica's six months pregnant)

Angelica was now off of bed rest. She was so glad to be out of the bed and able to do things around the house. Even though Angelica suggested sending the kids to her mothers, Roman insisted that they stay at home. Ever since Angelica was discharged from the hospital, Roman had been cooking breakfast, picking the kids up from school, cooking dinner, and entertaining. Angelica's mom would come over and help with the laundry and cleaning while Roman's mom watched the kids on the weekends. The kids would sometimes visit with Ian's parents, but since the attack and his disappearance, they kept their distance.

Angelica knew that the last couple of months had been hard on Roman, so she decided to take him away for the weekend to Miami, Florida. She had arranged for all the kids to stay with her parents for the weekend. Her bags and most of his were packed and ready to go. She even had Straight submit a leave request at the job for Roman for the weekend! Angelica glanced at the clock on the wall. It was about 5:15 p.m. as she dragged the last bag down the steps and into the dining room so that he wouldn't see the bags in the living room. She heard Roman walking on the front porch and hurried to open the door to surprise him.

"Hey….," Angelica's smile quickly dissolved as her face quickly turned sinister.

Monica stood at the door smiling from ear to ear with her thin frame, pristine hair, and glossy lips. "I'm sorry to bother you. I thought you were still on bedrest," Monica said cunningly.

Angelica was livid. "You better get the **FUCK** off of my porch," she said allowing the spit from her mouth to flick from her lips onto Monica's face!

Monica cocked her head to the side. "Or what?! What the *fuck* are you going to do fat ass?! You ain't gonna' do shit to me," she said laughing. "I guess that's why he's still fucking with me cause you sure ain't doing shit for him!"

Angelica felt her insides boiling, but she did not succumb! She tried to close the door, but Monica held it open. "Ms. Fat Ass, tell your man that I will be expecting him this evening at 12:45

A.M...Our usual time of dining!" Angelica slammed the door shut smashing her fingers in the door. As Monica screamed from the searing pain shooting through her fingertips, Angelica took pity and opened the door enough for her to pull her fingers out.

"Now get the fuck off my porch before your head gets stuck!" Monica ran off the porch. Angelica slammed the door shut and sat on the couch. She cried a little then stopped when she thought of the baby. She walked up the steps and ran a bath. As she sat in the tub, she closed her eyes and sang her heart out.

About 20 minutes later, Roman walked in the door and could hear her beautiful voice singing a sad melody. He hadn't heard this particular song before, but he knew exactly why she was singing it. Monica had called him and told him that she came to the house and paid Angelica a visit. Although he was guilty of speaking with Monica over the past couple of months, he didn't sleep with her. Roman did TELL Monica that he was going to come to her house around 12 midnight, but he just told her that to keep her from begging. He closed the door, locked up, and took off his shoes. Angelica immediately stopped singing. Roman felt so bad, but he was sure that they could get through this.

Roman walked up the stairs to the second floor. He passed the empty bathroom and went into the bedroom where he thought she was. On the bed there were two plane tickets wrapped in red ribbon labeled Mr. and Mrs. Callowhill. He shook his head and headed up to the third floor. Roman felt so bad that he stopped at the bottom of the third-floor stair and began to cry silently. Regardless of whether he felt lonely or not, he realized that he shouldn't have ever started speaking to Monica again. He was so scared of losing Angelica, but he knew he had to face her. He wiped his face, stood up, and went to the third-floor bathroom doorway. Roman looked in the bathroom, and Angelica was laying there with her eyes closed. Her body was buried in a bunch of bubbles. He smiled looking at her laying in the tub. He tapped on the door, and she opened her eyes. "Can I come in?"

"Sure." Roman came closer and sat on the edge of the tub. She turned toward him and just stared at him.

"Here, let me wash your back," he said reaching in the tub.

Angelica slowly pushed his hand back. "That's ok...I'll get it."

Roman looked at her. "We have to talk."

"Now?"

"Baby I know what happened with Monica coming over to the house." Roman stopped for a minute and gathered his thoughts. "Angelica, I'm sorry."

"So am I Roman."

"What do you mean by that?"

Angelica briefly closed her eyes and shook her head. Her voice was low and soft, but her words were clear. "I am a sorry ass fool for falling for all of your...bullshit." Angelica stood up and grabbed her towel. Roman looked at her huge stomach with their baby inside and smiled. He reached out to touch her. She slowly pushed his hand away again and spoke softly. "Don't touch me." Angelica stepped out of the tub, put on her slippers, and walked out of the bathroom. Roman silently followed her from the bathroom, down the stairs, and into their bedroom. Angelica looked in her drawer to grab a tee shirt and some panties. She didn't even bother to lotion up or dry her hair all the way.

Roman was petrified. "Angelica, please. I just talked to her on the phone. I never slept with her or anything like that."

Angelica stood in front of the dresser with her head hung low and eyes closed. She refused to look at him as she clenched onto the towel still covering her. "Roman right now, all I want to do is lay down and to be left alone. I don't want you touching me or talking to me," she said crying. "I don't want you near me Roman ok? Go ahead! Call Monica all you want and whoever else you want to talk to! Just leave me the fuck alone."

Roman went over to her. "Baby, I know you're upset, but we can get through this."

Angelica put the tee shirt and panties on top of the dresser, turned around, and stared at him. Roman could see the pain in her eyes. The way she looked reminded him of when he first saw her on that bottom step after being raped. He felt a tear fall from his eye. Angelica pointed a finger in his face. "You think I married you so that you could say the same shit Ian said to me? *YOU* wanted to marry *ME* Roman! I didn't rush you into this! If I wanted to hear these lame ass excuses, I would have stayed with Ian!"

"Angel...," Roman said trying to explain his self.

Angelica backed away from him and yelled, "Don't Angel me! Just leave me the fuck alone Roman!"

Roman shook his head. "I'm never leaving you alone! I'm sorry!"

Angelica dropped her towel to the floor and put her tee shirt on nice and easy. Roman looked at her stomach and reached out to touch her, but Angelica pushed his hand away. "Don't touch me I said!"

Roman felt her slipping away with each rejection of his touch. It infuriated him. "Angelica, calm down!"

Angelica stared at him. "Don't tell me what to do! That woman came to our home and spoke to me about *MY* husband," she screamed while holding her stomach. "My husband...who continues to lie to me over and over again."

Roman looked at her screaming while holding her stomach and knew that she needed to calm down. "Angelica, please just sit down for a minute and calm down."

Angelica pointed her index finger in his face again and snarled. "If you tell me to calm down...one more fucking *time*, I'm going to walk out that fucking door...and never come the fuck back!"

Roman knew she meant it and tried to calm her down. "Angel, if you keep it up, you'll be back at the hospital! Please calm down!" Angelica put her panties on, grabbed a bra from the drawer, some sweatpants, and socks from her bottom drawer. She put the clothes on and placed her hair in a ponytail. Roman yelled fearfully. "Where are you going?"

Angelica snickered. "None of your fucking business!"

"Angelica you need to stop before this gets out of hand!"

"It's already out of hand with you fucking around with Monica AGAIN," she said getting her purse together.

Roman pleaded. "Angelica can you please just stop for a minute so that we can talk about this."

Angelica raised her hands in the air surrendering to all the bullshit. "We *are* talking and to be honest with you Roman, there isn't anything to talk about! Let me see... you've been seeing Monica for... however long... doing who knows what! Ummm...let's see...you're sorry, and you'll never do it again right?!" Roman just looked at her and didn't know what to say. "I have done nothing but love you! You say I'm the only woman for you but you still...keep...fucking with her! I'm carrying our child! *OUR* child! The child you **begged** me for! With everything I've been through, you can't keep your fucking dick in your pants?!"

Roman gently grabbed Angelica's arm, "I didn't sleep with her!"

Angelica snatched her arm away, "Oh yeah, that's right! You were going over there tonight so she could just... suck your dick right?!"

He tried to touch her again, but she pushed him away. "Baby, I just told her that so that she could stop bothering me!"

"How could you do this to us Roman?! If it was something I wasn't doing why didn't you just tell me?" Angelica sat on the bed with her hands in the air. "What did I do wrong? Why can't I have a man who loves me and who wants to be with only me?" Roman went over to her and tried to touch her. "Do... not... touch... me... I said! It's over. I was never to hear that woman's name again...let alone see her at my front door telling me shit about my husband. It's over," she cooed.

Roman sat down next to her. "Angel...we married each other for better or worse. We can get through this!"

Angelica looked at him. "I know we married each other for better or worse Roman...but we also married with the understanding that there would be no one else in our marriage! Those are the words that **you** said to **me**! We haven't even been married for a year, and you're already talking to other women! What's it going to be... five years down the line and then you'll start having other kids with them?! I'm not going down this road with you! You obviously weren't ready, and I'm not going to live the rest of my life with someone who **said** they were sure about me... but weren't! Be confused by your damn self!" Angelica stood up and winced as she held onto her stomach. Roman reached out to touch her again. "I don't want you touching me so **stop** it!"

Roman caressed her face, and she knocked it away. "Angel, I'm sorry!" Tears fell from his eyes. "Baby, I'm sorry!" Angelica walked toward the bedroom door to leave while holding on to her stomach. Roman stood up and blocked the doorway. "Angelica! Please don't leave me! I'll do anything, just... please don't leave!"

Angelica looked at him. "I didn't want you to do anything for me! I just wanted you to love me like you said you did! I wanted you to just... be with me like you said you wanted to be with me! Now move out of my fucking way!"

"Are you just going to the house for the night," he asked quietly.

Angelica looked at his tear-filled eyes. "I'll be back to get the rest of our stuff over the next couple of days."

Roman slammed his fist against the wall, "NO!"

Angelica wasn't moved by his anger. "Roman move so I can leave!"

"NO!"

Angelica tried to push him, but he wouldn't move! "MOOOOVE!" She screamed in his face! Roman just stood there with tears falling from his eyes. Angelica held on to her stomach and winced. "Roman get the fuck out of my way!"

"I love you..."

Angelica walked up in Roman's face. "If you loved me, why would you let that woman back in your life? Why do you have the need to be with her if I am your everything?"

Roman held his stance in the doorway and stared at her. He didn't hesitate with answering. "I was selfish and stupid. I'm sorry."

"Me too," she said calming down. Roman reached out to touch her again and Angelica slapped his hand away. "Don't touch me."

Roman begged. "Please! Angel don't do this to me! I just want to hold you."

Angelica smiled. "No. Can you please step aside so that I can leave?"

"No." Angelica stood there staring at Roman while her eyes expelled streams of tears. Roman stared at her and quickly grabbed her arms. He held on to her and hugged her. "I'm sorry baby. I'm so sorry for hurting you." He felt her body trembling and looked at her face. "I swear on my life and our children's lives that I will never do anything like that again!" He grabbed her hands and got down on his knees. "Angel please forgive me! You will never hear about her again. I promise you...on my life!"

Angelica looked down at him. "Roman you told that same lame ass story before! You obviously have some feelings for her or else we wouldn't even have this problem!"

Roman held on to her hands. "You'll never hear about her or any other woman again! You have my word! Just don't leave!"

Angelica shook her head in disbelief and spoke in a defeated tone of voice. "Roman, my heart wants to believe you, but my mind can't! You're still involved with her. Take this time to find out why. Maybe she's the one you want to be with," Angelica said pulling away from Roman and walking over to the window. Roman walked over to her. "We all make mistakes right," she said chuckling while still crying. "I guess the dream had to end sometime huh?"

"You will *NEVER* have to worry about her again! You have my word! Or any other woman for that matter!"

Angelica stared at the glass. "You said that before Roman. You're repeating yourself."

Roman walked up to Angelica from behind and held her close while kissing her neck. "She will never bother us again." A chill ran up Angelica's spine as she heard the words come out of Roman's mouth. She turned to him and looked at his menacing face with his bright red puffy eyes. Angelica looked at him closely and frowned up her face. "NEVER." Angelica put one hand on her chest and the other on her stomach.

Roman put his hand on her face, "I told you that no matter what, we will always be together. I will never leave you!" Roman kissed her. "I love you and I married you to be with you and only you for the rest of my life! I'm sorry I crossed the line, but it will never happen again. She is **permanently** out of our lives...and I will *NOT* do anything stupid like that ever again." Roman kissed her lips again and instantly got hard. Angelica stood frigid not giving in to his advances. "Baby please kiss me."

Angelica stared into his eyes. "How can she be permanently out of our lives?"

"Because she is."

"Whatever Roman," she said pushing him aside.

Roman became infuriated again. "Stop pushing me away," he yelled. "Stop it!"

"You know what Roman!"

"What?"

"Move out of my way! I give you an inch and you fucking take a yard!"

"Angelica would you stop it! We have kids, we're having another baby, and you need to calm the hell down before something happens."

Angelica walked up to him, "What are you gonna do? You gonna get rid of me too Roman?" She said crying heavily. "You had your fill now you're ready to get rid of me too?"

Roman sighed and took Angelica's hand to kiss it, but she snatched it back. "I've come to realize that I don't know you at all." Roman looked at her and kissed her lips. He tried to pull up her shirt, but Angelica stopped him. "No," she said pulling her shirt down.

"Stop," Roman whispered in her ear. Angelica took his hands off her shirt as Roman quickly took control. He picked her up and placed her on the bed. Angelica immediately sat up. Roman sat next to her, put his hand up her shirt, and caressed her breasts as he kissed her earlobe. "Lay back." Angelica couldn't fight him. She did what was told and looked at him while he pulled her sweatpants and panties off. He placed his head in between her thighs and inhaled the scent he loved so much.

As he began to taste her, she moaned and clenched the sheets. "Roman stop it please."

"What's wrong?"

She pushed his head away, "I don't want to do this."

Roman was wounded. "What's wrong? You don't like it?"

"No," Angelica lied.

Roman looked up at her. "Baby, don't say that."

Angelica cried. "I'm a fat ass just like she said," she murmured underneath her breath.

Roman rose from in between her thighs and kissed her stomach, and then her lips. "Your stomach is big, and that's because you're carrying our baby! Everything else is the same!" Angelica stayed silent. She turned on her side and rubbed her stomach while smiling thinking of the baby. Roman spooned behind her and rubbed her belly, "Three more months to go."

Angelica kept on rubbing her stomach while Roman pulled her onto her back. He straddled her and began kissing her lips. "Roman, we need to separate."

"And when do you think we should do that and for how long," he said sarcastically.

"I think we should separate as soon as possible for at least six months so that you can think about what you want."

Roman got mad. "I think we don't need to separate as soon as possible. I don't need to think about shit! You're my wife, and we have four kids going on five! Angelica, we are not separating for NO length of time! We're going to work this out right here in this house or another house, but we're going to do it together."

Angelica turned her head toward the wall. "Yes we are."

"No, we're not," Roman said kissing on her neck.

"I can't do this!" Roman began to suck on Angelica's neck. "Stop it!" Roman kept on going making Angelica moan. She caught herself and pushed his mouth away. "Stop it," she yelled. Roman stopped and looked at her crying. "Why are you doing this to me? What did I do to you? Why did you do this to me?" Angelica cried hysterically while Roman just looked at her.

Tears came to his eyes once again seeing her in so much pain. "Baby, I'm so sorry. It'll never happen again! Please don't cry."

Angelica calmed down a bit and felt utterly humiliated from everything that had happened. "Excuse me! I have to go to the bathroom." Roman moved from over top of her and let her go to the bathroom. Angelica went to the bathroom and relieved herself. When she wiped herself, she was glad to see that it was just clear discharge coming from her vagina. With all the crying that she had been doing, she started to worry. She washed her face and blew her nose while looking in the mirror. Angelica tried hard to smile when her tears started to fall again. She looked at her hair and decided not to look at her horrible reflection. Angelica looked at her belly and began to hum a lullaby that she often sang to the baby which made her smile.

Roman, who was standing by the door, could hear her humming and smiled. Angelica put a headband on and looked at herself in the mirror again. This time Angelica smiled at the woman in the mirror. She remembered the most obvious, important things going on in her life: she's going to give birth to a healthy child, and she will then be a mother of five! God was with her! Angelica closed her eyes and prayed. She knew she would be ok regardless of what happened. She got on her knees and began to thank God for his forgiveness, love, and mercy.

"Angelica are you alright?" Roman entered the room, saw her on her knees, and instantly fell to the floor. "Angel, what's wrong?"

"Nothing," she said smiling. "Nothing. Everything is fine." Roman took her hands and kissed them. Then to his surprise, she kissed his. "Ask Him for His forgiveness Roman and mean it. Then and only then will I believe that you truly want me, love me, and are satisfied with me and only me like you said at the altar." Roman put his hand on her face and kissed her lips. "Roman while we are on our knees, ask Him for your forgiveness."

Roman closed his eyes. "God, I know that I'm not a perfect man. I humbly ask that you, please forgive me of my sins. Please forgive me for hurting my wife, Lord God! You know I love her with everything within me! Please forgive me! Please! Amen."

"Amen." Angelica kissed Roman on his lips, "Is this all out of your system? Are you sure about us? If you're unsure, tell me now and I'll give you time to think this through. I can't argue with you about this anymore."

"Baby, I'm more than sure about us Angelica. I would do anything for our family. I love you so much Angelica, and I'm sorry for everything that I have done." Angelica put her hand on his face and kissed him. "Do you forgive me?"

"Yes, but I'm not making love to you until after I have the baby."

"What?!" Angelica looked at him seriously but didn't say a word. "I know your joking right."

Angelica shook her head. "I'm not joking."

"Angel don't do this to me," he said standing up laughing. He held out his hand and helped Angelica up from the floor. They both went into the bedroom while Angelica laid on the bed. "Oh... so is this your way of punishing me for what I did?"

"I'm not punishing you. This is so that you can have time to get your game up and ready for me after I have the baby."

"Get my game up? What's that supposed to mean," he said looking offended.

"I'm just joking with you Roman!" He looked at her as if his feelings were hurt. "I was only joking with you! I didn't mean to hurt your feelings," she said smiling.

"Yes, you did."

"No, I didn't."

Roman laid down next to her and kissed her on her stomach. "How's my baby doing?"

"The baby's incredibly hungry right now! If you haven't already figured it out, we were supposed to go to Florida tonight for the weekend. I had Straight put in a leave request for you so that we could go away." Angelica got up off the bed and sat on the edge looking for her slippers. Roman laid there looking at the ceiling not knowing what to say. "Our flight was supposed to leave at 10:55." She put her slippers on and walked to the bedroom door to go downstairs.

"Baby let's go!"

Angelica turned around and looked at him, "No! After all that, I barely feel like cooking."

"If we don't go, I'm going to feel bad as shit!"

Angelica laughed. "You SHOULD feel bad as shit," she said laughing.

"C'mon baby, we do need to get away!"

She shrugged her shoulders. "Why don't you go by yourself and..."

"What? What the fuck I look like going to Florida by myself," he said laughing.

"You'll be relaxing and..."

"I'd be missing you and feeling bad as hell. All jokes aside," he said looking at his watch, "...it's almost a quarter to nine now. If we get dressed and pack what we need to pack, we can make the flight."

"I'm not really feeling the trip anymore," she said walking in the hallway.

Roman went up to her and hugged her. "Let's go so I can spend the whole weekend making it up to you."

Angelica sighed. "I'm going downstairs to cook us some dinner." Angelica continued walking down the hall and the stairs while Roman followed her in the kitchen.

"Don't you start cooking woman," he said jumping in front of her while laughing. Angelica smiled. "Now look, go back upstairs and get ready so that we can go to Florida! I'll cook us something quick, or we can get something before we get to the airport."

"We're already packed Spidey! I just needed you to pick out a couple of things in case you wanted to wear something else."

"You packed all of our things?"

"Yeah. This was supposed to be a surprise for you being such a supportive and loving husband and father."

Roman just looked at her and was lost for words once again. He put his arms around her and held her tight. "I'm so glad you're here with me! I am so glad you're mine." He kissed her and backed her up to the fridge. "I want you."

"Well, you're going to have to wait until the baby is born."

"Go upstairs."

"Ok," she said walking toward the stairs. Roman followed behind her until they got in the bedroom. "I'm hungry."

"I'll make you something in a few minutes. I'm about to eat right now!" Roman made her lay down while he ate her pussy. After a couple of minutes, she pushed his head away. "What's wrong? Why do you keep pushing me away?" Angelica didn't respond she just changed positions, pulled out his dick and began sucking it the best way she could. "Angel, you ain't never suck my dick like this before." Minutes later he was ready to come. "OH FUCK!"

"What you ready to come already baby," Angelica teased.

Roman looked at her and was about to explode. "Slow down baby please!"

"Why?"

"Because I'm gonna' nut all in your mouth if you don't slow down! Here it comes!" Angelica stopped just in time. "Don't stop baby! Don't stop!"

"Why?"

"Keep sucking it, baby! Don't stop!" Angelica started sucking again, and Roman was going off! He had one hand on the back of her head as she sucked the life from him. Ten minutes later Roman fell off to sleep, but Angelica didn't.

Chapter 22 – Lesson: Love ~~Excludes~~
INCLUDES Forgiveness!

Roman woke up smiling. He looked at the
clock. The bright red LED light displayed 10:49
p.m. "Baby," he said feeling for her in the bed.
Roman sat up and looked around. He could feel
that something wasn't right. The bathroom light
was on. "Angelica, you in the bathroom," he said
getting up and walking out of the bedroom. When
he reached the doorway, he saw that she wasn't in
there. "Angel, what are you doing," he yelled
thinking that she was in the kitchen. "Angelica," he
said yelling while running down the stairs.

He went in the kitchen with a smile on his
face ready to see her eating something while sitting
at the kitchen table. As soon as he entered the
kitchen, his smile dissipated. Roman put his hand
over his mouth and sat down at the table staring at
an envelope with his name on it. He took quite a
few breaths. He held the envelope in his hand and
stared at his name printed in Angelica's
handwriting. He was breathing heavily. Roman
opened the envelope with trembling hands. There

was a letter inside. Roman slowly unfolded the letter to read it:

Roman,

I love you so much...but I am hurting so bad inside about so much right now. I tried to wake you up so that we could go to Florida. While trying to wake you, you called me Monica. I know you're going to say that you didn't mean it because you always know what to say. Saying sorry or apologizing doesn't change the fact that she is, and has been, on your mind. I do not have the energy to fight right now while I'm carrying our baby. I'm EXTREMELY tired of this! Whether we moved too fast is neither here nor there because we are married! I honestly don't know what to do. I don't know what to do! I want to believe what you say to me but, I don't know! I don't know what to think anymore. I'll be back on Sunday. Just give me some time to think. I need some space and so do you. I think and feel that a separation is definitely needed at this point.

Roman threw the letter on the floor and ran upstairs to get his keys.

~

Angelica laid in the plush bed and rubbed
on her belly while singing a song. As she rubbed her
belly, the baby moved within her. Angelica laughed,
"Are you having fun in there?" She kept rubbing,
and the baby kept moving. Even though she was
mad at Roman, she wished that things were
different. Angelica looked for the remote under the
comfy hotel pillow. She turned on the television and
decided to watch the Law & Order: Criminal Intent
Marathon until she fell asleep!

The next morning Angelica woke up having
to pee awfully bad! She got up and practically ran to
the bathroom laughing! "You better stop kicking me
little one!" Angelica finished up in the bathroom
and heard her phone ringing. She got comfortable
in the bed before looking at her cell phone. Angelica
picked it up and saw that Roman had called her so
much over the night, that he filled her voicemail
inbox completely. She had so many texts that she
just called him.

Roman immediately picked up. "Angelica!
Are you ok? Where are you?"

Angelica was silent for a moment. Hearing his voice reminded her of the pain she tried so hard to avoid. "I'm fine. Did you get my letter?"

Roman sighed. "Yes, I did. I need you to come home! I need the both of you to come home. I'm sorry for what happened. Please come home!"

Angelica's voice was barely audible. "Roman, we need some space. I can't keep going through this with you. You need to make a decision about what you want. I'm not going to be second anymore to anyone."

Roman begged. "Angelica I need you! Please don't do this!"

"You need me when I try to leave you, but you don't need me when you have me," she snapped.

Roman was frustrated. "I always need you, Angelica! You know how much I love you!"

"So, what Roman! So, what! What about Monica," Angelica said through her teeth! Roman stayed silent. "Did she tell you about the pictures?"

Roman got real quiet. "What are you talking about Angelica?"

Angelica chuckled. "Oh...when you talked to her, she didn't tell you that she sent me pictures?"

Angelica heard something smash loud in the background. "What fucking pictures? What the fuck are you talking about," Roman yelled!

Angelica shook her head. "I guess when you all talked she forgot to mention that to you. Why don't you ask her? I'm quite sure she would love to rekindle the moments you all shared!"

Roman's chest felt like it was going to explode. "I need to see you. Where are you?"

"Away. When I get back, we'll talk about the next step."

Roman yelled. "The next step for what?" Angelica stayed quiet. "For what Angelica?"

"I'll call you tomorrow Roman."

Roman begged. "Angelica, please. Just talk to me then, please."

Angelica sighed. "What do you want to talk about?"

Roman sighed. He honestly didn't know what to say or where to begin. "I want you to come home."

Angelica laid down in the bed. "For what?"

Roman continued to beg. "I want you to come home so that we can talk and work this out. Please!"

Angelica tilted her head to the side. "Talk about what? Yeah, let's talk about why you took pictures of Monica sucking your dick...which she **proudly** forwarded me after she left our house. Or I know! Oh yeah...yeah...let's talk about all the selfies you all took while kissing in your truck! Or the other fucking pictures of you and her, in bed, kissing, fucking, sucking, having fun, eating dinner, traveling and shit!!" Roman stayed silent. "I can see that you're at a loss for words **YOU FUCKING ASSHOLE!**" Angelica hung up the phone and slouched back against the fluffy pillows. Twenty minutes later, she was fast asleep.

~

After Angelica woke up from her nap, she decided to take a shower and get some lunch! Since she was staying at the Ritz Carlton downtown, she decided to take full advantage of the scenery and food! Angelica walked to the Reading Terminal, enjoyed some ice cream, and oatmeal raisin cookies. She then had some soul food from Silvia's and bought some cheesecake from Termini Brothers for later! Angelica walked the streets, went to Macy's, and walked in the Gallery. She had a ball just being by herself!

About two hours later, she wore herself out and had to return to her room. She opened the door and immediately saw Roman sitting on the bed. Angelica took her shoes off, placed them by the door, and looked at him. He didn't look well at all. He looked as if he hadn't showered in a day or two. Roman stood up and walked over to her.

"Angelica, are you ok?" Angelica didn't say anything. Roman walked closer and hugged Angelica kissing her for dear life on her neck and face. "Thank God you all are ok? How's the baby?" Angelica partially smiled. "Baby I can't even begin to say how sorry I am for all of this. What can I do to make it right?" Angelica shrugged her shoulders and stayed silent. Roman fell to his knees. "I can't live without you! I have no purpose if you are not with me!"

Angelica backed away. "I need to use the bathroom." Roman just sat there!

A few minutes later, Angelica returned to the bedroom with her comfy-cotton night gown on. Roman was sitting on the bed, but then kneeled on the floor beside the bed while she made herself comfortable. She took her time getting comfortable underneath the comforter and leaned back onto the plush pillows. Roman stared at her. "Angelica please talk to me."

Angelica stayed calm. "Talk to you about what? What would you like to talk about?"

Roman continued. "I want you to come home."

"Then what?"

"Then we can talk and work this out."

Angelica looked down at him. "What is there to work out? You love me, but you love fucking Monica. There is nothing to work out. I worked it out already," she said calmly.

Roman took a hold of her hand but Angelica slowly pulled it back. "Angelica, please come home."

Angelica took a deep breath. "For what? Come home to you and keep living with you while you continue to be with other women?"

Roman shook his head. "Baby please. I don't want to be with other women. I fucked up! I know I fucked up! I won't lose you, Angelica!" Angelica sat up and looked out of the window. The room had a beautiful view of center city. She remained silent thinking of the clear blue sky outside of her window. Roman looked at Angelica. "I haven't slept since you left! I can't sleep or eat! I can't do anything! I need you to be with me Angelica."

Angelica stared at Roman while he talked and cried on his knees at her bedside. "I need you! I can't live without you! I won't live without you! We said until we die Angelica. You promised!"

"You said at the altar that I would be the only woman, but I'm not. You lied first."

Roman's face looked as if he was purely disgusted at the thought of being with another woman. "Baby, those pictures are old! They were taken a long time ago! Believe me, please! I wouldn't do that to us! That fucking bitch won't ever bother us again! I promised you that, and I meant it! Trust and believe me!" Angelica looked at him and shook her head in disbelief. "Baby please," he said shaking with his hands balled up to his face. He was distraught and consumed with fear.

Angelica listened to him crying profusely. He looked weak, frail, and broken. As his head was hung low, she could see a faint but existent ring-around-the-collar. How long had he been wearing that shirt? He even smelled musky! It was as if he hadn't put on any deodorant. He looked bad and smelled the same! "Roman."

Roman instantly raised his head while wiping his snotty nose onto the shoulder portion his shirt. "Yes baby. What is it? What?"

"Roman sit next to me," she said gently patting the bed. Roman slowly sat down next to her while she held one of his hands in both of hers. "Roman do you love her?"

"No," Roman swiftly answered.

"If you don't want to do this...If you don't want to be married for whatever reason, be honest with me and just tell me now. I won't be mad, vindictive, or anything like that. -Just be honest with me. Be honest with yourself."

Roman caressed her face. "I want you. I will always want you and only you."

"Roman if I come back, I need you to understand what will happen if this type of issue happens again."

"Angelica please..."

"Roman, I will leave you and never, EVER come back again. You will have to have someone pick up our baby for visitation because I won't ever want to see your face. We will never spend time together as a family. I won't ever speak with you...even over the phone. You will be dead to me. You will be dead...just like all the words and dreams that you shared with me. I won't need to divorce you because you will be dead to me! Do you understand me Roman? I will not go through this again...EVER."

Roman put his forehead on hers. "I understand. I get it! Can you please come home?" Angelica shook her head yes. Roman wrapped his arms around her and thanked her again and again. "I love you! I love you so much. Thank you for giving me another chance. Thank you."

Angelica stood up. "Let's get you in the shower." Roman looked at his shirt. "I think it's time for one."

Roman shook his head. "Ok." Angelica pulled his shirt over his head. Roman stared at her and kissed her lips.

Angelica looked down at her breasts and stomach and didn't feel desirable at all. After knowing what Monica looked like, Angelica felt like an ugly duckling. She looked down at her hands and knew that forgiving him for this was going to be hard. What if he speaks her name again while sleeping? Angelica closed her eyes feeling the pain resonate within her. "You can control your words and your actions but what about your thoughts? You will think of her. Maybe even dream of her."

Roman kissed her lips again.

Angelica cried. "I'm fat...and I'm not as young and pretty as she is."

Roman kissed her lips again. He then rubbed her stomach.

"What if you change your mind about her? What if you decide later to be with someone else or her?"

Roman kissed her neck, ear lobe, and then her lips.

"What if she...

Roman put his finger on her lips silencing her. He grabbed her head in his hands and kissed her. Angelica moaned and held on to him for dear life. "Do you love me?"

Angelica shook her head. "Yes."

Roman stared at her with tears in his eyes, "Do you promise to be with me forever?"

Angelica just nodded her head.

Roman kissed her again. "Do you mean that? Can you forgive me?"

Angelica cried. "I will try."

Roman smiled. "Thank you, thank you, thank you!" He held her close and kissed her again!

Angelica thought of Monica again and lowered her head. "Roman, if you change your mind about us or if you think that you would rather be with her..."

Roman silenced her again with his finger and kissed her. He smiled at her while tears continued to fall from her eyes. Roman kissed each one of them which Angelica loved. "Angelica I love you and only you." Angelica smiled and nodded her head. She looked at his disheveled state and knew he was speaking the truth. She knew right then and there that she would be able to do this. Angelica knew that he only wanted her!

Roman kissed both of her cheeks and held her close. He kissed her lips and looked into her eyes. "I don't want her and will NEVER want her. I don't want anyone else and will ONLY want you, Angelica! I love you and only you! Always. She will NEVER be...EVER be a problem in our lives. EVER!" Roman kissed her deeply and kissed her stomach. Angelica lovingly smiled back at him. Roman briefly closed his eyes and took a deep breath. He placed his hands on her face and kissed her softly on the lips. "You don't have to worry about her...EVER...

...because I killed that fucking bitch!"

www.ingramcontent.com/pod-product-compliance
Lightning Source LLC
Chambersburg PA
CBHW060750030726
47503CB00002B/228